Also by
LAURA VAN WORMER

TALK
JUST FOR THE SUMMER
JURY DUTY
ANY GIVEN MOMENT
BENEDICT CANYON
WEST END
RIVERSIDE DRIVE

The Sally Harrington novels

EXPOSÉ
THE LAST LOVER
TROUBLE BECOMES HER
THE BAD WITNESS

TH

KI

FE

LAURA
VAN WORMER

THE

KILL

FEE

MIRA

ISBN 1-55166-744-4

THE KILL FEE

Visit us at www.mirabooks.com

Printed in U.S.A.

First Printing: November 2003
10 9 8 7 6 5 4 3 2 1

For Michael Anderson
(Finish your book.)

ACKNOWLEDGMENTS

With heartfelt thanks to my friend Molly Savard,
my friend and agent, Loretta Barrett,
my friend and publisher, Dianne Moggy,
and my best in everything, Chris.

I

Stardom

CHAPTER ONE

"Oh, come on, Uncle Percy!" I cry, lowering my cards facedown to the table with my left hand and slapping my right on my forehead.

"The whole idea of playing hearts, Sally," Uncle Percy quietly explains, "is to maintain one's composure while using a strategy to win."

I sigh as I glance across the card table at my mother and then over at my great-uncle's friend, Mrs. Milner, who offers me a friendly wink. Of course Mrs. Milner has like zero points against her while I'm teetering around with ninety-one, and Uncle Percy has just passed the ace and king of hearts and the queen of spades to me.

"You're just rotten, I tell you," I growl at Uncle Percy, picking up my cards.

Mother laughs, picking up her glass to sip a little wine.

It is Saturday night at the Gregory Home in Castleford, Connecticut. My great-uncle, Percy Harrington, is eighty-four years old, and after a serious fall three winters ago, decided to move here. It is a remarkable institution, the Gregory Home, first started in 1936 by a wealthy industrialist to care for men and women in their later years. The endowment has been very well tended, and over the years the original mansion has evolved into something akin to a lovely feudal village.

The Gregory Home looms large upon a hill, lawns cascading beautifully down in front, and the interlocking buildings extend back and around, encircling to protect its vast network of common areas and residents' rooms, gardens and terraces, and most preciously, of course, its people. Today it can happen that a millionaire lives next door to a person of small means, and yet their quality of life will be indistinguishable. The only prerequisite to living in the Gregory Home, it seems, is to be nice. (As my mother always says, good manners will get you everywhere.)

Uncle Percy resides on the second floor—the party floor, he says—and after eating a light supper downstairs in the main dining room, the four of us moved up to the Turner Suite, where residents can privately entertain, to play hearts. My great-uncle is the only surviving Harrington of his generation. His eldest brother, George, was my father's father, the heir who married late in life, blew most of the Harrington family fortune and then blew his brains out in the pool house, leaving everyone somewhat at a loss about how to proceed.

For my father and grandmother, the consequences of my grandfather's behavior meant moving into a small rental house down the road before the banks foreclosed on the estate. For Uncle Percy, it meant watching the only company where he had ever worked, Harrington Fine Printing, abruptly slam the doors in the face of its longtime employees, cart off its presses and equipment and supplies piecemeal, and then auction the building itself in the bankruptcy courts. The huge redbrick building, with its large windows and decorative stonework, is now the home of twenty-four loft apartments. The only trace of my family that can be found is the name of my great-great-grandfather, Horace W. Harrington (the inventor of one of the earliest color-separation processes in printing), on the cornerstone.

Uncle Percy was never quite the same after the bankruptcy. Before the scandal and collapse of Harrington Fine Printing, he had been a rather dashing executive dandy of the old school, Mr. Rah-Rah Princeton, but afterward he became a quiet observer on the city sidelines. He had some sort of minor executive job in Hartford. His wife, it was said, couldn't bear children and so the couple drifted through life in their pretty, little house on Farm Hill Road, always pleasant, always the perfect gentleman and gentlewoman, but never the center of anyone's particular attention.

My father died more than twenty-two years ago, and it was four years later that Aunt Martha fell ill with cancer. Until then Uncle Percy had helped my widowed mother a bit financially, but the demands of his wife's care at home quickly curtailed that, and by the time Aunt Martha died six years later, Uncle Percy was mentally, physically and financially exhausted.

Uncle Percy was a proud man and when he said he was selling the pretty, little house to move into an apartment because, at his age, it was simply the wisest move to make, Mother believed him. But then, over time, Mother put it all together—the federally subsidized apartment, his never traveling, never buying new clothes, his car barely kept running—and realized that Uncle Percy had little or nothing to live on but his social security and the odd dollar he took in by addressing wedding invitations in his beautiful hand.

I'm still not sure how Mother convinced him to speak with Margaret Kennerly, the administrator of the Gregory Home. In Uncle Percy's day, the Harringtons were one of the largest benefactors of the Gregory Home, and certainly none of them had ever *lived* there. But after Uncle Percy's fall, it was evident that his health was at risk, and Mother and I ganged up on him about making a change.

We are so very grateful to the Gregory Home because since Uncle Percy moved in, he has come back to life in a way I never remember him being. Because, you see, living at the Gregory Home is really like living on a grand estate, which is exactly the way of life Uncle Percy had been brought up to expect. He is, in other words, after all these years, living in his natural element.

My mother, the former Belle Goodwin of Newport, often visits Uncle Percy. She also enjoys the atmosphere of the Gregory Home because it is reminiscent of a life that she, too, had been brought up to expect but was denied. Oh, yes, my father was a very good architect, and had, with his in-laws' help, designed and built Mother a beautiful home on the five-acre parcel of the old estate he had managed to hang on to. But then Daddy died so young, and so unexpectedly, and there Mother had been left with two small children and very little insurance. (She also had a brother draining her parents for all they were worth, but that is another story.)

No, I think, looking across the table at my blond (and gray) haired, blue-eyed, genuinely beautiful sixty-year-old mother, *she has not had it easy, either.*

"Who has the two of clubs?" Uncle Percy wants to know, snapping me out of my contemplations.

"I do," I sigh, tossing it on the table to start the hand. Sometimes I think I am Uncle Percy's favorite niece because I am his only niece.

After I get creamed and thrown out of the game, Uncle Percy asks if perhaps I can look at that letter he mentioned. I tell him sure, get up to pour myself a cup of decaffeinated coffee, retrieve the letter, settle back down at the table and look at all the commotion emblazoned on the envelope. NO SUCH

PERSON. RETURN TO SENDER. DECEASED. DEAD-LETTER OFFICE. The letter is addressed to Uncle Percy at the old Farm Hill Road address where he hasn't lived for years and years.

"Our new mailman brought it the other day," Uncle Percy tells me, playing a card. "Nobody seems to know where it's been all this time."

I open the letter. It's dated over two years ago.

Dear Mr. Harrington,

I am writing in regard to the five (5) acres of land you own outside Hillstone Falls, New York. The land trust wishes to explore the possibility of purchasing it from you. There may be many beneficial tax implications, and you will, as well, earn the deepest gratitude of every Connecticut and New York resident wishing to keep our air clear of toxic pollutants, our water clean and our landscape unspoiled.

Please call me at your convenience.

Sincerely yours, I am,
Harold T. Durrant
President
Western Connecticut Land Trust

The address is in Lakeville, a small, picturesque town in northwest Connecticut that has become popular with rather well-heeled New Yorkers.

"Do you know what he's talking about?" I ask my great-uncle.

"No," he says, tossing a heart onto Mother's suit of diamonds.

"Darn it," Mother says under her breath with a grimace. Then she glances over at me, curious about the letter.

"I wonder if you would look into it for me," Uncle Percy says, craning his neck over his cards to see what Mrs. Milner plays.

"Yes, of course I will." I slide the letter back into the envelope and put it away in my purse. There is a need for discretion. When Uncle Percy came into the Gregory Home, he signed over his assets to them—which were essentially his social security payments—to help defray the expenses of caring for him for life. Please understand, I do not wish to cheat the Gregory Home out of their rightful due, but I would like to know what this is all about before Uncle Percy comes forward with a newfound asset.

It's very strange, though. How can this land trust group know about the land, when none of us, including Uncle Percy, have ever heard of it? And if it's true, that there is a piece of the old Harrington empire still in play, who's been paying the taxes on it for all these years?

Mother is thrown out of the game next, so it is down to Uncle Percy and Mrs. Milner. In the next hand, Mrs. Milner has an inexplicable surge of good luck and Uncle Percy goes down. While I somewhat doubt that Mrs. Milner's strategy was quite as miraculous as it seemed, I do not doubt the caliber of a strategy that has nothing to do with cards. Uncle Percy is clearly sweet on her and he has purposely thrown the game to give her pleasure.

We pick up after ourselves and we all walk Mrs. Milner to her room to say good-night. Then Uncle Percy escorts us downstairs in the elevator, and in the lobby the receptionist reminds us to sign out. While Mother walks over to sign the register, Uncle Percy retrieves our winter coats from the closet. With Mother's coat draped over his arm, he helps me on with mine, and says, "Now, Sally, I don't want to conceal anything—"

"No, I understand," I quickly assure him, turning around. "We'll just scope it out first to see what's what."

"What's what," he repeats. "Exactly. That's what I would like."

"What are you two whispering about?" Mother asks, coming back.

"About how absolutely beautiful you are, my dear," he says, kissing Mother on the cheek and holding her coat out for her to slip on.

I smile, because for a second there I could see in Uncle Percy's eyes a slight resemblance to my father.

"Well, go on, my dears," Uncle Percy says, shooing us on our way. "Sally has a big day tomorrow and she needs her rest."

"What big day?" I ask, glancing back over my shoulder.

He raises a hand to his mouth to loudly whisper, "Lover boy is coming!"

"Mother," I say accusingly, turning around, but before I can find out what she told him, Mother has pushed me out through the automatic front door. As we cross the driveway, I can see through the window that Uncle Percy is laughing and laughing and waving good-night.

"I didn't call him lover boy," Mother says, defending herself.

CHAPTER TWO

Bradley International Airport is a Connecticut success story. It began as a small airport to service Hartford and Springfield, Massachusetts, in their urban heyday, but when the corporations of those cities stumbled on treacherous times, airlines drastically cut their flights and some considered pulling out altogether. Nobody, they thought, from central and northern Connecticut and southern Massachusetts would be flying anywhere anymore. *Wrong.* The truth was, most of us Connecticut and Massachusetts "nobodies" had always used Providence, Logan, La Guardia and JFK because Bradley had such crummy flight offerings.

Two airlines at Bradley experimented by expanding their flights, and lo and behold, the passengers came. In droves. And so did more flights and then whole new airlines and the urgent need for terminal and parking expansion. Today Bradley *International* is a very cool airport, big enough to get you everywhere, but small enough so that you almost always run into someone you know.

When I'm at Bradley I cannot help but remember how my father used to bring me here as a child. How in those days we could park at the end of the runway and stand right up against the fence, watching the planes taxi faster and faster toward us, bearing down on us, and then hearing and feeling the thunderous roar of the engines as they powered the jets over our heads into the sky.

The American Airlines flight has arrived on time, but Paul Fitzwilliam is so late emerging from the gate area I have begun to think he missed it. But no, there he is—I can see him approaching the barricade. He has a backpack slung over one shoulder and is carrying some lady's pet carrier in his arms, as aforementioned lady is walking sideways to talk to whatever it is inside. I smile and wave. He sees me and moves his head around the carrier to see better and to offer me a quick smile.

He is a cutie.

And he is young. Twenty-five years old to my relatively recent age of thirty-three. When Paul emerges from the barricade, a man hurries over to take the carrier from him, the woman thanks him profusely for carrying Smoochie—the Yorkie who has now emerged from the cage to be held in her arms—and then, finally, Paul turns to me with a tremendous smile. He is very tanned, so his teeth look very white. His brown hair is light from the California sun and saltwater; his eyes are dark brown.

It is only in this moment that I realize that he resembles my high-school boyfriend.

"Hi," he says, taking me in his arms and hugging me, then lifting me off the ground and holding me there a moment. He is five-ten, only three inches taller than me, but Paul is very strong. He puts me down, still holding me, but pulls back slightly to look at my face. "Hello, gorgeous girl," he says, kissing me squarely on the mouth. He lingers there and then releases me to take my hand.

"I brought you this to wear," I say as we head for the baggage area, holding up a blue down-parka with my free hand.

"January is very different in Connecticut than California. It's only twenty-five degrees out." He slides his arm around my shoulders, pulling me in close. It is not a terribly efficient way to walk, but it feels rather nice.

I met Paul Fitzwilliam last fall in Los Angeles while I was testifying in a celebrated murder trial—the "Mafia Boss Murder" trial. He was a police officer in West Hollywood. I work as a producer for DBS News in New York, but while I was out there, after I had finished testifying, DBS put me on the air as coanchor of a nightly news special about the trial.

After the trial was finished, I stuck around for a week and Paul and I got to know each other better. Then two weeks later, Paul flew east to look at Quinnipiac University School of Law and some law schools in New York, and we had a chance to hang out some more. Understand that there has been, from day one, such physical attraction between us, it is almost unbearable. And yet, we have not given in to it. Or Paul hasn't and so I have followed suit.

Up until now, Paul has been somewhat of a ladies' man. (He's already confessed to sleeping with four different women in the past year.) And although for years and years I was rather conservative in this department, it seems that in the last few I've become a bit of a—well, why don't we just call it a "sensualist"? (In other words, I seem to have awakened sexually in a way that has infinitely complicated my life.)

Paul is from an upper-middle-class California family who was horrified when he chose to, as his parents phrased it, "Throw the family back a hundred years to be a cop." But Paul is an active guy and I can understand the lure the streets hold for him. Prior to the police academy, he had been working the oil rigs of Montana and was an aspiring adventure novelist. After he started working for the West Hollywood Police Department, Paul finished his bachelor's degree at night at the University of Southern California and shortly thereafter began considering law school. He wants to become a prosecutor.

That's when we met in a rather startling fashion. And what very quickly happened in California, I think, was that each of us sensed that we could easily hurt the other. Whatever it is that Paul has in his personality, I have been falling very hard for it. And he, for whatever reason, seems even more taken with me. He is young, but because he grew up with an alcoholic father, he saw a lot and he saw it early. And whether a father is absent through booze or death, with Paul and me, it doesn't seem to matter, we both appear to be emotionally banged up in the same way—or at least in a way that enables us to understand each other.

"I finally heard from Fordham," Paul tells me in the baggage area, his arm still around me, watching the conveyor belt and absently running his hand up and down my arm. "The scholarship came through—"

"Really?" I say, eyebrows high.

"But I can't transfer into the NYPD," he finishes. "They're laying off people."

"Oh," I say.

"So Fordham's out, I'm afraid." He looks down at me, giving my shoulder a squeeze. "I know it would be nicer for us if I went to school in Manhattan, but I'm not sure I'm cut out to live there anyway."

That is where I live. Manhattan. I still have one foot in Connecticut, though, with a cottage in my hometown of Castleford, and I'm planning to buy my childhood home from my mother.

The luggage carousel has started to move and people start crowding in. I'm happy to see that Paul has chosen a spot where we can see the luggage as it comes out and that he's content to wait until he sees his bag before cramming into the crowd. (I don't think I could be with one of those people shoving each other up there.)

"But the New Haven Police Department is a go," he continues. He pauses for effect, knowing that I'm waiting to hear the rest. "In fact," he says, squeezing my shoulder, "I report tomorrow for orientation."

I blink. "New Haven?"

"Yep." He glances at the luggage belt. "And Quinnipiac's a go. The night school is a four-year program, but I can work full-time and have a shot at making the finances work." He stoops a little to get a better look at my expression. "It's okay," he laughs. "Don't be scared."

"I'm not scared," I say. "I'm just surprised that everything is moving so fast."

"I've gotta find a place to live," he says, gesturing with his free hand, "but, yeah—I'm here. Orientation tomorrow at NHPD and law school starts next week. Jack—you remember my roommate—got a U-Haul and is driving my car across the country." He breaks away from me, easing his way through the crowd to retrieve not one, but two huge suitcases.

I am more than a little taken aback. Pleased, I think, and happy and excited, but Paul's right—I am scared. He had been talking about the possibility of finding a job and going to law school next summer. But now, in the space of six weeks, he has committed to wholly relocating his life and dreams from California to Connecticut. And I would be a fool not to suspect why.

Paul returns with his bags, pulling them along on wheels. He releases one suitcase to place his forefinger gently on my mouth. "It's okay," he whispers, bending close. He drops his hand to kiss me lightly on the mouth. "Don't panic," he says softly. A kiss. "There will be plenty of space between us." A kiss. "You'll be in New York most of the time." A kiss. "And

I will be overwhelmed and freaking out in law school." He squints slightly, carefully studying my face. "Sally, I *want* to be in the East. I *want* seasons. And you never ever have to see me again if you don't want to," he adds with a laugh.

Actually, what I'm thinking about is how likely it is that Paul will eventually cross paths with my ex-boyfriend, Doug Wrentham, who is an assistant D.A. in New Haven. Interesting that I've been attracted to two men in law enforcement. More interesting, I suppose, is that the second looks a lot like the first when he was in high school.

CHAPTER THREE

As we near my hometown of Castleford, I relate the basic rundown on the history of the area to Paul—about the farming in the valleys, the valuable stone quarried from the Connecticut Mountains, the huge industrial boom in the late 1800s—until he gently reminds me I told him all of this on his last trip.

Paul is to meet Mother over Sunday dinner at her house, and I am a little nervous. I've told her about Paul, how much I like him, how much I admire his work ethic and how we're getting to know each other, but I didn't say anything about his arriving in Connecticut today for good.

"Wow. This is beautiful," Paul murmurs as we turn into Mother's long driveway. We had snow yesterday and the trees and house are at their winter best.

My father, Wilbur Kennett Harrington—known as "Dodge" from his football days—graduated from the Yale School of Architecture. Our handsome house of wood and stone was sort of a calling card for Daddy's specialty: adapting the best of colonial architecture to modern building practices.

The large brick mansion of the old Harrington estate, where Daddy grew up, is just next door, hidden behind a screen of towering pines. Today it is a Franciscan convent.

As we make the final bend, we see a police car parked on the snowy side lawn of Mother's house with its lights flashing. Behind it is an unmarked Crown Victoria. "Oh my God, what is this?" I say under my breath, slamming the Jeep into Park and jumping out.

My childhood friend, Detective Buddy D'Amico, is hurrying toward me across the driveway, holding up a restraining hand. "It's okay, Sally," he says quickly. "Your mother's fine. She's not in danger."

I look past Buddy to see that a man is sitting in the back seat of the patrol car. One officer is standing next to the car talking into his radio mike while the other is watching us. Somewhere deep inside the house I can hear Abigail, Mother's golden retriever, barking. "What's going on? Who is that?" Buddy's eyes dart momentarily to Paul, who has been just a half step behind me. "He was trespassing, Sally, that's all. He was standing out here for hours, apparently, just staring at the house."

"Where's Mother?"

"She's inside, she's fine," he says. "She called the station because she didn't know what to do about him."

"He must have done something that finally made her call," I say. Mother is notorious for giving everyone the benefit of the doubt for far longer than is healthy.

"She said he was here yesterday, too, for a while. Standing over there." He points to the bend in the driveway.

"And she just called you *now?*" I say, angry.

"Less than an hour ago," Buddy says. "I was at home when I heard the call on my scanner so I came over to see what was up."

I notice, then, that Buddy is standing out here in the cold dressed in nothing but a paint-covered sweatshirt and windbreaker.

"What is he *doing?*" Paul says in such a voice that it makes

Buddy and me whirl around to look. The guy in the back seat of the patrol car is on his knees, pressing his hands and forehead against the back glass, yelling something. And there's no doubt about it, he's looking straight at me. He starts making a grabbing motion with his right hand against the glass, crying something.

Paul steps in front of me to block the view while Buddy barks, "Get him out of here!"

I look to the house and see that Mother is standing at one of the living-room windows, watching. I start toward the house and then think better of it, not wanting the creep in the police car to necessarily link me with her. While the squad car spins and starts off the snow-covered lawn to turn around and pull out, Paul and Buddy say something to each other and shake hands.

"As you might have been able to tell, Sally," Buddy says, "he was hanging around here in hopes of seeing you."

I grimace. I'm never going to shake the image of that guy groping the back window with the look that was on his face.

"These nuts can't find you, Sally," Buddy says, "but they can find your mother." He sighs. "It's an issue we have to address. Ever since that trial, they've been showing up around here," he adds to Paul.

"You mean these are like," Paul says, "*fans?*"

Buddy nods, offering a small smile. "Sally's our very own hometown celebrity. Complete with sick fans from out of town."

After my national exposure as "The Bad Witness" (as the *Los Angeles Times* so happily nicknamed me) and my stint as a coanchor of the nightly trial-recap program, DBS learned that I have a certain appeal to younger viewers *and* an unusually strong following with social misfits, sexual miscreants and generally romantically inclined crazies. And while it is almost impossible to track me down at my sublet apartment in Manhattan, or to penetrate security at the West End Broadcasting Center, or learn where my isolated cottage is here in Castleford, Mother is openly listed in last year's telephone book.

It's so weird that I should end up with this problem. When I graduated from UCLA and worked at *Boulevard* magazine in Los Angeles, I used to *cover* stuff like this, the stalking of celebrities. But then my mother fell gravely ill and I came back to Castleford to help care for her and I took a job at the Castleford *Herald-American*. Mother got better, but I ended up staying on at the paper and then I lucked into a freelance magazine assignment which, in turn, led me to a job with DBS News. In other words, I've gone from hiding behind newsprint to write about celebrities, to becoming a celebrity of dubious stature myself.

"Buddy," I say, crossing my arms over my chest against the chill I'm starting to feel inside, "what are we going to do about this?"

"Your mom has an alarm system," he says.

I nod. "Yes. I put it in six months ago."

"So maybe the next step is a fence," Buddy says. "With an electrically controlled gate. Or maybe—" He shrugs. "Another dog might help. If *your* dog had been here, Sally, rest assured that guy wouldn't have stuck around."

True. My Scotty is a big gorgeous mutt—collie, German shepherd and retriever—but his junkyard-dog toothy smile and barrel-chested bark scare the hell out of everybody. He is a gentle giant by nature, but if anyone comes near me that I don't like, I know for a fact he will intervene. He would behave the same on Mother's behalf, for he often lives here when I'm away and considers her an integral part of our pack.

"Maybe I could help," Paul says, speaking up.

The front door of the house opens and Mother's golden retriever comes happily bounding out. Then Mother herself appears on the front step, "Please come in, people!" she calls, sounding like the schoolteacher she is. "I can see you shivering from here, Buddy, and there's nothing you can say to Sally you can't say in front of me. So let's move it! *In.*"

"I can't stay long, Mrs. Harrington," Buddy says, dutifully walking to the house. "I left Alice with a screaming toddler and a broken playpen."

Paul has to run back to shut off the Jeep. He jogs back, hands me the keys and escorts me up the walk. "One thing we could do right away," he suggests, "is post some signs about your mother's alarm system. And a Beware of Dog sign wouldn't hurt either."

"That's an idea," I say, watching Buddy disappear into the house. "Mother," I say as we near her, "I can't believe you let that creep hang around for two days and you never said anything to me!"

"It's nice to see you, too, dear," Mother says, sort of pushing me to the side when I reach the step. "You must be Paul," she says warmly, holding out her hand.

"And you are certainly the beautiful Mrs. Harrington," Paul says, receiving her hand to shake it. "Sally warned me that no one pays attention to her when you're in the room."

Mother sort of pooh-poohs this and gently places her left hand on top of his. "I hope you'll excuse our rather unusual reception for you today. We don't often have such an exciting Sunday dinner."

Paul laughs and picks up on Mother's cue for him to pass on by her into the house. As soon as he does, she turns to me, widens her eyes and mouths, *He's very young!,* and then sweeps into the living room behind him.

CHAPTER FOUR

Buddy D'Amico will be staying far longer at Mother's than he knows, for while we are sitting around the fire in the living room, eating dip and crackers, I can hear Mother on the telephone in the kitchen. Shortly thereafter she reappears with a cutting board of cheeses. "Buddy, it's all settled," Mother says, swooping the board down to hold in front of him, "Alice and Jenny are joining us for dinner. They'll be here in about ten minutes, so why don't you tell Sally what you'd like to drink."

"Please," Paul says, jumping up, "let me help, Mrs. Harrington. I've been sitting all day on the plane." He takes the cheese board from Mother and starts taking drink orders. When he puts the cheese down on the coffee table and follows Mother into the kitchen, Buddy looks over at me, plucks his ratty, paint-covered sweatshirt—as much as to say, *Not even your mother can pretend I'm not wearing this*—mutters something about a preppie Californian cop and takes out his cell phone.

While Buddy is waiting to talk to the desk sergeant at the station, I get up to cut a small piece of cheddar to give to Abigail, and think maybe I should run over to my house to get Scotty. I have to go back to New York tonight to make a meeting at DBS in the wee hours (with the newsroom night shift), and the plan is for Paul to stay at my place. He specifically asked that Scotty stay so he and my dog could get to know each other better (yes, I should have seen the signs that things were moving more quickly in Paul's mind), but I feel badly about Scotty being there all alone now when there are all of these nice people here.

"Yeah," Buddy says, shifting his cell phone so he can shovel another cracker with spinach and artichoke dip into his mouth. He swallows, eyes moving to the window. "Then just let him sit there until he feels like telling us." Pause. "Trespassing." His eyes move over to me. "I'll be there in about—" He looks at his watch. "Hour and fifteen." He clicks off his phone, sticks it in his back jeans pocket and absently rubs his chin.

"So?" I ask, smiling slightly as Abigail gently lays her head on my knee. This little retriever is awfully sweet sometimes.

"He refuses to give his name," Buddy says, sounding tired, "has no ID on him, but he does have seven hundred and eighty-two dollars in cash." He pauses. "And a picture of you, cut out of a newspaper."

I frown. "Yuck."

Mother and Paul are in the adjoining dining room, moving silverware and glasses and candlesticks. They are chatting amiably, preparing to pull the table apart to insert more leaves. Buddy glances over at Mother and then leans forward toward me. "I don't like your mother being here alone. Not with this creep around."

"I don't either," I say. "But I've got to go back to New York tonight and Mack's at a conference in Houston." Mack is my mother's fiancé, a retired scientist who teaches astrophysics at Wesleyan University in Middletown.

"Then why don't you leave Scotty here," Buddy says. "He'd scare the hell out of anybody."

I nod. "I was thinking the same thing." Laughter spills into the living room from the dining room, which fades as Mother and Paul go back into the kitchen.

"He seems like a nice kid," Buddy says, reaching for more dip. "He said something about coming East."

"He's transferring into New Haven PD," I explain, rising to stoke the fire.

"New Haven?" he says, surprised. "After southern California?"

"He's starting law school next week, at Quinnipiac," I say, putting the tongs back and opening the wood box to fetch another log. "He's going to try the four-year night program."

"Good for him." The log I put on spits sparks onto the hearth, so I have to sweep it. After a moment, Buddy says, "So are you guys friends with his parents or something?"

"No," I say, putting the broom back and replacing the firescreen. "I met him during the murder trial."

"Oh, was he working for you guys?"

"He's the one I was on the motorcycle with," I say, crossing the room to my chair. I'm referring to Paul and me being run down on a motorcycle during the "Mafia Boss Murder" trial. We were on what would later be a very highly publicized dinner date. I sit down, happy to see that the fire is blazing merrily again.

Buddy appears openly puzzled, trying to put what I said together.

"On the Pacific Coast Highway," I add, reaching for a small piece of smoked Gouda.

"Oh," Buddy says, blinking. Then rapidly blinking. "*Oh.* You mean?" He abruptly turns away, as if to hide his thoughts. Then he looks back at me.

"*What?*" I ask him.

He leans forward. "How old is he?"

"Twenty-five," I say. "And count yourself lucky I don't dump that dip on your head."

There was a time, years and years ago, when we were in high school, that Buddy D'Amico was sweet on me. Well, maybe it was all of high school. I'm afraid the feeling was not mutual.

"He looks a lot younger," Buddy says, sitting back against the couch and raising his right ankle to rest on his knee.

Buddy has stuck by me in recent years with incredible loyalty, so I let the comment pass.

Mother and Paul come back into the living room, with Mother alerting us that Alice is pulling up. While Buddy hastens to the front door, I make a covert study of Paul. What makes him look so young, I decide, is that he has beautiful skin and doesn't have a terribly heavy beard. Kind of a Pretty Boy Floyd, I guess. His khakis and blue-and-white pin-striped shirt are classic prep, as are his Bass loafers. And in this light you can't see the crow's-feet the California sun has started around his eyes.

And those dark eyes. I don't think Buddy is the type to want to try to peer into Paul's soul, but if he looked deep into Paul's eyes, he would find the sagacity and slight world-weariness of a good man.

I haven't seen Alice in a while, so when she comes in through the door I am shocked by how pregnant she is. The baby, I hear her tell Mother, is due next week. As if in response to this announcement, two-year-old Jenny gives her mother's hand a vicious yank, nearly pulling Alice over and prompting Buddy to leap to the rescue.

I walk over to kiss and hug Alice hello. She was at Castleford High with me and Buddy, too. Alice has always been warm and lovely to me, despite the fact that while she dated Buddy in high school she knew he had a thing for me. There was once a horrible moment at a party following our high-school prom, when Buddy had had a great deal to drink and he cornered me to confess his undying love. When he tried to kiss me, I managed to fend it into a hug, and over his shoulder I saw Alice standing there, watching. So I patted Buddy on the back, loudly told him I loved him, too, he would always be my friend and then I growled in his ear that Alice was standing behind him and either he pulled himself together or I would never speak to him again as long as I lived.

Of our graduating class of three hundred twenty-one, there are maybe fifty of them who still live in Castleford. And of our classmates who graduated from out-of-state colleges, I think I am like one of three. This distinction, of having left the area for Los Angeles and then moving back, seemed to draw some kind of invisible line between me and what's left of our class. The only way that I perceived there's a line is by comparing the easy camaraderie between me and the D'Amicos and the arm's length at which I'm held by the others.

"You said you were looking for a place to live?" Alice asks Paul over Mother's Sunday dinner of roast beef. Mother always makes far too much food and to stretch this dinner all she had to do was double the mashed potatoes and add a couple cans of LeSeur peas.

"I have some leads," Paul says.

I see Alice nudge her husband before turning her attention to the mess Jenny is making of her food.

Buddy puts down his fork and sips some ice water from his crystal goblet. "So where are you staying in the meantime?"

"At Sally's," Paul answers.

"Sally is going back to New York tonight," Mother can't help but explain. After everything Mother's been through concerning my reputation, it seems ridiculous at this point for her to try and protect it, but she is, after all, my mother.

"I would sleep a lot easier," Buddy says, reaching for a roll, "if I knew you were staying here for a couple of days."

Both Paul and Mother look at Buddy.

"He means with that creep around, Mother," I say.

"Oh, him," Mother says quietly. She doesn't eat the piece of meat on the end of her fork, but gently eases it off with her knife instead and carefully places her silverware on the edge of her plate.

"We're not going to be able to hold him for very long," Buddy says.

In the silence that follows, Paul looks embarrassed and wipes his mouth with his napkin. "I wouldn't want to make Mrs. Harrington uncomfortable."

"But you wouldn't, Paul," Mother assures him. "My son's room is empty and it has its own bath. But the point is—" She turns to Buddy. "If the Castleford police can't handle this, there's no point of poor Paul doing this unless he moves in here forever."

If Paul and I were further along in our relationship, I might actually go for that. I worry about my mother in the winter alone in this house. It's a lot to take care of. I had hoped, as a matter of fact, that Mother and Mack would have been married by now.

"Until Buddy finds out exactly what's what with this guy, Mrs. Harrington," Alice jumps in, "I think it's wiser to err on the side of caution." She neatly intercepts her little girl's wrist before Jenny can *fwang* some mashed potatoes across the table at me.

"I agree, Mother." I look at Paul. "I mean, it would be nicer for both of you to have your privacy, but certainly it would make me rest easier this week if I knew you were here. And, Mother—" I look at her "—you could help orient Paul with directions and apartments and things. He doesn't know the area very well at all." I offer him a smile. "And I don't want him to be lonely or go hungry. He only just got here."

Paul is smiling back.

Mother clears her throat.

Mother, you should understand, is the perfect hostess, so long as it is understood that everyone who is not immediate family leave the gathering afterward. After meeting my eyes, though, Mother glances down at her plate, smiling a little to herself, and then raises her head to look at Paul. "*Danger* aside, Paul, you are most welcome to stay here. But I do not want you to feel obligated. I've been the only adult living in this house for almost twenty-three years, I think I can handle one more week."

"Bail me out and feel obligated," Buddy whispers loudly to Paul.

We laugh.

"Seriously, it would help me out," Buddy says.

Paul is biting his lower lip and bows his head slightly before speaking to Mother. "I think it would probably be for the best, Mrs. Harrington," he says, sounding sincere. A smile. "And I would love it." Then he shrugs, asking the table, "Who wouldn't want to stay here? This house is gorgeous."

He is so good-looking, I think. And he can be such a love. Like now.

"Then it is done," Mother announces, picking up her fork. "Paul is now officially a part of the Harrington Homestead."

Ah-ha, I think. So Mother *was* nervous about the creepy guy. I look gratefully across the table at the D'Amicos.

My home in Castleford is the isolated caretaker's cottage on what's left of the old Brackleton Farm. The farm for generations had been famous for barns filled with fine dairy cows and a small stable of thoroughbred horses. The farm's vast fields, over the course of each year, would produce alfalfa, hay, strawberries, green beans, tomatoes and a variety of squashes, corn, oats, brussels sprouts and pumpkins. Even the acres of woodland had produced crops of chestnuts and maple sugar and syrup, and, maybe every ten years, a cash crop of oak or maple hardwoods.

The cottage I rent—which is really more of a bungalow, with a charming pillared porch, living room/dining room with a stone fireplace, bedroom, bath and kitchen—was built in the 1920s. I am surrounded by woods, but have a large yard and shed, and the only unfortunate reminder that the Brackleton heirs are only interested in crops of cash, are the occasional dynamite blasts from a massive project to "build" a lake, which is, in actuality, a dodgy method of defying zoning regulations to strip-mine for rock.

When we drive up, the motion detector turns on the front lights and I hear Scotty barking inside. We walk over the frozen ground, past the big granite rock on the left, and step up onto the porch. I unlock the door and turn off the burglar alarm. On his way out, Scotty pauses to carefully sniff, greet and confirm that he knows Paul already, and then continues, first whizzing a little on the big rock to let trespassers know this is his house.

I pack a briefcase in the alcove that was meant to be a dining area, but which I use as my office, and thank Paul again for staying at Mother's. "It's the least I can do," he says, watching me. "And it's really nice of you to let me use your Jeep this week."

"I don't need it if I don't have Scotty," I explain, scanning the labels in my disc file and selecting the one that says NIGHT SHIFT to put in my bag. I glance over my shoulder. "And he'll love being with Abigail."

Paul smiles and walks over to stand near me. "I had hoped to come into Manhattan at least once this week."

"It's probably just as well if you can't," I say, closing the briefcase and turning to face him. He is looking at my mouth.

Finally, his eyes come up. "You need to get your bearings around here." Smile. "You've got a pretty full dance card coming up, my friend."

"I'll say," he murmurs, sliding his arms around my waist and stepping in close to kiss me.

After we part, I glance at the desk clock and grimace. "I'm going to have to hustle if I'm going to make that train." I ease out of his arms, walk over to drop my briefcase at the front door and head to the bedroom. "I bought some Coors for you," I call. "You should take it with you to Mother's." I throw a few things into an overnight bag and notice how, because I knew Paul was coming, the cottage is cleaner than clean. Since I started commuting between two homes, it isn't often this way. The orderliness makes me look forward to coming back.

I zip up the bag and head for the living room, flicking off the light and checking my watch—and crashing into Paul in the hallway. I laugh. "Sorry."

He takes my bag from me and kisses me on the forehead, but then pauses, bringing his eyes down to look meaningfully into mine. He draws a long, slow breath and then lets it out. Then he leans forward to kiss me. A moment later he drops my bag (I wince at the sound of a perfume bottle clinking with a bottle of nail polish) to put his arms around me. The kiss deepens and he pulls me into a full-body embrace and I can't help but feel the growing sign of his sexual desire. "I'm glad you're here," I murmur, kissing his ear softly. His hands slide down to my lower back, pulling me even tighter against him, and his mouth slides lightly over my cheek and then falls to the base of my neck.

If I miss the Amtrak train out of Castleford, we're going to have to rush to New Haven to catch an express.

His mouth is moving, and one hand sweeps lightly over my breast. His touch and embrace are tender. I sigh a little, moving my arms up around his neck. He smells good—a kind of citrusy-masculine smell, if there is such a thing.

I don't know what he is doing to my breast, but it feels divine.

Paul knows women well. He knows how to explore and find out what is pleasing and what is not. We've gotten to this point several times, entwined in sexual longing, but we have always remained standing, as if to be even remotely horizontal would spell the end of civility.

"I don't want to let you go," he sighs, lessening his grip. He pulls back slightly, bringing his right hand up from my breast to look at his watch. He shows it to me. "How much time do we have?"

"Six minutes. Tops."

Paul dutifully releases me and bends to pick up my bag.

"No," I tell him, pulling him back to me.

"But you've got to go," he says quietly.

"There has to be something I can do for you before I leave," I hear myself whisper in his ear. "I can't leave you like this." I'm not quite sure what I'm thinking about, or maybe I am, but if I am, I also know I don't know him nearly well enough to do it. But now I've said it, because, I guess, I feel as though I should do *something* to reward and relieve this love-struck young man who is moving three thousand miles away from home.

He shakes his head. "No," he says, sounding hoarse. He swallows. "There's nothing you should do."

I slide my mouth down from his ear to his neck. "What about something we can do together?" I whisper, hiding my face. "Can you think of something we can do in five minutes?" I bring my mouth back up to his ear, swallow, and whisper, "Something I've longed for since the day I met you?"

I feel his body tense, but he says nothing.

I raise my head to look at him and I press my lower body

against him; his hands slide down around my hips. He closes his eyes, making a sound in his throat. "Sally," he says, opening his eyes. "Maybe—"

Looking into his eyes, I reach down to his belt buckle. After a moment of fumbling with it, I bring my other hand down to help undo it.

"Are you sure?" he whispers, eyes half-closed.

I unzip his pants as an answer, which is enough to make him cave, and as he moves us sideways into my bedroom I remind him we don't have very much time at all before we have to leave. He lowers me on the edge of the bed and in the light from the hallway I watch him pull down his pants and then straighten up, revealing boxers badly swollen to the left. I reach for his waistband, pulling him closer, and with both hands, tug them down, down, lowering my eyes with them until they reach his pants, which are around his ankles.

I raise my eyes—he is gorgeously distended, and as I slide my hand over to touch him, he bends from the waist suddenly, rummaging in his pants pockets and pulling out his wallet. He straightens up, his longing swaying, and I take the foil packet from his hand. I glance up to see that his expression is almost one of pain. I carefully tear open the packet. Before I think about it, I reach out to hold him, softly kiss him there, and then I back away to gently negotiate the condom to cover him. When I'm finished, he eases me back on the bed and pulls off my panties and slacks in one motion, tossing them to the floor. He slides his palm over my stomach, down my groin, and then swiftly and wholly between my legs. He makes a sound deep in this throat at what he finds there and then abruptly pulls me farther across the bed, stretches to grab a pillow, lifts me with one hand and slides the pillow under my hips. He crawls over me, his face hanging over mine, and I feel him positioning himself.

I can feel that he is where he should be and I smile, whispering, "We have all of two—" Paul pushes his way into me with an easy but large slide that makes me cry out softly, and then he lowers himself, sliding his hands under me, holding me, and finishes his entry saying my name.

"God, yes," I moan, sliding my hands down his back. He makes a small sound deep in his throat, pulls back slightly, and, testing, pushes his way back in. I groan and feel myself twist into him. He takes it as a signal because in the next instant he's effortlessly driving himself into me with a steady and strongly athletic rhythm, and I know I'm making sounds—because it's so good, so very, very good. He starts making noises, saying my name, over and over, thrusting and hurriedly pulling out to thrust again. I feel this endless tide rising fast in me, swelling up from way down inside and I am up and off the bed, clinging to him, my back arching as I cry out, and I peak and crash back down, the waves of satisfaction making me convulse around him. His rhythm falters, and then his body stiffens and with one last thrust he cries, *Sally!,* gives a tremendous shudder and collapses.

He's breathing heavily, his face buried in my neck, and I hold him, kissing the side of his head, my legs tightening around him.

After a moment, I hear him swallow and whisper, "I've got to—" He rolls slightly to the side and pulls out of me, making me want to cry, *No, stay like this.* But I don't. Instead, I reach down to gently take the condom off him, and then I reach back over my head to toss it in the base of the potted palm.

He chuckles, looking at me, undoing the top button of my blouse. "I've come to a decision," he says, moving to the next button.

"Oh? What's that?" I ask, tracing his mouth with my finger.

"If we get to take our shirts off this time, I'll drive you into Manhattan." He pulls my blouse apart and suddenly reaches under me, struggling to undo my bra. He gets it undone, pulls it loose, freeing my breasts and bringing his mouth down.

I thought I was spent, but what he does brings on a new sensation, different but ever so welcome.

I can't get enough of this man.

CHAPTER FIVE

I'm down in the newsroom when word reaches me that Alexandra has blown into her office and would like to see me. It is a little before noon and being Monday there's nothing odd about this request, for our star anchorwoman often begins the week with a mile-long list of things she's been thinking about over the weekend.

It is important to understand that regardless of any less-than-flattering things you hear about her, Alexandra Waring is the indisputable heart and soul and financial backbone of DBS News. The youngest of five children of the legendary Congressman Waring from Kansas, Alexandra grew up on her family's farm, where she attended public school, but also spent a significant amount of time in Washington D.C. She attended Stanford University, where she began her broadcasting career by mopping the floor of a local radio station. Eventually she started reading the news at that radio station, jumped to an independent San Francisco TV station as a news writer, then became a reporter, and finally, only six months after her college graduation, became a weekend news anchor.

From there Alexandra headed home to begin a triumphant five-year reign as an anchor and investigative news reporter at a network affiliate in her hometown of Kansas City. Then she moved on to New York City, where, as a nightly coanchor of the local news, she doubled the WWKK ratings and within eighteen months had whipped the crew into something that resembled a proper news team. At twenty-eight she was hired as the Capitol Hill correspondent for one of the Big Three news networks, and two years later, when Alexandra was shot on the steps of the Capitol Building by a so-called fan, she came to the attention of media magnate Jackson Darenbrook.

Darenbrook, the CEO of the family-owned-and-operated communications empire, was angling to launch a fourth broadcast television network. Darenbrook Communications owned a satellite and had developed a highly sophisticated transmission system in order to orchestrate cost-effective methods of publishing their chain of daily newspapers, national magazines and small-town weeklies. The plan for DBS was to link, by satellite, the newsrooms of independent TV stations around the country, from which a nightly news hour could be created in New York. That finished newscast would then be transmitted back to the stations along with an hour-long talk show that was also produced in New York. Those two hours of programming would establish a foundation upon which the network could grow.

Alexandra Waring was hired as the face of DBS News and a western media sensation named Jessica Wright was engaged to launch the talk show. The idea was to offer affiliates the opportunity to run the earliest "late" newscast in their market, at nine o'clock, followed by the talk show with a late-night feel, at ten.

Alexandra recruited an old friend, Cassy Cochran, president of WST—the largest independent TV station in the country—to build the news division, but Cassy did far more than that. She ended up recruiting the DBS affiliates herself, thus building the very network and producing both *DBS News*

America Tonight with Alexandra Waring and *The Jessica Wright Show.* She became the first and only DBS president, and also married Jackson Darenbrook in the process.

The rest, as they say, is history. *The Jessica Wright Show* did well from the start. And despite the fact that the affiliate newsrooms of DBS were, in those first few years, wildly uneven resources at best, the audience studies and focus groups on Alexandra Waring were proven correct: younger baby boomers, brat packers and GenXers absolutely loved her. Critics immediately gave it the nickname "The Yuppie News."

Today, the critics rather like our newscast and we may well be the only broadcast network in the world whose national nightly newscast actually makes money. (The Big Three don't.) The critical and financial success may be in part due to our having a whole hour and that Alexandra, as managing editor, insists on a reporting approach that treats the United States as a local market, giving the newscast a kind of this-is-what's-happening-to-your-neighbors feel. Yes, we cover international news, but every news hour almost always has a breaking story from each of eight regions of the United States.

Our major weather segment—from 9:26 to 9:34—has consistently had the highest ratings. Each night our meteorologist, Gary Plains, explains what creates the phenomena that is currently taking place somewhere—snowstorm, hurricane, tidal wave, flood, earthquake, lightning, wildfires, etc.—which is always accompanied by spectacular footage and computer graphics. Then we cut to the affiliates for the local weather forecast and reports of possible transportation hazards for the morning commute.

We have four regular "editors" who appear—weather, business, entertainment, international—and 192 affiliate newsrooms, which translates into 203 possible reporters. We also have spun off the highly successful *DBS News Magazine,* and produced a lucrative and well-reviewed line of videos, DVDs and CD-ROMS on aspects of American history.

But make no mistake about it, Alexandra Waring is the center of it all.

Some say that Alexandra's core audience is younger because they are the first generation to accept a woman as an authority figure. Whatever the reason, advertisers are wild over our demographics of up-and-coming men and women with above-average incomes who evidently like to catch the news early and go to bed.

The drive to success, however, has taken its toll on Alexandra. As her right-hand producer, I've seen the damage her career has wreaked upon her personal life; I've seen the sacrifice and the denial of human limitations, and I've seen the pounding her body has taken from stress. On the other hand, this is a woman who genuinely seems happiest on the air. She watches what she eats, works out mercilessly, bypasses alcohol and simply goes all-out until she near collapses, at which time she retreats into seclusion at her farm in New Jersey.

This is—at her farm—where her personal life struggles to exist. Alexandra's love life has centered around another woman for several years now, a fact that is widely known but never openly acknowledged and which is hindered further by the fact the woman in question is a movie star in her own right, who has, no less, a Scottish lord as a father and a 1950-60s sex symbol as a mother.

Alexandra's is not, in other words, an uncomplicated life.

I hustle out of the newsroom and take the elevator up to ground level. The West End Broadcasting Center, whose entrance is on Twelfth Avenue at Sixty-seventh Street, is built in a gigantic U, facing out over the West Side Highway to the

Hudson River. In the center of the complex is a park for employees to enjoy, a play area for the day-care center and a dog run originally set up for me (long story). The center building, Darenbrook I, houses the corporate offices, cafeteria, day-care center and security headquarters. The far wing, Darenbrook II, houses the print offices. The other wing, facing south (where I am going now), is Darenbrook III, which houses the broadcasting division.

Below the outer span of the complex are two floors of offices, electronic laboratories and technology centers that have windows looking over the vast canyons of Television Studio A (news) and Studio B (talk and entertainment), which sink three floors below ground level. On that lowest floor are the functional rooms that catacomb around the studios (props, carpentry, film editing, conference rooms, newsroom, dressing rooms, hair and makeup, and on and on).

Alexandra's secretary, Korean-American Benjamin Kim, tipped me off that the star anchorwoman is not in a great mood. (His code is "BSA," which stands for Beware of Stormy Atlantic—a warning that rather well describes both the temperament and blue-gray color of our boss's eyes in this mood.) I pass one security guard outside the elevator in Darenbrook I and meet another at the elevator in Darenbrook III. When I emerge on the third floor, I notice yet another security guard as I walk quickly down the hall and turn into the outer area of the second to last office.

Benjamin looks solemnly up at me from his desk. "Is she in there?" I ask him.

As an answer, he covers his face with his hands.

Uh-oh.

"I don't give a damn!" I hear Alexandra yell in her office. "Not only do I think it's unfair, I think it's an outrage! I think it's dishonest! I think it's stupid, foolhardy and a complete violation of trust! *That's* what I think!" Her office door slams shut and we can hear her continuing to yell behind it.

"Whoa," I say to Benjamin. "This is a first."

"Hmm," he says, cinching his mouth to the side. "I've seen it once or twice before." He meets my eyes. "I'm afraid this could be about you."

"About me?" My stomach flip-flops. What could I have done? I put down my clipboard and cross my arms, resting them on top of Benjamin's computer monitor. I need grounding. "Who is she talking to?"

He checks over his shoulder to make sure we're alone. "Cassy."

Uh-oh. The president of the network. Not good.

"Do you know what about?"

He shakes his head. "She asked that Alexandra call her when she got in and—" He gestures to illustrate that things just—abracadabra!—exploded.

The door to Alexandra's office suddenly swings open and Benjamin and I jump to attention. The raven-haired anchorwoman is wearing her usual kind of outfit when she returns from the farm, a navy blue turtleneck, blue jeans and flats. Even with simple silver hoop earrings and no makeup, she looks fabulous. Well, that's what unbuttered popcorn and carrots and celery sticks will do for you.

"Come in," she says to me.

I take a breath, pick up my clipboard, glance at Benjamin, and go in.

"Have a seat," she says quietly, walking around her desk.

The farm girl side of Alexandra becomes more obvious in this greenhouse of an office. While all the functional things are in here—desk, computer, TV monitors, couch, conference table—plants are everywhere. It smells green, too, like my yard in Connecticut after a heavy spring rain.

I take a seat, cross my legs, and rest my clipboard on my knee.

"Did you meet with the weekend shift?" she asks, sitting down.

"Yes, at ten o'clock last night," I report, remembering how narrowly I made it here in time. Poor Paul had to turn right around then and drive back to Castleford, at best an-hour-and-forty-five-minute ride.

On the other hand, if last night left him feeling the way I do this morning, he is tired but happily amazed. We are good together, no doubt about that.

I clear my throat, recross my legs in the other direction to fend off further memories of Paul, and recap the newsroom meeting for Alexandra. I met with the weekend night shift in the newsroom; I explained the changes in their responsibilities that would come with our new collaboration with the British International News Service for more intensive foreign coverage. I also explained the possibility of broadcasting a late-night international-news hour anchored from London.

"Any complaints?" she asks, sifting through her mail folder.

"A little concern about the British viewpoint," I say.

Alexandra makes a sound to acknowledge that she's heard me, but continues going through her mail.

"I explained how we're going to work the editing process," I add, "and how it will work to our benefit."

She doesn't respond and is scanning a piece of paper.

I notice the lines between her eyebrows. And around her eyes. At thirty-nine, she is doing pretty well. Her high cheekbones, generous mouth and knockout eyes will save her from plastic surgery a little while yet.

She tosses that piece of paper and picks up another.

I know better than to ask Alexandra what's wrong. If there's something she wants me to know, she'll tell me.

"Okay," she finally says, glancing up. "Thanks. I'll see you later."

Blink. I have been dismissed. Well. I rise from my chair.

You may be surprised to learn that Alexandra and I are fairly close, which gives me a very good idea of how upset she is.

And Benjamin says he thinks it might have something to do with me.

"Wait—" she says as I approach the door.

I turn around.

She meets my eyes. "Have you talked to Cassy?"

I shake my head. "No. Not today."

She looks at me a moment longer, nods, and then waves me away. "Okay. Thanks. Close the door behind you, will you?"

I do as she asks and when I reach Benjamin's desk he comments that I don't seem to have broken legs.

"Something's up," I say quietly to him. "She's not a happy camper." I look at him. "You really don't know what it's about?"

He shakes his head. "No."

I walk next door to my considerably smaller office. Still, I have the floor-to-ceiling wall of glass that overlooks the park, and if I lean back in my chair far enough, I have a nice view of the Hudson. I slide into my chair and pick up the phone to check my voice mail. It is the usual stuff for the broadcast day—Do this, Do that, Tell Alexandra this, Tell Alexandra that, Where is that? Where is this? Can you get this and that yesterday?—but then there is an urgent message from my agent, Saul Michaels, which surprises me. Saul never calls, basically because I am at the bottom of his agency list that includes a ton of top names in TV news. My contract isn't up for over a year, so for him to deign to call must mean he wants a favor.

My second line rings and I push a button to answer it. "Sally Harrington."

"Hi," Paul says.

"Hi," I say, smiling and sitting back in my chair.

"Do you have a minute?"

"As it happens, I do," I say, swiveling around to look out at the park.

"I got my uniform," he tells me.

"You're kidding, already?"

"Yep. And they want me to start tomorrow."

"My gosh," I say, sitting up. "That was fast. And you have everything? To start work?"

"Blues, badge, nightstick, gun, bullets, handcuffs, walkie-talkie—I am the *man*, ma'am."

"Make sure you model it for Mother, she'll love it."

"I gotta tell ya, Sally, your mom is one cool lady. I really like her."

"Yes, she is," I agree. I've already talked to Mother this morning. She said the night was uneventful, but Paul was a perfect gentleman, offering to put Christmas stuff back in the attic for her, taking the trash and recycling out and throwing a tennis ball for the dogs.

"Have you heard from Buddy?" Paul asks.

"No, not yet."

"I called him about an hour ago," Paul reports. "They let your creep go this morning. He's some sort of mental case from Massachusetts."

"Great," I mutter.

"They took him to his car. It was in some park near your mother's."

"Probably Kreske Park," I say.

"And they fined him for trespassing, he paid it and then they had to let him go. With money in his pocket they can't treat him like a vagrant, although Buddy says they followed him out of town."

"Did he leave Castleford? That's all I want to know," I say.

"Well, for now. They also checked with the police where he lives, and he's supposedly harmless, but a pain in the neck. You're not the first woman he's followed."

I sigh. "Well, as long as he stays away from Mother." I switch the phone from one hand to the other. "So should I be worrying about this guy coming back?"

"Not for now. Buddy rattled him."

"Good."

Pause. "So how are you feeling?"

I laugh a little. "Uh, happy. Maybe the tiniest bit sore—"

He gives a warm and knowing laugh.

"But basically, pretty good," I finish. "And I can't thank you enough for driving me in so I could make that meeting."

"You're thanking me? I've never felt so good in my life."

This touches me and I wonder if it's true. Or even remotely so. "I'm glad," I finally say.

After a moment, he says, "Hey, so guess what? Your mom's making homemade stew, salad and garlic bread tonight. Maybe I shouldn't tell her creepo's left town—she might kick me out."

"She likes you, Paul. Stay. She doesn't like cooking for one anyway." I can visualize Mother happily throwing everything into the Crock Pot this morning before leaving for school and planning to pick up a salad and fresh bread on the way home.

Besides, my younger brother Rob flew in and out so fast over the holidays, she's still feeling a little lonely.

Paul and I talk about what NHPD is doing with him tomorrow and his initial schedule: days, seven to three-thirty, Tuesday through Saturday.

"So you have Saturday nights off," I say.

"And Sunday and Monday to prepare for school on Tuesday and Thursday nights," he says, sounding pleased. "They were pretty accommodating. Being the new kid on the block, I felt sure they were going to give me nights."

"It's still a lot, though," I point out.

"I miss you," he suddenly says. "And I can't believe how wonderful you are. How beautiful, how smart, how funny, how absolutely drop-dead gorgeous you are."

I think I'm blushing. After a moment, I say quietly, "Right back at you, Officer Fitzwilliam."

When we get off, I try to focus on the rundown sheet for tonight's newscast. While I'm trying to remember what we did with the footage of a hailstorm we didn't use last week, I see the copy I made this morning of Uncle Percy's letter about the land in Hillstone Falls, New York.

I look at my watch and decide I can give this five minutes. I call up the DBS News database on my computer and run the Western Connecticut Land Trust through it and come up with the same address in Lakeville that is on this letter. Then I try "Harold T. Durrant," the name of the man who wrote the letter, and come up nil. So I call information, but am told there is no telephone number for him. "Not even unlisted?" I persist. "No listing in Lakeville, Connecticut, under that name whatsoever," I am told.

I go into our telephone database, go back two years and find him: Durrant, Harold T., Pheasant Run Lane. I call the num-

ber and get somebody named Mickey Bickford at the Min-
uteman Insurance Agency. That's it, I don't have the time for
this. I call down to Edith, my slightly "out there" ally in research, and ask her if she can work on something for me on
her own time. "It's a personal favor, it's family business," I
explain.

"Thank you for the opportunity to, in some small way, repay
your many kindnesses," she says. (I told you, she's a little, uh,
"out there.") I tell her I'll bring down a letter I want her to see.

Then I try to find a listing for the town hall in Hillstone
Falls, New York. Hillstone Falls, it turns out, is covered by
the larger township of Hillstone. When I call the Hillstone
Town Hall to inquire about access to land records, I am told
I must appear in person to register first and then I may request
to see records. When I explain that I am doing this on behalf
of my aged great-uncle, that I would simply like something
looked up, the lady tells me that's nice and informs me once
again that I must appear in person at the Hillstone Town Hall
to register. They are open from nine to one on Saturdays.

I make a note on my calendar, and get back to work. I grab
my production stuff for the newscast and head down the hall to
the spacious offices of our executive producer, Will Rafferty.
"He just called," his secretary informs me. "He's not coming in
after all." In a lower voice she adds, "Jessica's not doing so hot."

"I'm sorry to hear it," I say. Jessica Wright is one of the
neatest people I've ever met in my life. Bright as all get-out,
funnier still, she is a kind and warm and eccentric voluptuous
kind of cowgirl talk-show host who brightens the halls of
DBS, both spiritually and financially. Three years ago she and
Will Rafferty were married, and three months ago they an-
nounced she was pregnant.

Two weeks ago, however, while taping her show, Jessica's

blood pressure skyrocketed to nearly stroke level and she almost passed out, and she was hospitalized in an effort to help her hold on to the unborn child. DBS, in the meantime, is running "best of" shows, and because the tabloids have run wild with the story, her ratings have ironically moved higher.

Jessica, I know, has miscarried twice before.

"So everything is to go to Alexandra's office," Will's secretary summarizes. "Or actually, Will said to you."

"Great, I can ask myself questions," I mutter, thanking her and walking back to Alexandra's office. No wonder the anchorwoman's in such a horrible mood. It's not me she's upset about, but on top of worrying about Jessica—for they have been best friends for years—we're missing our executive producer yet again, a happenstance that last week created havoc all week.

I find the anchorwoman standing over Benjamin at his desk. She glances up and then down at the tape on the top of my production stuff. "What's that?"

"A seventy-six-year-old saved a thirty-year-old guy from drowning in Biloxi. The visuals are good. It's that Goggen guy? Remember the reporter who covered the oil tanker fire in Gulfport last year?"

"Great, give it to Bix," she says. "Look, I need you to get down to the newsroom and get some order in there—please. We've got seventeen know-it-alls and nobody to make a decision. *You* make the decisions today and tell them they're mine."

"I'm on my way," I say, shoving off. The transference of power is easy; all I have to say is, "Alexandra wants—" and everyone jumps.

"And could you see what's going on with the staging, please?" she adds. "Those microphone plugs blew out again Friday."

I know, I was there, I think to myself, but say, "I'll make sure they're squared away."

"And find out from Milwaukee what their lead is, please."

"Okay," I say, edging away as I make a note in ink on the back of my hand.

"And see if Rachel's on time. And if she's here, check to see what she's doing and make sure it's something constructive."

"Okay," I call, slowly progressing down the hall.

"And remind Bix I want that hail footage in the weather segment tonight, so he better find it."

"Right," I say, neglecting to mention I think I might have been the one to misplace it.

"And check with Stephen to see if he needs help. I sent a truckload of stuff down to editing on Friday."

I know, I was there. "Will do!" I call. Then I hesitate, listening. Good. No more instructions. By now I'm only a hop skip from the elevator, so I hurry into it before I'm handed the responsibility of the entire Ottoman Empire.

People are running in circles downstairs and I start throwing Alexandra's weight around to synchronize their efforts toward a coherent newscast. I am often walking chaos in my personal life, but my professional life is another matter. For whatever reason, working under the strain of pending deadlines, a fast pace, tension and rapid-fire demands makes me feel strong, vibrant and alive.

To understand what the formation of a newscast is like, it's helpful to visualize an auditorium filled with unruly children and jealous parents—all being asked to produce a variety show by nightfall. The unruly children are developing news stories and the parents are the reporters and field producers. The idea is to rely on your best experience and judgment to quickly assess which children genuinely have talent and which parents can get a passable performance out of them. So, say, by noon, we've picked forty kids and sent the rest packing. Some children simply won't sit still, or their parents are so out of it you know they'll never get the child ready in time, and so you let them go, too. Now we're down to thirty kids, but then ten of them, by nightfall, have fallen asleep and can't be awakened. So we have twenty, but then four run away, but then one from the first batch that we let go in the morning comes back and turns out to be the star.

The thing is, even when we get down to the twelve children we're pretty sure we can use, we still need to arrange their performances in an order that works; we need to rehearse them and time their performance and we need their parents to dress them, comb their hair and give them instruction and coaching all the way to the stage.

And then it is time for the actual newscast and the stories are trotted out for Alexandra to introduce to the world. Although the newscast shifts and changes even while we're on the air, it has to look as if we've had all the time in the world to prepare, and the writing, the graphics, the feeds, the live reports, everything needs to be paced and presented in such a way that the general population can readily understand. And there can be no errors, not in fact, not in production. That's our goal, to report the news, and to do so faithfully.

I have had a relatively brief and bizarre tenure at DBS News, but I possess two things that command a great deal of respect: one, Alexandra's trust. And two, I am blessed with a natural gift for cohesive narrative, written or visual, and can tell within moments if a story is structured properly, and if it is not, I am perfectly capable of whipping it into shape myself. The staff and crew also knows, from experience, that if the world were to blow up tomorrow, I could also go on air and do a reasonably good job. I have a union card to appear on camera; I have a different union card to write; I have yet another union card to be allowed to edit film in a pinch; I have no union whatsoever when I am in the position for which I was hired, a producer, aka management.

But let's face it, this is not a normal job and I am kind of nuts, but you almost have to be to thrive in news. And you cannot possibly imagine how gratifying it is when all goes well. There is an undeniable high and a deep sense of satisfaction like nothing else when you realize that at the end of the day, millions of people across America are a little bit smarter, a little bit wiser and a little bit better off because you did your job well.

God, I love news.

I am at the top of my game today and know the newscast is going to fall together well. When we're fifteen minutes from airtime, I feel relaxed enough to take a call from my agent in the control room.

And that's when I find out DBS wants to hire me as a replacement for Jessica Wright.

CHAPTER SIX

"**S**o the offer," my agent, Saul Michaels, says on Tuesday morning as he looks down at his notes, "is one million for one year, no bonuses, no guarantees, no discussion."

My stomach hurts. No wonder Alexandra was upset yesterday. She must have known about this.

Saul and I are sitting in Cassy Cochran's office. Cassy is leading the meeting, and also present is Langley Peterson, COO of Darenbrook Communications, and Denny Ladler, vice president and executive producer of *The Jessica Wright Show*.

"Essentially, yes," Cassy says lightly, taking her reading glasses off to look at us both. First at Saul and then at me. Cassy is somewhat of a legend in television—the natural blond beauty from Iowa refused from day one to appear in front of the camera. She has that elegant long-blond-hair thing going, always worn up on the back of her head, à la Judy Collins, and has beautiful blue eyes. High-WASP looks tend to do well in TV news and yet Cassy refused to use hers. Instead, she worked behind the scenes, first in TV news production with her first husband, Michael Cochran, in Chicago, and then in New York she rose through the management ranks at WST to president and station manager. Then she came to

DBS, where Langley Peterson made her president and Jackson Darenbrook made her his wife.

Actually, Langley is married to a Darenbrook, too, the youngest heiress, Belinda. (I used to think maybe I should try to marry into the Darenbrook clan, too, since everybody seems to be doing so well, but this morning it appears I might be doing just fine on my own.) Some credit Jackson with the success of the Darenbrook empire by capitalizing on the original newspaper chain left by his father, while others credit Langley for it by developing the electronic side of the media giant and switching corporate emphasis. In my book, I think it's fair to say that both men had an equal share in pushing Darenbrook Communications onto the next level.

I look at Saul. "May I ask a question?"

I'm asking permission because I have been instructed not to open my mouth, but to merely sit there because Cassy requested I be present. Saul says to leave the agenting business to him because, "You've got too much relationship crap between you guys to keep your priorities straight."

Saul nods, yes, I can ask a question, but throws in a cautionary look.

I turn to Cassy. "The contract is for one year. Does that mean Jessica is definitely not coming back for at least one year?"

Cassy glances at Langley and leans forward slightly. "We don't know." Her blue eyes look a trifle sad; her mouth is pressed into a line. Cassy is extremely fond of Jessica and I'm sure she is worried about her. We all are. And, of course, she's worried about the future of the least expensive program for DBS to produce—the program that also happens to make the most profit.

"So she might come back before the end of a year," I say.

"It's possible," Cassy concedes.

"And if she does, what happens to me?"

Langley clears his voice; Cassy sits back and throws the ball to him. "Then you'll still be paid the million over one year's time," he says.

"But then I'll also be out of a job," I say, turning to look at Saul, who nods gravely.

"That's right, for a lousy million your career will be finished," he summarizes.

"Saul," Cassy protests.

Now Saul leans forward to gesture with a meaty hand. "Let's get down to brass tacks here, Cassy, shall we? Even a month from now, Jessica Wright could come back, and not only will Sally be out of a job, but *she'll never be able to work in news again.* Her legitimacy will be gone." He lets this sink in. "So what does a lousy million bucks compensate her for?" He shrugs. "Three years?" He turns to me. "How old are you?"

"I just turned thirty-three."

"Thirty-three," he nearly shouts. "With brilliant career prospects and then—" He snaps his fingers. "She's finished. She'll have to crawl back to Bridgeport."

"Castleford," I say out of the corner of my mouth.

"Castleford," he says with emphasis.

"A million dollars, Saul," Cassy says calmly, "compensates for *five* years of Sally's current salary."

Saul throws up his hands. "So now she's not only out of a career, you want her to be broke and destitute by thirty-eight?"

"Saul—" Cassy says, looking tired suddenly.

"Forget it!" Saul says, vigorously shaking his head. "Forget it! This is a terrible offer!"

"What is the show going to be called?" I ask, trying to divert attention away from my agent, who is shouting forget it to a million dollars.

Besides, I'm getting rather taken with the idea of being a

national talk-show host. I love research, I love interviewing people, and then there's all that money, and, golly, just think of it, I'd have normal and predictable working hours for the first time in my life.

"You're Jessica's number-one choice, you know," Denny Ladler says to me. "She made us promise we'd offer the slot to you first."

I smile, so deeply flattered I can't tell you. Jessica Wright is a personality and phenomenon unto herself, but I do understand why she thinks I might work as a pinch hitter. Our temperament, personalities and upbringing are not terribly dissimilar and I bet management sees something in my TV-Q ratings from the trial program that makes them believe it could work, too.

"What would the name of the show be?" I ask again.

"Forget it!" Saul shouts.

"Until we know what Jessica's situation is for sure," Cassy says to me, "it will remain *The Jessica Wright Show.*"

"Sally!" Saul snaps at me.

"So everyone would know from the start that I'm a substitute," I say, "and that DBS is hoping Jessica will come back."

"Shut *up,* Sally!" Saul tells me.

"Essentially, yes," Cassy says candidly.

"And when would I start?"

"As soon as possible," Cassy says evenly, meeting my eyes.

It is hard to read what message Cassy is sending to me. I know that she is fond of me; I know that she is well aware of the fact that my crazy tenure at DBS has somehow managed to invigorate part of the news group (while irritating the other part into doing better work); and I know she has been very grateful to me for my support of Alexandra. On the other hand, if *The Jessica Wright Show* should plummet in the ratings, DBS is in big trouble and Jessica Wright herself thinks I might be the way to avert disaster.

I don't know, though. Jessica Wright has this legendary bosom and wears miniskirts and what she calls cowgirl boots and the raciest I get is to change from a Liz Claiborne suit into a DKNY.

And then there is the point that Cassy is offering me one million dollars to try hosting a talk show. One million to change career tangents—with regular hours and national exposure—or I can stay at two hundred thousand dollars off camera, schlepping around for Alexandra.

I don't know what telepathic message Cassy is trying to send me, if any. Clearly the decision is mine to make.

I turn to Saul. "You forgot to tell me to shut up again," I say, prompting everyone to laugh, breaking the tension.

"My client has to leave now," Saul says, gesturing for me to get out of here. As I stand up, he says to Cassy, "If we can have a minute more, there are a few things I would like to go over with you."

I shake hands and thank Cassy, Langley and Denny. "I'm afraid you'll have to make a decision by eleven on Friday," Cassy tells me. "We have other candidates to consider."

Translation: *If you don't want the million, we'll give it to someone else.*

I am feeling very strange and oddly alone as I walk back to my office in Darenbrook III, the pluses and the minuses of the proposal boomeranging in my head:

One million dollars; national exposure; regular hours.

Never be in TV news again.

It's still early for the news group—it's only ten in the morning—and our floor is quiet. I walk down the hall and turn into my office, wondering who I can talk this offer over with. The father of my college roommate is a possibility, Levi D. Rubin, who's worked in television for thirty-five years. He could assess this deal for me. And he knows me pretty well.

"I'm sorry," a male voice says, making me jump. Sitting on the small couch in my office is a man, briefcase open on his lap and papers all over my coffee table. "Alexandra told me to park myself in here." He is fumbling with his briefcase and papers, trying to stand up. I'm just standing there, watching him.

The man is tall, about six-two, with neatly cut dark hair flecked with gray and wonderful blue-gray eyes. Just as I'm thinking he looks familiar, that he might be an on-air talent from one of our affiliates, he says, "I'm David Waring, Alexandra's brother." He finally just heaves the briefcase and papers on the couch and steps around the coffee table to extend his hand. We shake and I note with satisfaction the firm dryness of it and the nice cut of his pinstripe suit.

He's in his forties, I would guess. Handsome. Doesn't have the sizzle of his sister, but possesses a quiet sense of authority. I wonder which brother he is, the doctor, the lawyer or the rock singer turned investment banker. I know there is a sister and Alexandra was the afterthought, but which Waring brother this is I have not a clue. I smile. "It's very nice to meet you," I tell him, thinking that later in the day, if I decide to take the talk-show job, there will be two Warings around to break furniture over my head.

"You're Sally Harrington," he says. "My sister speaks very highly of you."

"That's nice to hear," I say quietly, smiling.

"She didn't think you'd be in until later," he continues, "so she stuck me in here while she's doing something."

"Please, sit down," I say, gesturing to the couch. "If you can endure me talking on the telephone and reading aloud to myself, I certainly can endure you reading quietly."

"Thank you," he says. He waits, however, until I circle my desk and sit down before he sits. "My sister reads out loud all the time," he adds.

"As do you, big brother," Alexandra announces, sweeping into my office. David stands up again. This is a very polite family, I am to assume, and I find myself standing again also.

Alexandra is wearing a dark blue suit today, looking very *very,* if you know what I mean, complete with Tiffany pearl earrings and necklace. She is five-eight, but standing next to her brother she looks amazingly small. She is thin, whereas he is strapping. Athletic-looking. He might have a paunch somewhere I can't see inside that suit, but I doubt it—although I'm willing to bet *he* doesn't eat raw carrots and unbuttered popcorn.

Well, maybe the carrots.

Wedding ring, naturally.

"I'm sorry to stick him in here," Alexandra says, "but I didn't expect you in so early." Her eyes traveled down my body, taking in, I know, the fact that I, too, am dressed to the nines. "What's up?"

What am I to say? The truth, I suppose. (Half the time Alexandra already knows the answers to the questions she asks, which sometimes makes you wonder what her real purpose is in asking them.) "Um," I say, "Cassy wanted to see me."

A spark of anger flashes in the anchorwoman's eyes, but she contains it without comment. She turns to her brother, looking at her watch. "We need to get going."

"I'll get my stuff," he says.

I'm standing there, waiting for Alexandra to look at me again. She doesn't. She simply waits for her brother to finish stuffing his papers in his briefcase and then walks him out, calling over her shoulder, "I should be back by one if you want to talk to me."

CHAPTER SEVEN

"**Y**ou must be joking," Mother says, using her lunch break at school to return my phone call.

"I'm not joking," I assure her.

Pause. "I don't even know what exactly to say, Sally. It's a great deal of money. And they're probably right, dear, you probably could be a very good talk-show host."

"And I could very well bomb," I point out, swiveling my office chair around to look down at the park. "And if that happens, I'm out of a job."

"That was going to be my next point," Mother says. "All that money aside, Sally, the question is, do you want to leave news? And you are making a very nice salary now."

There is a part of me that is irritated with Mother. It is the part of me that would like to see my face on the billboard on the West Side Highway instead of Jessica Wright's; it is that part of me that sees how many inconveniences in life will be solved with that kind of money. How much more I could give. Heck, with a million-dollar salary, I might even go into therapy.

Well, let's not get carried away.

"Darling," Mother says in that tone of voice I know means

she is going to try to subtly push me in a certain direction, "what did Alexandra say?"

"Nothing yet. I saw her this morning, told her I met with Cassy, and she didn't say anything. Her brother was here and they went off somewhere."

"Well, I would be very interested to hear what she has to say," Mother says. "Of course she has a deeply vested interest in what you choose to do, but knowing her, I think she would try very hard to be fair and tell you what she honestly thinks. And you never know, darling, she may be able to do something for you. To keep you."

"A lot of people think she's done far too much for me already."

"Of course they do. There are always jealous people, Sally. Envious of your talent, of your intellect, of your youth."

"People who have worked very hard, Mother, and for a number of years, and who perhaps should have gotten the breaks instead of me."

"Darling heart, if they were supposed to get those breaks, they would have gotten them," Mother counters. "There's no way Alexandra would have passed over someone who was the best person for whatever—I can only go by what you tell me, but it would seem that Alexandra is a fanatic about the right people being in the right job."

I think about this for a moment; Mother has a point. I take a deep breath. "So deep down inside, Mother, what do you think I should do?"

"I think you need to hear what Alexandra has to say and take it from there." Pause. "And I'm so proud of you I could just scream."

I smile.

"By the way, young lady, I spent the most wonderful evening with your friend Paul last night. He's just a darling.

He brought home flowers for me, ate everything I put in front of him, washed the dishes, and then we just sat and talked in front of the fire. Then I corrected papers and he studied his handbook."

"I'm glad you like him," I say.

"And the dogs absolutely love him. For the last two nights, Scotty's been sleeping right outside his door."

"That could also mean that Scotty doesn't trust him," I laugh. "Which reminds me, what's the word from Buddy?"

"No sign of the trespasser. Oh—and Paul went out and got some Beware of Security System signs and put them out."

"Good," I say, my mind veering back to the job offer. I can't help it.

"Mack's coming home tomorrow," Mother continues.

"That's nice."

Mother didn't go near men for nineteen years of her widowhood and then it was like she flipped a switch—*Okay, now I'm ready.* Some friends introduced her to Mack, their relationship blossomed, they started spending nights together last summer (I don't like to think about it), and now they are to marry this summer.

They want to build a house on the water in Essex and were supposed to have started building it by now, but then Mother got nervous, I think, and said she thought they should wait until they've been married a year before finalizing the plans. Now where she and Mack are supposed to live during that year, I have no idea, because he says my father's presence in our house is overwhelming and Mother says the same of Mack's home, where his wife died three and a half years ago.

Mother has to get back to her class and I need to get started on the rundown sheets for tonight's newscast. Will's out again today.

I pull my production stuff together and walk out of my office, finding David Waring again. He is sitting at the desk of my nonexistent secretary. He stands up. "Do you mind?"

"Not at all," I tell him. "In fact, I'm going to be in the newsroom all afternoon and evening, so please—" I gesture "—use my office. I won't be using it."

He ducks his head a little, looking hopeful. "Are you sure?"

"Positive," I tell him, moving on, nervously wondering where the rundown sheet is that should have been delivered to me by now. I get my answer when I see Alexandra standing outside her office with a distinguished-looking black guy.

"Sally," Alexandra says, waving me over, "I want you to meet Haydn Cooke. Haydn, Sally Harrington."

"Hi," he says good-naturedly, shaking hands. "I've heard about you." His eyebrows shoot up. "Seen you, too, at that wild trial on the West Coast."

I smile. "Very nice to meet you, too."

"Haydn's just coming on board today, Sally," Alexandra explains. "He's going to be our special projects producer."

"Oh," I say, surprised, basically because I've never heard of such a thing before. "Congratulations and welcome aboard."

"Thank you."

I have heard of Haydn Cooke, though. He was recently fired from one of the networks as the scapegoat for the increasingly despondent ratings of their vastly overpaid anchor. The anchor has six years left to run in his eleven-million-a-year contract, so somebody else had to be sacrificed to pretend the problem is other than what it is.

Haydn holds up Will's copy of the rundown sheet that I

was worrying about. "We were just going over the preliminary story lineup."

"It's very different, isn't it, with a whole hour to work with?" I ask him.

He grins. "An unimaginable luxury."

My smile expands.

"Haydn's going to pinch-hit today for Will," Alexandra says. "Rick is going to help him." Rick is normally the producer in charge of the business, sports and entertainment segments.

It would appear that Alexandra has already set about to replace me.

Or Will. Or both of us.

"Haydn, why don't you go into my office to wait for Rick. I need to talk to Sally for a second."

"Sure. Good to meet you, Sally."

"Same here," I call.

Alexandra glances at Benjamin at his desk, and guides me by the elbow down the hall a few paces. "Could you meet with me at three? In my office?"

Her face is so close to mine, I feel that I'm either about to be threatened or kissed.

"Sure," I tell her. She releases my elbow and steps back. "So what do you want me to do today?" I ask her. "Since you and Haydn have intercepted my duties."

"I'd like you to take my brother to the cafeteria for lunch."

"You're kidding, right?"

She shakes her head.

I roll my eyes and walk back to my office. I've been benched.

CHAPTER EIGHT

There is no executive dining room at the West End Broadcasting Center; everybody eats together and we eat very, very well. The cafeteria in Darenbrook I is an eatery with vaulted ceilings and skylights, a gigantic wall of glass looking out over the park and Hudson, and the other walls are ever-changing galleries of paintings, drawings and photographs, either by DBS employees or their families, or of DBS personalities and events.

There is, for example, on the far wall, a portrait of Alexandra that is being inducted into the Museum of Broadcasting later in the month. (She was, and still is, the first woman to regularly anchor—by herself—a national newscast on a broadcast television network.) There's also a picture of me and Scotty, drawn by a four-year-old in day care that we have become friendly with at the dog run. (To others, the drawing merely appears to be a banged-up circle and a Picassoesque spider.)

The food is just terrific. From a carton of yogurt to filet mignon, from Thai vegetables to deviled eggs to sushi, the food is subsidized by the company and is unbelievably cheap to us. It's like the gym and the showers and the bikes you can borrow here; the Darenbrook family view themselves as parent and provider, and West End as the home for their large family.

David Waring, I quickly find, is a gentler version of his sister. Of course, I'm pretty sure he hasn't had the giants to slay that Alexandra has, and that does make a difference. He is an attorney, he explains to me over his lunch of broiled salmon, boiled potatoes and garlic spinach, and a partner in a general-practice firm in Santa Barbara, California.

"What is your specialty?" I ask, eating a forkful of Oriental chicken salad.

He finishes chewing and swallowing before answering. "Trusts and estates."

"And what brings you to New York?"

"My sister," he says, cutting a potato in half with his fork. "And one of my kids. She's in prep school near here and I'd like to see her."

I'm about to ask him which school, when I become aware of a presence standing next to me. I look up to see Edith from research. She is wearing one of her gray skirts and white starched shirts and a baby-blue cardigan that looks almost like cashmere. And, of course, as she does every day, Edith has tied a piece of yarn in her graying hair that matches the color of her sweater. Baby blue, yellow, pink, pale green, white, lavender, I know them all.

"Hi, Edith," I say. "I'd like you to meet Alexandra's brother, David Waring, who's visiting from California. David, this is our crack researcher for DBS News, Edith Pease."

By now David is on his feet, holding his napkin with his left hand and offering his right. "How do you do?"

Edith tentatively gives him her hand. "Hello," she says, looking down. Once her hand is released, she looks at me. "I'm encountering some difficulty in the independent research project you gave me."

She must be referring to the mystery of Uncle Percy's letter.

"I was just trying again, during my lunch period," Edith says, speaking slowly, rolling her head slightly from side to side as she does, "and I cannot seem to find any proper source for the land records of Hillstone Falls."

"Oh, I know," I say. "They told me I have to be there in person to register and see them."

"No," Edith says. Then she looks at David, who is still standing there, licks her lips and then bites the lower one, indicating she doesn't feel free to speak in front of him.

"It's okay, just tell me," I say.

She shuffles a little to the side, as if to shield her words from David by blocking them with her body. "I had Dr. Kessler's group look." Her eyes widen slightly and she gives me a hesitant wink.

Oh. She means she had the Nerd Brigade hack into the Hillstone Falls computer system. *"Really,"* I say.

"Highly unusual," Edith says. "There should be *some* kind of entry. But there isn't. Very strange."

"Huh," I say, thinking about this. Then I thank Edith and send her on her way so David can sit down and finish eating his lunch.

A little while later, he pats his mouth with his napkin. His mouth is a lot like Alexandra's, although her lower lip is fuller. "I think my sister relies on you far more than you know."

I draw back slightly, surprised.

"Georgiana was talking about you this morning, how great you've been for Alexandra."

Now I put down my fork and pat my mouth with my napkin. "Really."

He nods, his mouth twitching a little. "Lexy and I are pretty close," he says next.

I wait and wait and he doesn't say anything.

"And?" I finally ask.

"That's all," he says, shrugging. "I don't know how much you know, or don't know about—" He seems to be searching for a word, suddenly unsure.

"About Alexandra's private life?"

He nods, reaching for his water glass.

"I know as much about it as I do about any boss and their other half," I say carefully.

He swallows, putting his glass down. "So you know about them, right? Georgiana led me to believe you did."

I suppress a smile. "Not to shake up your world or anything, David, but most of the world knows about your sister and Georgiana Hamilton-Ayres."

"Yeah, right, I guess that's right." He looks out the window and I wonder what he wants to say. The silence becomes a little prickly.

"Did you always want to be a lawyer?"

He turns quickly and smiles. "No. I wanted to be a crop duster. And the doorman at the Ritz-Carlton in Washington. I liked the hat."

I laugh.

"My dad was a lawyer before he went into politics," he says, pushing his plate ahead slightly to lean on the table. Within moments a busboy comes by to pick up our dirty dishes. "Why, do lawyers bother you?" As he asks this question, his blue-gray eyes focus on me in a way that makes me feel vaguely uncomfortable and I divert my eyes.

"Gosh no," I tell him. "In recent years I seem to have nothing but lawyers in my life."

"Oh yeah? How's that?"

Just like a lawyer, he wants to know exactly what I mean. "I went out with a prosecutor for a couple of years. Before he was a prosecutor," I add for no reason save I suddenly feel nervous and don't know where else to go with this conversation. "He was a corporate tax lawyer."

David's head kicks back slightly. *"That's* a change."

"Hmm," I agree, looking around. "Would you like some coffee?"

"No thanks."

A moment passes. "What other lawyers have you had in your life?" he asks.

"Well," I say, sipping my water and putting the glass down, "in November I was surrounded by lawyers in the 'Mafia Boss Murder' trial." I look past him, thinking. "My coanchor on the trial-recap show was a law professor." I hazard a look at him again and this time I feel something churn inside me. "A friend of mine starts law school this week, in fact."

He nods once, his eyes still on mine. "He or a she?"

"He." I force myself to look away.

God, what is going on here?

"He's a cop," I add.

David is nodding and finally looking elsewhere. I look down at the table, to his arms on the table, to the wedding ring on the hand that is cradling one elbow. I wait until I am certain he realizes what I am looking at, and then I check my watch as a cue.

"What are the chances of Lexy and Georgiana lasting, do you think?" he suddenly asks.

I look at him. "I think you should ask your sister."

"I don't think my sister has a clue," he says, raising a hand to hold his chin while he picks at the surface of the table with the other. "She's so smart about so many things." He raises his eyes. "But she's so dumb about everyday living it blows my mind." He lowers his hand. "It's like she's on another planet."

"Planet DBS News," I tell him sympathetically. "I'm afraid we all live there."

"*You* do?" he says, looking amused, settling his arms down on the table again and openly looking at me.

What the hell is the matter with me? *Stop looking back at him!*

"In my family," he says, lowering his eyes slightly and then sweeping them away altogether, "we were the poster children for Congressman Waring's never-ending reelection campaigns. We had the right look, the right behavior, we went to the right schools..." He pauses, reflecting a moment. "And the right spouses." He frowns. "I think the idea was to throw everything so fast at us that we never had time to think of doing anything other than what our parents wanted us to do." His eyes come back. "It didn't happen fast enough with Lexy, though. She was supposed to marry this jackass from home, you know."

"No, I didn't know."

"Yeah. Tyler. Oh my God," he groans, "what a pompous ass. She called it off, thank God. By then, I think she had begun to understand some things about herself." He looks at me. "Later she was engaged to my best friend, did you know that?"

"I didn't know he was your best friend. You're talking about Gordon Strenn?"

He nods. "He was my roommate at prep school. All four years." Pause. "She broke his heart. But she had to." He adds, "My parents were upset all over again—they had sent out the invitations, had her dress made—" He offers a wry smile. "And they didn't have a clue about what was really going on with Alexandra." He lowers his head, slowly shaking it. "Our family is still fighting over her."

I wonder where this is going, why he is telling me all this.

Suddenly he looks up. "My sister really needs you, Sally. Please don't take that other job."

So that's it.

I scoot my chair back, stand up and toss my napkin on the table. "I trust you can find your own way back," I tell him before leaving.

CHAPTER NINE

After being broadsided by David Waring, I storm back to my office. You know, it drives me crazy when guys pull this kind of thing. Can you ever imagine them doing it to another man? Have lunch, flirt a little, tell him all about his family's problems and then plead that he turn down a million-dollar job to help out his sister in her tormented life?

Achhh! Makes me *nuts*.

"Sally Harrington," I say, snapping up my phone as it rings for the second time. I sound every bit as friendly as I feel.

"Hi," Paul says.

I glance at the clock. "Hi. Sorry I sound so cross, but somebody has just ticked me off big-time."

"Brrr," he says. "Glad it's not me, ice lady."

I smile a little. "So how's your beat?"

"Really something. There was a knife fight outside the soup kitchen across from Barnes & Noble. It ended okay, though."

"How so?"

"I took their knives away and brought them in," he says. "One of them has had a warrant out for his arrest since 1999 and he's been hauled in twice in the past year and nobody seemed to notice." He sighs. "It's a funny city, New Haven.

One block pristine, historic, dignified, the next, slum city. I'm beginning to worry that more than the streets may be the same way. No, check that," he says quickly. "It's just frustrating to know there's a certain kind of paperwork no one ever wants to do, so they just don't do it and *I* end up doing it. So what's up with you?"

How do you tell a police officer making thirty-seven thousand dollars a year you've been offered one million dollars to become a national talk-show host? Could there be a problem?

"Something interesting has come up—a job offer—but I'll tell you about it this weekend," I promise.

"Knock, knock," I say in the doorway of Alexandra's office at exactly three o'clock.

"Hi," the anchorwoman says, finishing reading something and then tossing it aside to look across her office at me. "Close the door and come in, Sally." She stands up. "If Will was here," she says, gesturing to a seat, "he would be having this conversation with you."

"He would be having this conversation with my agent," I say, correcting her. I say this perhaps a little more coldly than I intended and Alexandra looks vaguely startled.

After a moment, she says, "I suppose you're right." She slips off her blazer and hangs it on the back of her leather chair. Then she picks up a legal pad and pen and makes her way around the desk to sit in the chair next to me. She crosses her legs and says, "You're angry. Why?"

Her blue-gray eyes are somewhat subdued. And she seems tired.

"Your brother asked me not to take the job because he thinks you need me."

"He's right, I do," she says without hesitation. And then she lowers her eyes to the pad, adding, "Which has nothing to do with anything." She writes something down and flips the pad so I can see it.

YELL AT DAVID

"Now," she says, flipping a page and looking up to smile, "this conversation is off the record. Okay?"

"Saul said you would probably try to play on our relationship."

"Oh? And what relationship is that?"

I shrug. "I don't know, but everyone seems to think we have one." After a moment, "Whatever relationship a handmaiden has to a queen, I guess."

The look I get back would wither lesser people. Then she looks down at her pad, tapping her pen on it a couple of times. Suddenly she throws the pad across her desk so that it crashes and falls. Then she gets up to walk over to the couch. She slips her shoes off and drops onto the couch, bringing her legs up under her. Finally she plunks her elbow down on the arm of the couch and rests the side of her head on her hand to look at me.

I have to get up to turn my chair around in her direction.

There is a knock and Benjamin appears. Before he can say anything, Alexandra says, "No calls, please, and no interruptions."

"But it's Georgiana."

"Find out where she is and tell her I'll call her back. Thanks." She waits for the door to close behind him. "Which reminds me," she says, turning toward me, "that regardless of your decision, DBS needs to do something about Castleford."

I have no idea what she's talking about.

"Your mother," Alexandra says, "or her house—or your house—whoever's house, but we have to do something. My suggestion would be a fence and electronically controlled gate."

I think my mouth may have dropped open.

"What?" She does look tired.

"How do you know about that?"

"About Luke Jervis?"

"*I* don't even know what his name is!" I complain.

"It's security's job to keep on top of our employees' safety," she says, dropping her arm. "Heaven knows, Sally, you'd never tell us."

I wave it off. "Buddy ran him out of town and—" I am about to say that Paul's staying at Mother's, but I'm not sure I want her to know about him yet.

Alexandra rests the side of her face on her hand again and says, "Paul can't stay there forever."

"Honest to God, Alexandra!" I fume, slapping the arm of my chair.

"What?" she says, sitting up. "What's your problem? Buddy D'Amico told us he was there. No big deal, we're not spying on you." There is the smallest hint of a smile. "Though I must confess, I was a little surprised to hear that he was here. I was under the impression he lived in Los Angeles."

"He's going to the Quinnipiac University School of Law. The four-year night program so he can work his way through." I rise from my chair, never taking my gaze off those inquisitive eyes that are boring in on me. "Just stop it, Alexandra!"

Now she is openly laughing. "All right, all right," she finally says, waving me back in my chair. "I'm not going to say another word."

"*This* is why Saul doesn't want me to talk to you," I say, getting up and walking through her jungle to stand at the window with my back to her. I rest my forehead on the glass, looking down at the square. "Because we don't have very businesslike conversations."

Pause. "So what am I supposed to do?" the anchorwoman

asks me. "Just sit around and wait for them to tell me the deal is sealed? That they're taking my best person away from me?"

Best person? This is new. I turn around.

"Yes," she accentuates, nodding. "My best person. So sit down and let's talk a minute."

Feeling a bit numb, I do as I'm told and return to my chair.

Now Alexandra is sitting up straight on the couch, her legs still tucked under her, mouth absently working at her thumbnail. She throws her hand down and says, "First off—they should be paying you a lot more than a million dollars to trash your news career."

The words hang in the air a moment.

"You're thirty-three, and I know it seems like the biggest pile of money you can imagine and yet I'm telling you, Sally, in the long run, it's no windfall." She changes her position slightly, and starts gesturing with her hands. "There are also a couple of things you may not realize and your agent certainly isn't going to tell you. But you need to know them before you make this deal."

I wonder why I am bristling at the notion that, yet again, Alexandra knows far more than I do.

"First," she begins, shooting out an index finger, "odds are three to one you'll fail. And the problem is, it will have very little to do with your talents and capabilities. It's simply the situation—viewers are bereft at the idea of not seeing Jessica and you're not like Jessica in some key ways."

I want to say *nobody* has bigger breasts than Jessica Wright.

"Second—" her middle finger joins the index one "—Saul's agency also represents Marianne West, the person who is most likely to succeed as Jessica's replacement. Everything points in her direction, and everybody knows she's the better fit."

"The stand-up comedian?" I used to see her at The Strip in

L.A. years ago. Now that I think of it, she *might* have breasts as big as Jessica's.

"Third. DBS is offering you the slot first out of courtesy to Jessica, who has recommended you as her replacement. If I had to guess, Jessica's thinking is, that if she ever comes back, the two of you would be different enough so that you could have your own show." Pause. "The problem is, DBS has no intention of producing more than the one talk show."

She takes a breath. "So this is what you have to think about, Sally. If you sign that contract, Saul will take a hundred thousand of it. If you're fired in, say, two months, DBS will be frantic to save the show and so they will move on to Marianne West. Saul's agency will triple her normal price—probably up to six, seven, eight million dollars, and DBS will pay it because they have to, and Saul takes home six to eight hundred thousand a year. And if the show fails, we lose *millions upon millions.*"

"So you're telling me that my agent is sacrificing me to sweeten the deal for another agency client."

Looking grim, Alexandra nods. "Yes. If DBS goes first round with Marianne they'll only give two million."

I drop my head in my hands, letting out an expletive. I raise my head. "Then why is Cassy doing this?"

"Because it's her job to give you the opportunity," Alexandra says. "Think about it, Sally, if she gives you the chance, and you manage to beat the odds and garner a decent rating, DBS is going to be in fat city and it will have cost them almost nothing." Pause. "It's a gamble, but it's also a huge compliment to you." Her eyes narrow. "But it's the risk to your career and the damage it will do to the news division if we lose you that I take exception to. To say nothing," she adds, "of the monetary ramifications for the network if the show fails with you. You know how they keep trying to cut our budget as it is."

If the show fails with you. I can't shake that from my head. The whole thing is giving me a stomachache.

How an offer for a million-dollar job on national television can so quickly turn into a potential nightmare is beyond me. I didn't even get one day to enjoy it. "All right," I say, "so we've got points one, two, three, a little summary and some explanation. Anything else?"

"Yes, your agent's a son of a bitch," she says matter-of-factly. "He used to be mine years ago, but I fired him. But I understand he is your representative and so we will formally go to him to make a counteroffer."

My ears perk up and I feel a small glimmer of hope.

"You know the numbers in the news division better than almost anyone," Alexandra says, "so you know we can't compete with the entertainment division by offering you a million dollars." Pause. Eyes blazing blue. "But I can play to your talents, Sally, and I can play to your heart, because you are news—through and through, you know that—and I know how hard it will be for you to abandon your career."

She's playing you like a violin, I caution myself.

"You think fast on your feet, you move quickly, you write superbly, you have an excellent grasp of what we're trying to accomplish here and I'm not sure how it comes into play, exactly, but your personality seems to—" She searches for the words. "You get people going, Sally. Good, bad or indifferent, you get them off their duffs and you get them moving, which is something I've had trouble doing in the last two or three years. So yes, my brother was quite right—I *do* need you, but we *all* need you, Sally. You wrestle with the affiliates better than any of us. And you clearly have an ability to charm audiences. Now, in hard news, as you know, we've got to ratchet down that charm of yours and bring up the volume on facts and figures."

Where is she going with this?

"At this point, I can only offer you three hundred thousand for this next year."

My hopes are slipping.

"But I will give you a national newscast."

We look at each other in silence.

"One hour, early morning, six to seven, coast to coast. I want to try Emmett Phelps as your coanchor."

I blink. Emmett was the law professor who did the trial-recap program with me in L.A.

"It's essentially going to be an update of the nightly news, but because it is early morning, the newscast will be lighter and more personable than mine. You get top billing, of course."

When I guess I must have looked confused, Alexandra says, "And you have to know going into this, that the critics will hammer you in the beginning. With everything that happened at the trial, they'll give you some kind of nickname, or they'll—" She looks up at the ceiling for words. Finding them, she looks at me again. "They'll say something like, 'The last of The Flying Wallendas has somehow landed in the anchor chair at DBS News.'"

I laugh. She's right. They will.

"So that's what I am going to propose to Saul," she says. "He'll go absolutely ape and scream at me, so before I call him, I wanted to know if you're interested."

It's a fabulous idea. There would be very little updating on the stories from the night before (how much happens between

10:00 p.m. and 6:00 a.m.?), more on international because of the time difference, but the new deal with INS will take care of that, which means the production costs will essentially be a wash. After start-up costs, a news hour broadcasting before the Big Three roll out their 7:00 a.m. shows would essentially be a profit machine, a cost-effective vehicle to carry advertising.

"What are you, on drugs?" I ask her. "I'm sitting here having a heart attack. Of course I want to do it! Have you talked to Emmett?"

"After I finish talking to you. He's been offered a true-crime show on A&E, but he came to me first to see if there was anything he might be able to do with us."

"I just can't believe it," I say, bringing my hands up to the top of my head.

She's beaming over there.

I bring my hands down. "You're not expecting me to do this on top of what I already do for you, are you?"

"Absolutely not," she says, swinging her legs to the floor and standing up. "I'd expect you to be here by 4:00 a.m., go on the air at six, and then stay on until noon, by which time you will have gone over the preliminary rundown sheet for the evening news."

"But you know what will happen, don't you?" I ask, turning my chair back around to follow her as she moves back to her desk. "I'll end up being here all the time."

"You're getting a dressing room, so fine, you can sleep in there if you want," she says absently. She extracts a thick sheaf of papers from her briefcase and thunks it down on the desk in front of me. "Here. This is for your eyes only. Take it home with you tonight."

On the top page, it says:

DBS NEWS AMERICA THIS MORNING
with
SALLY HARRINGTON
and
EMMETT PHELPS

Looks good.

I start flipping through the pages. This is essentially a bible for the newscast, A-Z, who, what, when, where, and then fourteen pages of numbers: Budget, DBS News Current Fiscal, Advertising Projection, the studies on my and Emmett's TV-Q (mine's higher). There's no way a document like this could have materialized in such a short period of time. I realize that Alexandra must have been working on this for a while. "Who wrote this?"

"I just followed the format Cassy used for the nightly news," she replies, as if the effort was nothing.

There is absolutely no question in my mind whatsoever about this. I want to do this. Hell, Alexandra could slash my salary to fifty thousand and I'd do it. Five thousand and I'd do it. I'd pay her.

Anchor a national newscast. Mine.

There is a knock and Benjamin opens the door. "I'm sorry, Alexandra, but the line to see you is so long it's starting to look like auditions for *American Idol* out here."

Alexandra laughs and tells him it's okay, we're finished.

I stand up, clutching the proposal and Alexandra comes back around her desk to see me out. "You'll be in the morning and I'll be at night, the yin and yang of television news, how 'bout that?"

"Yeah, but *I* have to share the set," I point out.

"Sally," she deadpans, stopping to address me, "how could anyone *recognize* you without a man in the picture?"

CHAPTER TEN

There really wasn't much to consider; I knew I wanted to coanchor *DBS News America This Morning* with Emmett. I had the good sense, however, to keep quiet and work as I normally did through the nightly news and only afterward, at home, have I allowed myself to study Alexandra's lengthy proposal.

There is one burning question I have. I look at the clock, think it might be okay, she should still be up, and call Alexandra at home at one-thirty in the morning.

"Hello?" says a voice with the flourish of the United Kingdom.

"Hi, Georgiana, it's Sally," I say. "I'm sorry for calling so late, but I have a rather important question for Alexandra."

"Oh, I bet you do," the actress says knowingly. "Hold on, love. Alexandra?" I hear her call. "It's Sally. She's got a question for you.... Okay. Sally? She'll be right here. She's just getting out of the bath."

Bawth is the way Georgiana says it. Something exotic and special.

Alexandra picks up and seems pleased to hear from me. "So what's up?"

"I have a question," I say. I'm sitting up in my big round bed (I'm subletting, I tell you, I did not choose this bed), with the proposal in small piles around me. "How much of this proposal has Cassy seen?"

"None of it," she replies.

My heart sinks. "Does she even know about it?"

"She knows something is coming," Alexandra says. "By the way, I had a long talk with that jerk Saul tonight. He's going to talk to you tomorrow. I told him I needed an answer by eleven on Friday." Interesting. It's the same deadline that Cassy gave me.

"So what happens," I say, "if I accept your offer, and then Cassy and Langley nix the whole thing?"

"Then I guess neither one of us will be working there anymore. I'll go to another network and I'll take you with me."

I blink. "You'll *quit* if they don't go along with the proposal?"

"I certainly felt like quitting yesterday when Cassy told me what they were up to."

Huh.

"So I was angry." She clears her throat. "Anyway, in my contract I have guarantees about how much new programming I'm allowed to develop. And trust me, this is a project DBS will want us to do."

"The numbers certainly look good," I say.

"And we'll save them a lot more money by forcing them to go with Marianne West from the get-go."

It is only after I hang up with Alexandra that I realize she has been talking as if the deal had already been closed.

"Good heavens," Mother says when I call her with the headlines first thing in the morning. Then she is silent for a moment. "Good heavens," she suddenly says again, "my little girl." And then she laughs. "Darling heart, what is there to think about? Of course you should do it!"

"That's how I feel," I admit. "But the talk show—"

"Don't even give it a second thought. You love news, you always have. You were publishing a newspaper when you were nine years old, spilling everybody's secrets in the entire neighborhood—and getting paid to do it."

"It's not quite the same thing, Mother," I laugh.

"And it's obvious that she's had this in mind for you," she says. "That's what makes it so special. Alexandra's been planning this for you all along."

"I doubt if it was all along, Mother."

"And while I think the world of Cassy," she continues, "and you know that I do—who's to say that she really wants you to fill in for Jessica? As Alexandra said, she has an obligation to offer you the opportunity whether she wanted you to take it or not. And certainly she had to offer it to you if Jessica Wright herself picked you as her substitute."

When I don't say anything, Mother keeps going. "I don't know a lot about television, sweetheart, but I do know that when you were covering the trial in California, people loved you. And well they should have! You think well, you talk well, you look well, and you can handle anything anyone throws at you. And what could be better for television than that?"

There is a noise on her end of the telephone.

"Oh, Paul, good morning," Mother says. "Wow. You've got everything now." Pause. "Don't you look *won*derful. Oh, Sally, you really should see Paul in his uniform." A laugh. He's saying something. "Hold on, Sally, Paul would like to say hello." The phone gets transferred.

"Hi," he says brightly. "How goes it in the big bad city and what are you doing up so early?"

"Extremely well, as a matter of fact, I'm talking to my mother and just how good do you look in this uniform?"

"I'm hoping I'll soon receive your opinion in person," Paul says. Then a laugh. "In the meantime, know that it's good enough to have your mother and the dogs circling me."

I smile. I can imagine it perfectly.

"And guess what? I think I might have found an apartment. In North Haven."

"That's good for work, how far is it from Quinnipiac?"

"It's not too bad. It's off Route 22, which cuts over to Hamden. Do you know it?"

"Oh, yeah, I know it."

"It's another cop's house. It's a basement apartment with its own bath and entrance. The price is certainly right. Five hundred bucks a month."

"It sounds great, Paul." There's no way I can tell him I was offered a million dollars yesterday.

"And Buddy thinks things are cool here—"

I hear Mother say, "Very cool."

"So I was thinking of moving over there tomorrow. And Jack should be here on Saturday with my car and stuff."

I visualize Jack, Paul's old roommate, and smile. I can remember him standing in the kitchen with a towel around his waist, drinking milk out of a carton. Jack has some sort of money from somewhere, which means he doesn't work overly hard and plays a lot of sports.

"So my plan is to leave your car here tomorrow—"

"But you'll need it on Friday," I point out.

"I can get a ride to work."

"But you'll have a million errands to run and I'm not even

going to get out of work until after eleven. So just keep the Jeep, and I'll get a ride out with a DBS guy who goes up to Vermont on Fridays, and I'll pick it up. I've got another set of keys here. Just leave the car in the driveway."

"You're not even going to come in?"

"You will have had a very long day and a long week," I say. "And I wouldn't make it there until twelve-thirty, if I'm lucky. So just go to bed and I'll talk to you first thing Saturday."

"I could nap," he says suggestively.

I smile. "What are you going to sleep on, by the way?"

"Your mom's loaning me a sleeping bag. And a pillow and a couple of towels. Jack's bringing everything in the U-Haul." I can hear my mother saying something. "So really quick, Sally, tell me about this job offer."

Briefly I outline what happened at work, about the talk-show offer, and about Alexandra's offer, all without mentioning numbers.

"You'd be fantastic in either," he says.

"But one pays over three times the other," I explain.

"That's like saying IRS auditors make better money than police officers. What difference does it make when you know the kind of law enforcement you want to do?"

Good point.

"I'm assuming you want the newscast," he adds.

"Yes."

"And that's the one, of course, that pays less than a third of the other—right?"

"Yes."

"Come on, Sally, it's TV, you're still going to make more money than the rest of us could ever dream of, so go for what you love. Or you'll be miserable. Rich and miserable. Which is better than being poor and miserable, I suppose, but what is the point of all the years you've put into news already if not to take it to the next step?"

I smile. He gets it. Good for him. *Good for us.* There is a reason why I like him so much.

"I'll look forward to Friday. And if you're not up, Saturday."

"Me, too."

"Oh, and Paul, the job offer—"

"I'll keep it under my new hat," he promises.

He gives me his address and says he has to get moving and hands the phone back to Mother. I ask Mother about Scotty, how he's behaving, and in the middle of her answer she says, "Well, your young man just drove off. I must say, Sally, he is a *very* nice young man. And *very* attractive. I can see what you see in him."

"I'm glad, Mother."

"Still, darling, he is young and at a different stage in his life…"

I let Mother share her wisdom a bit before I get off. Then I sink back into the pillows of the big round bed knowing there is no way I'm going to be able to go back to sleep.

So I roll out of bed, make a pot of coffee, grab a container of yogurt from the refrigerator and sit down at the table with Alexandra's proposal, determined to read every word of it yet again.

When Saul Michaels reaches me at the office to hit the roof, I am forced to turn my headset way down and then to take it off altogether so I can hold the phone away from my ear.

Alexandra should never have talked to me! It's completely unethical! She's taking advantage! The offer is absolutely unacceptable! This is an outrage!

So then I take a turn at hitting the roof, saying that Alexandra is my boss and she was discussing a promotion and who the hell else should she talk to first to find out if I'm interested? "So go down the hall, Saul, and tell your guys, sorry, but we have to offer up Marianne West to DBS the first time around."

At this, there is a grunt. "What did you say?"

"I said you'll have to offer Marianne West the first time around. I know it won't be nearly as lucrative as if I bomb out in the job first, but it still will be a big step up for her. Get her on TV, anyway."

Silence. "What are you talking about?"

"I'm talking about the fact I don't want to substitute for Jessica. I want to do the newscast. So your agency should proceed with Marianne West and I want you to seal my deal with DBS News."

A sigh. "Unbelievable. You're going to walk away from a prime-time vehicle and a million dollars to start."

"I'm taking my career in journalism to the next step," I tell him. "The opportunity's awesome, I want it."

I have a pretty good idea what he's thinking. *They come crawling in the beginning, begging for my help, and at the first sign of success, it's the YOU work for ME crap, as if they ever could have gotten this far without me.*

I rattle off to Saul some odds and ends I would like in the contract: a full-time assistant, clothing allowance for the newscast, a car to and from work each day, at least one story a month for *DBS News Magazine.* Also, a fence and remote-control gate at my mother's house in Castleford.

"What, no flea powder for the dog?" Saul growls. "Look, appearing on the newsmagazine is *extra.* You should be compensated for it."

"They—*we*—don't have the money. You can ask, but don't push it," I tell him.

He makes a sound of disgust. "You haven't given me jack-shit to work with here. And let me tell you, Her Highness is a royal pain in the ass to deal with."

"And as soon as we have a deal in principle," I tell him, "I want you to call Cassy and formally decline her offer. They need to get moving on Marianne."

"Why do you keep *saying* that?" he demands.

I answer a question with the question. "Well, what client *would* you have offered after I failed as Jessica's substitute?"

"This is stupid," he says.

"Yeah, well, whatever—just make a deal with Alexandra for the newscast." And I hang up on him.

CHAPTER ELEVEN

I do my work as usual on Wednesday, waiting for some word from somebody that Saul and Alexandra have talked. Or Cassy and Saul have talked. Or anybody has talked to anybody. It is not until almost seven-thirty, when I'm down in the newsroom going over some stuff with our new guy, Hadyn, that I'm called to the phone. I snap up the wall phone. "Sally Harrington."

"No to the fence and gate," Saul's voice says, "but DBS will provide you with an overall security plan and get you a discount on the fence and the gate and the installation by placing the order through them. Yes to the car—coming and going from work, including out-of-state if that is where you are staying. Yes to at least one story on *DBS News Magazine* each month, and generous woman the high priestess is, she'll kick you ten thousand for each appearance, zero on rerun, fifty bucks each run in syndication. No on the full-time assistant, but she'll give you someone twenty-four hours a week, plus an intern."

That stinks. I need a real assistant, somebody who knows something.

"There's a hiring freeze," he adds, "and even the high

priestess can't add any personnel at more than twenty-four hours a week."

"They just added a full-time producer," I say, looking across the newsroom at Hadyn.

A bitter laugh. "She said you'd say that—and when you did I was to tell you he is the reinvention of the sales rep who retired."

Yeah, I guess that's right. The freeze is for any new personnel requiring benefits, which at DBS is anyone over twenty-four hours. "All right, what else?"

"I got you the clothing allowance, and I got you first-class airfares, a so-so expense account, and let's see..." He sucks his breath in through his teeth and I imagine him scanning his notes. "Oh, the car service includes the dog, by the way."

I smile, starting to feel enormously happy. I can't believe this. I take a breath, my stomach starting to flip-flop as I look around the newsroom and visualize myself in here before the morning newscast. *My* newscast. *DBS News America This Morning with Sally Harrington and Emmett Phelps.*

"So let's do it," I tell him, watching one of the writers as he absently touches his stomach. *Great, another ulcer in the newsroom.*

"I'll make the call," he promises. "And then I will find Cassy and tell her no to *The Jessica Wright Show* and yes to the newscast proposal."

"Good." Pause. "Listen, Saul, thank you. I know it's not what you would choose to do."

"Sally—"

"Yes?"

"Congratulations."

Slightly begrudging, but at least he said it. I get off. Twenty minutes later one of the gaffers comes cruising through the newsroom. "Sal, you're needed in Alec Aldridge's office, stat. Underline *stat*."

I frown. Alec's the head of publicity. "But I've got things to do here," I say, holding up the mess that is currently our special report on alien registration in the United States.

The gaffer throws his hands up. "You gotta get there, that's the word. Go, go, go."

I take the alien-registration mess with me and two minutes later I'm knocking on Alec's office door. His office is a square room decorated with piles of newspapers, magazines, videos, CDs, DVDs and posters. Alec is young, very bright, very gay and completely overwhelmed by trying to orchestrate publicity for the broadcasting group. Publicity, you see, means free advertising. He talks as though he's on speed, but isn't, and is known to continue moving after all other mere mortals have collapsed and died.

"Thanks for coming up, have a seat, Sally-oh-Sally-oh-Sally-oh," he sings cheerfully, picking a pile of magazines off a chair and dropping them on the floor. As I take the chair, he swivels his designer-covered derriere around many obstacles to reach his desk chair. Today's outfit consists of black slacks, red shirt, silver tie and silver belt. "So congratu*laaa*tions, go-go girl," he says, folding his hands on his desk and blowing his light brown bangs out of his eyes. He offers a full smile, revealing orthodontically perfect teeth.

"Thank you."

"So I'm to have you everywhere yesterday," he says, blowing at his bangs again. "Queen Alexandra speaks, you know how that goes."

"Yes, I do."

"So, go-go girl, we must zero in on magazines this very second. It's a four-month lead time, you know, and this show's supposed to go on—"

"Newscast," I say.

"Yeah," he says a bit breathlessly, shaking his head up and down in high-spirited agreement, "newscast." Then he reaches his hands out, fingers extended, to rest his palms on top of his desk, as if to keep the desk from floating away. He takes a deep breath and lets it out slowly, ballooning his cheeks as he does so. "*Good Housekeeping* owes us. We can probably get a fashion shoot in *Harper's Bazaar*."

I must have made a terrible face, because he says, "Oh, you'll be fine, go-go girl. We just get you there and they'll slap some gorgeous rags on you and everybody will see how beautiful you are." He closes one eye, as if looking at me through a telescope. "You look gre*aaa*t," he confides, opening both eyes.

"Thanks."

Alec throws himself back in his chair. "The big enchilada that everybody's afraid to talk to you about is *Expectations* magazine." He winces, closing one eye to look at me again. "I know you hate them, but they want to do you. And to be honest, we need them." He scoots his chair closer to his desk. "They want to send a writer out this weekend. To Castleford. To spend the day with you."

I am blinking rapidly, trying to understand this. "We only made the deal a half hour ago."

"You know how Alexandra is," he reminds me, drawing a pad of paper toward him and picking up the pen that is lying on it. "She's foaming at the bit."

I laugh at the mixed metaphor and Alec looks up, startled. "Oh, well, you know what I mean." He reaches ahead to flip pages on his calendar. "Do you think you could do it on Sunday? Say, nine o'clock?"

I am at a loss. It's not that I hate *Expectations* magazine, it's the fact that the publisher, Verity Rhodes, loathes and despises me that is somewhat troubling. I wrote the profile of Cassy Cochran, which ultimately brought me to DBS News, for Verity. We didn't, shall we say, agree on slanting the piece in a certain direction; Verity tried to intimidate me into doing it and I was forced to do an end run around her. And then there is the minor matter of a bedmate we shared, but that's another story.

I try to think about this weekend and all I can remember is Paul. But then I remember I wanted to run over to Hillstone Falls to register in person with that flaky town clerk and check out Uncle Percy's letter. "Sunday is actually better for me."

"It's going to be Roderick Reynolds," he says, writing something on a sticky.

"I've never heard of him."

"Nor have I, but who cares as long as we make you a household name?" He rips off the sticky and offers it to me. "Here's his number. I'll e-mail you the details to remind you."

"It's going to be a disaster, you know," I say seriously.

"What is?" He looks like a disappointed child.

"The *Expectations* piece. You know Verity's going to do a hatchet job on me. But if you think that's going to help people place their faith and trust in me as a news anchor, then okay."

"Oh, go-go," he says, waving my comment off, "Alexandra talked to Verity herself, everything's set. Everything's fine. Nobody's going to slam you, baby." He scrunches up his shoulders. "You're too irresistible."

Alexandra talked to Verity? Huh. So this is that day hell freezes over.

Alec cocks his head slightly, looking concerned. "So you'll do it, right?"

I nod. "If Alexandra wants me to, of course I will."

"Cool," he says, writing something down. "In the meantime I'll get started on *Good Housekeeping, Harper's,* and maybe we can do something with *Cosmo,* you never know. You're single, that helps." He makes another note and then throws down the pen. "Okay! We're done!"

When I return to the newsroom, I immediately sense a change. The rather listing advancement toward airtime that I've become accustomed to lately has given way to the decided hum of smooth operation. I discover the reason why: Will Rafferty is here. We talk for a minute—Jessica is stabilized—I tell him how glad I am, and how glad I am to see him, and then we hustle off our separate ways to pull the final elements of the newscast together. When I swing into makeup to hand Alexandra her final rundown sheet, she thanks me, as she always does, but then quickly turns her attention back to Cleo, who is finishing her eyes.

I'm puzzled. I was expecting a smile, a wink, some acknowledgment of what has come to pass. But nothing. Or was I supposed to say something first?

The newscast goes fairly well, although we lost a live feed from Seoul and didn't have a clue what went wrong. At first, when the image went snowy and then altogether black, we feared the worse, that something bad had happened to the reporter and cameraman, but then the reporter called in the rest of his report, which we patched through to Alexandra and over the air, so we knew it was some kind of equipment failure.

The rest of the newscast is uneventful, but after we wrap, Will and I head to engineering to talk with the Nerd Brigade. It takes until nearly eleven-thirty, but they finally figure out what happened: the problem was not with the transmission from Korea, or with the Darenbrook satellite, but with a receiving dish on the roof of Darenbrook I. Water had somehow gotten into it, froze and then exploded a receptor element while we were on the air.

That problem solved, Will asks me if I will have a cup of coffee with him in the cafeteria and bring him up to speed on what's transpired in his absence. I am so tired at this point, I can think of nothing worse. I feel sure he's going to want to talk about me substituting on his wife's show and— Ach! Not tonight!

"Sure," I say and then we set off. I tell him my initial take on Hadyn—which is good—and by the time we are riding up the elevator I'm running through my mental checklist of everything that went wrong in his absence and how we addressed the problems.

"You have no idea how much I appreciate the hours you've been putting in to cover for me," Will says as we approach the cafeteria. "There's no way I could have taken the time unless you were here. Jessica and I really appreciate it. Not just now, but, you know, before, too."

He's referring to their miscarriage last year, which devastated them.

"We're all just saying our prayers," I tell him, giving his hand a quick squeeze and releasing it.

Since I am the only DBS News employee who reports directly to Alexandra and not to Will, we have had some rather tenuous moments between us. Alexandra has a habit of suddenly yanking me from daily operations for a special project, you see, an action that always leaves Will scrambling, and since nobody likes to get mad at Alexandra, Will and everybody else gets mad at me. (Don't worry, it's okay; that's what I was hired for.) But we like each other and we respect each other.

I wonder how he's going to take my refusal to substitute for his wife, though.

"That's weird," I say as we approach the cafeteria. "I've never seen those doors closed before."

"They shouldn't be," Will says, reaching ahead to pull one open.

Almost everyone from the news division is in the cafeteria, standing around eating off platters and sipping from plastic cups, scarcely noticing our entrance. When I see Alexandra and Cassy and Langley standing together, I wonder if maybe this is a little party for Will. But then I see Jackson Darenbrook walking toward us with my fair-haired and mild-mannered law professor colleague from the West Coast, Emmett Phelps.

And then I know. It is a surprise party for us.

"Congratulations, Sally," Will says in my ear.

I look at him. "When did you—?"

"I've won five bucks from my wife," he says. "I told her you wouldn't leave us in the lurch." He grins and kisses my cheek. "It's going to be great."

I can feel myself beaming.

"Creepin' crickets, the kid's a star," Jackson Darenbrook cries, picking me up like a rag doll and hugging me. Jackson is a dashing kind of Southern gentleman, once a distraught widower turned playboy, but now the decidedly well-grounded, albeit eccentric, husband. Over his shoulder I can see that Alexandra and Cassy are laughing.

When Jackson puts me down again, Langley is there, shaking my hand and putting his other on top of mine. "I admit it, Sally, I wanted you in the entertainment division. But I've also got to admit, I'm very, very glad you decided to stick with the news division. It's a tremendous boost for morale and this newscast sounds super."

I know what sounds super to Langley—the numbers. Low overhead, recycled material and lots of advertising slots.

"Thank you, Langley. I'm going to try to do a really good job for you."

"And I'm sure you will."

Langley steps aside to clear the way to Cassy, who is feigning that she is about to drop. "Quite a day," she says, smiling.

"She was in bed, you know, when the call came," Jackson pipes up. "Got dressed and everything to come down."

Cassy rolls her eyes at her husband's indiscretion, but I can plainly see how tired she is. Even her hair looks tired, seriously starting to slip from her barrette. "I'm very proud of you," she says quietly, giving me a brief hug and then stepping back to hold my arms. She seems to want to say something else, but closes her mouth, gives my arms another squeeze and steps aside to make room for Emmett.

"Hey!" I say, hugging him.

"Who knew?" he says, hugging me back.

Certainly neither one of us saw this coming.

"Here," Alexandra says, handing me a fluted glass of champagne. She slips off her shoes and steps up to stand on a chair.

"See?" Will says to me and Emmett. "This is star treatment. You get a real glass while everyone else gets plastic."

Meanwhile, nobody is paying much attention to Alexandra up on the chair. "You may have taken a little too long," she says, looking down at Will. "They're all half in the bag."

I smile. Free booze will do it every time with this crowd.

Jackson Darenbrook raises his hand to his mouth and lets out an ear-shattering whistle that stops everyone in their tracks.

"I think all of you know," Alexandra begins, "how terribly, terribly proud I am of everything we have accomplished in such a relatively short period of time. And it is with heartfelt gratitude to you—and to the *suits*—"

There are some hoots at her reference to corporate management.

"That we are, this spring, once again expanding the hours that DBS News is on the air."

"Yippee," a dull voice says somewhere in the back. "More work, just what we wanted." Laughter.

"But when have you ever known the news to stop?" Alexandra asks the crowd.

"When the president of the United States decides to take a nap," Will says. More laughter.

"Ladies and gentlemen, my friends, I wish to make a toast." Alexandra raises her glass high. "To Sally Harrington and Emmett Phelps, may you be the happy and healthy faces of thousands of newscasts."

"Hear! Hear!" Jackson cries.

As I've explained before, not everybody in the news division is overly fond of me, but everyone does come over to congratulate me and Emmett. Regardless of how irritated they may be at my admittedly spectacular climb at DBS News, they know another newscast means more revenue, which brings with it the possibility of raises, promotions and bonuses.

Another glass of champagne is pressed upon me; I am handed a cracker with cream cheese and caviar on it. While one of our camera guys is telling me how he thinks I should be lit on the set, I see David Waring edging over and talking to Will. I find myself making excuses to leave the cameraman and walk over to him.

"I took your advice," I tell him.

"Advice?" David says. "It was a plea." He looks at Will. "Alexandra went absolutely off the wall when she found out they were making Sally an offer."

"So, older brother, here, blurts out over lunch he knew about it before I did," I add.

David points a thumb at me. "And she walked out on me."

Will laughs, looking at me. "You did?"

"Yes, I did."

"That's our Sally," Will says, raising his glass in salute and moving away.

"So congratulations," David says, clinking his Amstel Light bottle with my champagne glass. We both take a sip. "You excited?"

"Thrilled," I admit. "Everything's happened so fast, though, it's hard to take it all in."

"That's the way it happens, isn't it?"

His eyes are warm and inviting and for a moment I wonder if he's talking about something else. I shake off the thought, turning away slightly. "I can't believe they got this party together," I say, scanning the room. "It's very sweet."

"My sister's *very* happy."

I smile into my glass, sipping again.

"Generally speaking," David says, "I find there is no such thing as overnight success—only overnight recognition. And in this case I think it's very well deserved."

I glance at him. "I've done nothing compared to your sister."

"Alexandra never moved back home to care for our mother when she was sick."

Jarred, I look at him.

"Alexandra told me about that." Pause. "She seems to think it's indicative of your character. It's a kind of loyalty she highly values." Pause. "I do, too. And I appreciate what you did for Lexy when she was sick."

I turn away again because I feel uncomfortable. Nervous. Hideously aware of what looking into David Waring's eyes is doing to me. "It wasn't hard. I wanted to do it."

We just stand there awhile, watching people. Finally he says, "I should let you get back to your friends."

"What I should do is go home and go to bed. I'm about ready to drop."

"Cassy and Jackson are leaving," he points out. "Maybe you can use them to get out of here." He nods toward our technical crew guffawing in the corner. "The diehards might be here awhile."

"Free food and drink gets them every time," I say. I turn around suddenly and hear myself ask, "Are you going to be here tomorrow?"

"As a matter of fact I am." He smiles, ducking his head slightly. "You wouldn't happen to want to let me buy you lunch, would you? Or dinner? Or whatever kind of meal it is people who keep vampire hours eat?"

"Sure," I say, trying to make it sound casual. "Lunch."

"One o'clock?"

"Twelve would be better," I tell him.

"I'll pick you up at your office." He smiles.

I smile.

Alexandra appears at my side. "Let's take some of this food down to the newsroom."

"We'd better put it in the conference room or they'll drop kaiser roll crumbs in the keyboards," I say.

We walk over to the tables and combine a couple of platters of food to take downstairs. Will comes over to heft a couple cases of Snapple.

As we walk out, I turn to look back.

Yes, David Waring is watching me. Our eyes meet and he smiles.

Don't be a fool, I think, turning away.

But somehow this feels as though it could be something different.

CHAPTER TWELVE

Yesterday flew by, but today, Friday, has gone on forever. Our audio director, as I hoped, was going up to Vermont tonight after the newscast, so I hitched a ride with him to Connecticut. Any hope of making good time by leaving Manhattan after eleven at night, however, has gone up in smoke—or, as it happens, stretched sideways across the road in front of us.

Where the Hutchinson Parkway swings east toward Connecticut, where 287 peels off to the north, there is long, narrow curve with an inside concrete wall that even in daylight and good weather is worth slowing down for. As we took the right-hand lane into the curve, nervously aware that daytime melting was starting to refreeze as black ice, a Chevy flew past us and started to slide. The back end of the car swung into the wall first, bounced off, the front end hitting next, and then the whole car spun around, finally coming to a stop across both lanes.

We were maybe twenty feet from the car by the time we could stop. "Say a prayer, Sal," Joe said then, looking in the rearview mirror at the next car coming around the curve. That car, too, thank God, was able to stop in time, although it had to slide into the left lane beside us to do it. The next two cars were able to stop, so then we were reasonably safe. While Joe called 911 and fumbled around for his emergency road kit, looking for flares, I got out—nearly falling on the ice—and half walked, half slid up to the Chevy.

The windshield was still in place, but both driver-side windows were blown out and the doors smashed in. Amazingly, the driver was okay. He was maybe sixteen or seventeen and his younger sister, if you can believe, had been napping in the back seat with no seat belt on. And yet she seemed relatively unharmed, although covered in shattered safety glass. It was cold, but since there was no smell of gas or sign of smoke, I encouraged them to stay where they were until a medic arrived, and then I stood by the smashed-in side of the car to make sure they did.

Joe finally found his stupid flares, but by then the cars had backed up all the way around the curve out of sight. A state trooper arrived, and not long after, an ambulance from Rye.

So here we are, just sitting now, the Chevy stretched across the Hutch, and the emergency vehicles on the shoulder. We are unable to go forward and we can't back up against the ten million cars that are jammed behind us. So we watch, and time passes—midnight, twelve-thirty—a tow truck arrives at five to one, pulls the car away at one o'clock, but now we have to wait for highway workers to sand the oil and ice on the road. It is one-fifteen before we get moving.

We follow the directions I printed out from MapQuest, although based on Paul's description, I have a very good idea where the house is. We exit the Merritt at North Haven, Route 22, take a right, cross three lights—passing over Route 5— and take our first left on Basil Drive, looking for the third house on the right, a gray split-level.

"There's the Jeep," I say, checking my watch—2:32 a.m. No wonder there aren't any lights on in the house. Someone left the garage light on, though, so the area is well lit. Joe waits as I unlock the Jeep door, climb in and start it, and then he takes off. As I wait for the engine to warm a bit, I notice the back seat is down and I think, of course, Paul's been moving stuff, but he's left something—I turn around to get a better look, see something moving and in two seconds, I kid you not, I am out of that car and backing up to the house.

"It's me, it's me," a voice says. The back door opens. "Sally, I'm sorry. I didn't mean to scare you."

"Paul," I gasp, slapping my hand to my chest.

"You didn't come and you didn't come," he says, stumbling a little, finally kicking a blanket off his foot. "I didn't want to miss you."

Tentatively I walk toward him. "You scared me to death," I scold him.

"Sorry," he whispers, sliding the puffy sleeves of the down jacket I gave him around me, hugging me close. "I was so sleepy and I didn't want to miss you, so I thought—"

"You'd freeze to death," I say, my heart still pounding. I pull back slightly. "You're nuts. Don't you people from California understand about cold?"

"I know you've got good reflexes, girl," he says approvingly, kissing me on the mouth. "You were out of the car and halfway to Castleford."

"Don't let your assailant get you into the car," I recite from our security classes at DBS.

"Do you want to come in for a minute?" he asks, shivering suddenly. "See the place? It's not much but—"

"I'd love to see it." I follow Paul around the side of the house to the back, where he unlocks a door, reaches in to flick on a light and then holds the door open for me.

Blinking against the light, I have to laugh. It is definitely battle conditions in here, no luxuries like furniture allowed.

It is a large oblong room, clearly a finished basement, with two open suitcases on the floor, and in the corner, a sink, small refrigerator, hot plate, a standing cabinet, and that's it. "This is a nice space," I say, walking in and turning around.

"Sixteen by twenty."

"And, look, a fireplace," I say, pointing to what looks like an upside-down metal funnel in the corner. "Does it work?"

"Yep," he says.

"And you have a nice wood floor," I notice under our feet.

"With a cold, cold slab of concrete underneath it," he adds.

It's not bad. For five hundred dollars in a nice residential neighborhood, it's excellent. There are two windows, and no sign of damp or mold. "And you can make something to eat," I point out.

He laughs. "Make 'something' is right. I've decided to call it the snack bar."

"Don't be like that," I protest, walking across the room. "You've got what you need. Refrigerator, two-burner hot plate, good, large sink, and even this counter thing." I turn around. "Was that your microwave in your kitchen in California?"

"Yep."

"So you'll have that," I continue.

"Come see in here," he says, encouraged now, waving me over to the open doorway. He flicks on another light. Inside is a smaller area, maybe ten by ten, but which has clean light green wall-to-wall carpeting. A sleeping bag and pillow are in the middle of the floor. Another one is rolled up in the corner. "In case I have guests, your mother said," he laughs, pointing to it.

I walk over to open a door on the other side of the room. Inside are a sink, john and shower. Tiny but will do the job. I smile, recognizing the towels. "This is great, so you have your own bathroom."

"Shower room, you mean."

I open the last door. A closet the size of a phone booth. I close this and turn around, considering. "So you'll put your bed…?"

"I thought this way, with the headboard there."

"That would look nice."

"No windows in here, though."

"I bet you sleep better."

"I think I'm going to have to put my dresser in the other room," Paul says, leading me back in there. "And then I've got a couch. Which pulls out into another bed."

"Which you could put along that far wall," I suggest. I move over to the short wall next to the fireplace. "That easy chair and ottoman from your bedroom could go here." I pass the fireplace. "Put your TV here. Or maybe on the other side of the door." I think a moment and then turn around. "You need to have a dedicated study space, though."

"I need to get a desk or something," he agrees.

Immediately I think of one of those armoires that open out as a mini office, with space for computer, monitor and printer, and a pull-down desk for writing and studying. "Please let me give you a house present," I say, excited by the idea. It could go right in that corner. It could close up if he needs the space and when he's using it, it will almost be like a separate study.

He smiles. Then he walks over, takes my hands and simply holds them. "Thank you, but you don't have to."

"I want so much to," I tell him. "I'd like to think I can do something that might help you in some small way. It's not easy, what you've set out to do."

He lets go of my hands, sliding his hands inside my coat and around my waist, knitting them together in the small of my back. "You're absolutely beautiful, you know that?" He kisses me.

I know I shouldn't have let the other night happen, because now Paul has every reason to expect the same thing now. Paul is a young man who enjoys an active sex life, I know, so either I'm going to have to get on the same wavelength pretty quick, or be prepared for him to take his sexual energies elsewhere until we get to know each other better and see where this is going.

But how do you go backward? How do you have sex and then start dating?

He is holding me, his breath warm on my neck. I can also feel him against me below, waiting. But he says, "Your mother said I could cut some dead wood at her place and split it for the fireplace." He leans back to look at me, his lower body not moving even a fraction. In fact, I think he is pressing slightly harder as he looks into my eyes.

"That's great," I say.

"It would take the chill out of here."

"And it would be lovely."

"You're lovely," he murmurs. And then he inhales sharply, kicking his head back slightly. "But I don't want to push anything on you and I get the feeling I might be."

I don't say anything because I'm trying to figure out what, exactly, I want to do. I have, to be honest, a great weakness for simply getting right down to things while fully dressed like this. That's how the other night happened. If I think about things too long, I can never do anything. And if even for a moment I imagine us making love right now, the pull to do so is unbelievably strong.

"I am awfully tired," I say. I feel him recoil slightly and I feel bad. Or disappointed, because I know my body has already started to disagree with me. I have been fighting thoughts of a certain kind for over twenty-four hours, and I'm not sure what to do about them now, or if there is any reason to worry about not doing anything at all.

You see, David Waring and I took a cab to Michael's yesterday, a terrific midtown restaurant where I can usually get a good table because of Alexandra's patronage. They like famous people in Michael's and I couldn't help but wonder, after the maître d' had seated us, how long it would be before Michael's knew that I had gone from periodically infamous to genuinely famous.

I'm still not sure why I agreed to have lunch with David. I mean, obviously I like him, and he is Alexandra's brother, but it's not as if anything can come from this, either personally or professionally. We live in worlds apart.

We talked for a while about his law practice. Rather, he told me all about it, to the point where even he wondered out loud how I could possibly still be interested in what he was saying. I only smiled, remarking it was refreshing to listen to someone who loved his work. He asked me a few questions about my career and I told him about it.

It was easy to talk with David. It was fun to talk with him. It was fun to be with him, talking easily, laughing, looking at each other and then carefully making sure to look away at the right intervals.

Because I didn't want to look away and I sensed he didn't either.

By the middle of lunch, I knew the sense of connection I felt was mutual. David did most of the talking, telling me about his personal interests: flying (he, like Alexandra, has flown since he was fourteen), week-long trail rides, skiing, tennis, golf and trapshooting.

From this I gathered he did very well financially.

To put the brakes on where I felt we were heading, though,

I asked him about his children. And while he talked about his twenty-year-old son, Kyle, at Duke, and sixteen-year-old daughter, Tory, at Choate-Rosemary Hall, I studied David's face, its lines, eyes and mouth, and I thought about Paul being twenty-five, and about David being forty-four, and that David was, in fact, old enough to be Paul's father.

But not old enough to be mine.

I drank some water then, trying to ignore a new feeling I felt stirring.

I felt scared.

David's beeper went off and he excused himself to make a call. I watched him confidently cross the restaurant and noticed that other people watched him, too, trying to figure out who he was. He's got that kind of commanding self-possession.

While he was gone, I dropped my fork again and drank more water, trying to figure out what was going on with me. What was going on, period.

He was probably just looking for a roll in the hay while he was away from home, I decided. Certainly it was possible he knew enough about me to consider me a likely volunteer, and thought I was probably a discreet one, considering my relationship with his sister.

Yeah, I thought, sighing to myself. *What else could he want? What else could he be after? My scintillating MIND?*

When David returned to the table, I was pleased that after glancing over his body on his journey back, I didn't feel anything in particular. Sexually, I mean. But then when he sat down, put his napkin back in his lap and focused his blue-gray eyes on me, I felt this slightly hollow feeling in my stomach. Butterflies.

Fear.

"Penny for your thoughts," David said, glancing across the table as he picked up his fork.

"I was wondering about your wife," I said.

He paused, slowly put his fork down and looked at me, turning his head slightly to the side. "What do you want to know?"

"What is she like?"

"Pretty, very smart—a Smithie—a great mother, good athlete, active, interested in many things." He narrowed his eyes slightly. "Why?"

His eyes didn't waver as he waited for the answer. This entire exchange should have been telling me something, but I didn't know what. Either he had no intention of hitting on me, or he was simply pretending lunches like this are normal for him, that he always takes out single women and gazes meaningfully across the table for no reason at all.

Oh, hell, I thought, *I'm imagining the whole thing.* "I just wondered," I said, shrugging, reaching for my water glass.

"And what is your boyfriend like?"

Now it was my turn to look across the table. "What makes you think I have a boyfriend?" I say before sipping.

"A woman like you can pretty much have whoever she wants."

I nearly choked on my water, spilling some down my chin. *"Hardly,"* I say, laughing.

He watched me as I wiped my mouth, and his eyes, I noticed, lingered on my mouth long after my napkin was taken away.

I averted my eyes, but at that point I couldn't even make a pretense of trying to eat. I felt sort of sick.

"So what is he like?" he persisted.

He wasn't, I noticed, eating either.

"Well, I think I told you he's starting law school," I say. "A second career," I add.

David nodded slightly.

The conversation just sort of died at that point. Our dishes were removed, and we were asked if we wanted coffee. He looked to me and I said I was sorry, but I needed to get back to West End. We rambled on about something—the Middle East?—until David paid the check, we got our coats and went outside. The icy blasts of cold air helped to clear my head and stopped the burning in my cheeks.

I felt so strange. Like I had been broadsided by something very big. David flagged a cab and as we rode back to West End, I felt the space was too small, too intimate. I needed to get out of here. I think we talked about Mayor Bloomberg.

When we reached West End we signed in at the security desk and he came up with me to see his sister. There were some newspeople in the elevator and I smiled and said hello, feeling David's eyes on me, and I realized how much I wanted his eyes on me, but I also wanted this feeling to stop. Like I needed to say or do something before—

Before—

I didn't know what.

But I told myself to just *stop* it. *Stop thinking about it. You don't flirt with married men, you never have, and you will not start now, or ever. It's wrong. Absolutely wrong.*

By the time we walked down the hall of Darenbrook III and saw Alexandra outside her office, I was feeling somewhat better.

"So where did you guys go?" Alexandra asked us.

"Michael's," David answered.

"I love that place," she said.

"It was very good," he said.

"Well," I said, turning to David, "thank you for lunch. I've got to get a move on."

"Yes, you do," Alexandra said. "I left the nightmare that's supposed to be breaking news from Washington on your desk."

So I walked to my office, turning back around to call,

"Thanks again," and as I was turning back around, I suddenly had this panicky thought that I might never see him again. But I forced myself to continue into my office, hang up my coat and sit down behind my desk. I picked up the notes on the Washington story—and stared at the pages but saw nothing.

I was thinking about what we had talked about at lunch, about certain parts of our conversation and then I started to feel strange again. Anxious. I looked at my hand and couldn't believe it; there was actually a tremor in it. So I lowered my hand to the edge of my desk to steady it and sat there awhile.

When David appeared in my doorway, at first it didn't register. It was as though I saw him through a haze. "I don't mean to interrupt," he said, coming in. I noticed how becoming the navy blue overcoat was on him, and that the gray scarf around his neck looked very soft. He walked right up to my desk to stand before me. "I'm sorry if I made you feel uncomfortable."

"You didn't," I told him.

He bit his lower lip a moment and then said, "I'm not—" Then he dropped his eyes, hesitated, and brought his face back up. He offered a small smile, said, "Thank you for coming with me to lunch," and walked out of my office.

I heard and saw nothing of David today, but he was very much on my mind—and that's why I don't know how to respond to Paul.

Paul has released me and is walking me toward the door. "You should get a start before you get too sleepy to drive."

I don't move.

He opens the door and looks around for me. He turns around, sees my expression and closes the door. "What's wrong?"

"I'm tired, but I don't really want to go."

He comes over and takes my hand. "Come on. It's better that you do." He kisses my hand and leads me outside. "I've got a big day tomorrow. Did I tell you? Jack was in Pittsburgh this afternoon. He's actually going to be here when he said."

"It will be nice to get all your things."

"And my car."

We walk up to the Jeep. "So tomorrow night…" I begin, opening the Jeep's door, the dome light coming on.

"I don't know," he says. "Let me find Jack and then we'll take it from there." He helps me up into the Jeep, as if I need it. "I definitely want to see you. Have dinner. Whatever."

"You can't just ditch Jack after he's driven your stuff three thousand miles across the country."

He's squinting against the dome light. I reach up to shut it off.

"Thanks," he says, moving closer, shivering slightly and holding my hands in my lap.

"Let me start the car so you can get warm."

"No, don't," he says.

"Why on earth not?" I ask. In the light from the garage, I can see the earnest look on his face.

"I don't know," he says. "Just please, don't." And then he gently lays the side of his face on my lap, still holding my hands. We stay like that for a while, quiet, our breath making clouds in the cold.

Then Paul clears his throat, raises his head and brings my hands up to his mouth to kiss. "I'm so glad I'm here," he says quietly, lowering our hands. "I'm so glad we found each other."

It is my turn to kiss him and I do. There is an awkward moment when David appears in my mind, but I push him out and concentrate on the wonderful young man right here.

My guy. Paul Fitzwilliam.

The kiss has deepened and his left hand has slid inside my coat.

I am starting to waver, particularly as I feel his hand brush gently over my breasts. He pulls away from my mouth, whispering that I need to go.

I take a breath, murmuring I am the best judge of what I need, and what I need right now is him.

As we twist around a bit, his hands quickly work inside my coat, and we're kissing again and I'm half falling out of the seat, but I don't care. His hand has moved downward and I tense, waiting, wanting, *willing* him to touch me there.

This is crazy, I think. *We're in the driveway.*

"You have to go," he mumbles in my ear, touching me.

"Let's go inside," I say, breathing heavily.

"No, you have to go," he teases in a whisper, his hand sliding between my legs; I close my eyes, groaning softly. He continues and it feels *so* good, and I know I'm losing any will whatsoever to behave. Ever. *Ever,* if it feels like this.

My head falls back against the headrest and I groan again, my legs tensing.

"Did you say you were on the Pill?" he whispers.

I make a sound of acknowledgment, yes, but I've involuntarily begun to move against his hand. I feel his body jerk a little; I hear the sound of his parka rustling, and then the jingle of his belt buckle.

"Here?" I say, my eyes opening, but he fondles my concern away, making me groan again. When I feel his hand withdraw, I feel like screaming at him not to take it away—is he crazy?—but he has me pulled sideways in the seat and he moves in between my legs, pushing up my skirt and yanking off my underpants. Then he pulls me off the seat, catching my derriere in his hands, and I wrap my legs around him, seeing my high heels behind him and thinking this is—

Oh my God.

II

Attention of a Different Sort

CHAPTER THIRTEEN

"I'm leaving in about a half hour, Uncle Percy," I say over the telephone, pouring myself another cup of coffee. It is a beautiful Saturday morning and while I have only had a little over four hours' sleep, the sunshine that is flooding through the bay window of my kitchen is most definitely of the inspirational variety. "Are you absolutely sure you don't want to come? It's a beautiful drive, even in January."

"I'm old enough to have learned by now, Sally," he says, "that if I'm feeling a little off, it's best I stick close to home and take it easy."

"All right, I just wanted to make sure." I stifle a yawn. "I'll call you as soon as I find out something."

The doorbell rings and inwardly I groan, wondering if I can just pretend I'm not home. But if someone is all the way out here at the cottage, either they know me well or someone is dreadfully lost.

Aye yie-yie.

I get off the phone with Uncle Percy and walk to the front door, wishing Scotty was here because not only would I have received early warning, but the nature of his bark might have given me a hint of how well we know whoever it is. Possi-

bilities: Mother; Paul; FedEx, RPS or Priority Mail; the oil-
man; my handyman; or the snowplow man.

It isn't any of them. It is a heavyset man around fifty or so,
wearing corduroys, Oxford shirt, loosely knotted tie, leather
jacket and leather hiking boots. He has a Yankee hat on his
head, a leather carryall bag in his hand and a purplish nose in
the middle of his face. "Hi," he says, openly looking me up
and down through his glasses. "Roderick Reynolds." He sticks
a hand out.

I try to think. *Is today Sunday? Didn't the confirmation say
Sunday, 9:00 a.m.?* "How do you do, I'm Sally." I shake his
hand, making a slight grimace. "I'm afraid our appointment
is set up for tomorrow."

"Well, I'm here now," he says, looking past me into the
cottage.

Uh-oh, he's one of those. This is a typical strategy out of
the Verity Rhodes playbook: arrive a day early to catch the
subject unprepared.

The best way to play this is not to raise a fuss, I decide, but
to kill him with kindness, seem to hide nothing by answering
his every question, make innuendos that he will find out too
late are dead ends, and yet offer enough interesting new information to make the piece salable.

"Please come in," I say graciously, backing away to open
the door to him. Thank heavens I'm showered and dressed.
Nothing special though, just jeans, turtleneck, sweater and
clogs. Earrings, bracelet. On second thought, I decide I'm
good to go. "Did you have trouble finding the house?"

Roderick Reynolds doesn't respond; he's too busy looking
around.

"Would you like a tour?" I ask him.

He nods, regripping the strap of his bag as though I might

try to steal it. The fact that he hasn't taken off his hat, of course, has classified him in a certain way in *my* playbook.

"You live here alone?" he asks when I take him back to the one and only bedroom, just before he sticks his head into the bathroom.

"Yes," I say, shifting my weight from one foot to the other. The jeans I have on are too tight and are hurting me right *there*.

Back in the living room, Roderick is intrigued by what was supposed to be a dining area, set off by a couple of square wooden columns and archways in the corner of the living room, but which I have always used as a home office. When I was a newspaper reporter, the area consisted of bookcases, a computer, printer and file cabinets. Since the advent of DBS, however, it has a twin video/DVD deck and two monitors, in addition to my computer screen. A lot of books had to be shifted as well, to make room for a couple scores of CD-ROMs and videotapes.

"You can work this?" he asks, pointing to the slight daunting array of electronics.

"Yes. I can even do some rough-cut editing of video out here. Which enables me to come out here some weekends." I watch him scrutinizing the equipment. "The newsroom can send a video feed through my computer. I can use the editing deck and then zap it back to DBS."

"High-speed access?"

"Yes."

"No shit," he says. As if I have passed some kind of test, he drops his bag on the floor and takes off his coat, which I hang up on the coat tree next to the front door. He keeps the Yankee hat on.

I did my homework on Roderick Reynolds and I cannot pretend to be surprised Verity selected him, or be particularly happy about what the outcome will surely be. I was told he had been on the magazine scene for twenty years, but I had never heard of him before. Then I found out why from friends at *Boulevard*. Reynolds, until recently—like even maybe a few days ago when he was given this freelance assignment—had spent his career writing under a number of names, abandoning one for another in order to gain access to a new subject as a so-called first-time but promising major-league interviewer.

Roderick Reynolds had been the first to smear Princess Grace of Monaco after her death, to savage Connie Chung, vilify Sherry Lansing, hammer Sharon Stone and defame Hillary Clinton. And while perhaps his raging ridicule of such public figures as Diana Ross, Barbra Streisand, Madonna, Martha Stewart and Rosie O'Donnell might somewhat be expected, his attack of such a diverse list of beloveds—Lucille Ball, Helen Thomas, Meryl Streep, Gwyneth Paltrow, Jane Pauley and Dame Maggie Smith—was almost unreal.

The point is, the guy gets paid very well and often for targeting very successful and widely admired women and assassinating their characters.

So, in a way, I suppose, I should be deeply flattered Verity has gone to so much trouble.

I offer Roderick Reynolds something to eat and drink. He asks for herbal tea and after I make a show of going into the kitchen to prepare it, I sneak a peek back around the swinging door to watch him open my desk drawers.

Ha. Already beat him to the punch. Anything that's anything I keep in a fireproof safe located in the kitchen with my pots and pans.

Uh-oh, I remember. *The bathroom.*

I make noise to warn him I'm coming back out, which I do,

and then excuse myself to change into some more comfortable slacks. I close the bedroom door and zip into the bathroom to hastily go through my cabinets. I take out my birth control pills and a box of disposable douches. Rummaging around further, I find an unopened box of condoms (that I'm not at all sure how they got here) and take those. I look in the drawers of the bedside tables and under my Bible, thank you very much, I find an ancient issue of *Penthouse Forum* (from my ex, the book editor). Then put all of those things in a suitcase in my closet that has a combination lock. I change into khakis and *ta-dah*.

When I come out, Roderick is reviewing the titles in one of the floor-to-ceiling bookcases that frame the stone fireplace on the far wall. The teakettle whistles and I promise to return. When I do, I bring with me a small tray that includes two buttered English muffins, sliced in quarters, a jar of strawberry preserves from the Franciscan convent, a bone china teapot with matching cup and saucer (from my grandparents) and a mug of coffee for me. He ends up eating seven of the eight pieces of muffin—thoughtfully leaving the one sort of crummy piece for me—while firing questions, his recorder spinning its tiny reels on the coffee table.

Yes, I was born here in Castleford. My father was an architect, specializing in adapting colonial architectural plans to modern building methods and materials. Most famous projects? The Mercantile Library in New Haven, the Zemke Building in Wallingford, the mansion and outer buildings of Blessings Farm & Stables in Durham. (I show him photos.)

Mother is a schoolteacher. Grade-school English, grades five and six.

No, I have nothing to add to the published stories and news tapes about the murder of my father. Yes, I confirm again, he was murdered. That's right, the murderer is somewhere in Europe. No, I'd rather not talk about it.

Yes, I went to UCLA, majored in English and journalism. Actually, I got a full ride on an academic scholarship. Well, almost; worked and relied on student loans for the rest. *Boulevard* magazine. Castleford *Herald-American*, part-time at WSCT in New Haven and then full-time at DBS News in New York.

Specialty? Feature writing, newspaper and broadcast journalism. Love the longer form—the series in newspaper, the documentary in TV—but am very comfortable with the short form. Yes, I will be a contributing reporter to *DBS News Magazine,* as well as coanchoring the morning news.

I offer Roderick a box containing copies of articles I've written and videos of the kinds of stories I like to write or produce or cover, adding that at some point I will need them back.

"Is the sex tape in here?" he asks, setting the box down to paw through it.

My heart sinks. "I'm sorry?"

"That tape that was sent everywhere," he says matter-of-factly. "You and Spencer Hawes doing the nasty."

"As it happens," I say smoothly, "I didn't keep a copy of that." Believe it or not, someone once videotaped me having sex with my ex Spencer Hawes, and then sent the tape all over everywhere. (No, it was not Spencer, although he was my first suspect as I had just broken up with him.)

Roderick meets my eye and finally seems a little embarrassed, lowering his eyes and switching tracks to ask if I'm happy about the time slot of *DBS News America This Morning*.

I tell him, yes, I'm happy with it, look at my watch and then explain that I must go to Hillstone Falls, New York, just over the state line, and he can either accompany me and continue this in the car, or come back tomorrow when he was scheduled. I briefly explain the familial nature of my mission, underscoring that I promised my great-uncle I would go today on his behalf.

"So you're his heir or something?" Roderick asks.

"As a matter of fact," I say, "no." I am Uncle Percy's executor, although all of the assets of his "estate," as it were, were signed over to the Gregory Home.

He asks to use the bathroom before we leave and he is in there for a while (which is understandable since there's a medicine cabinet, the under-the-sink cabinet and a whole linen closet for him to go through).

So we move on, my new acquaintance and I, in the Jeep, heading northwest. Now he wants to talk a little about my exes, starting with Manhattan book editor Spencer Hawes.

"I should warn you," I tell him as we turn off 84 onto Route 8 north, "Verity won't appreciate a lot about Spencer in the article." I glance over. "He's part of her husband's suit in their divorce."

Roderick looks down at his notepad, considering this.

"So if, for example, you want to write about that videotape you asked about before," I add, "you'll have to interview Verity about why her husband made that tape and who the other woman was he was filming. And why."

Roderick sighs, irritated. "Is this really mixed up with Verity?" (*The woman who has promised to make me respectable by letting me write for* Expectations *under my own name?* I can imagine him adding.)

"With Verity, Corbett Schroeder and Spencer. It actually had very little to do with me."

"Except you were the starring attraction, I hear."

I pretend to concentrate on my driving for a while. "So what's your kill fee on this article?"

He shuts off his recorder. "Ten thousand, why?"

"Just wondered. In case Verity refuses to run the story."

"So you're advising me to fuck the editor who was fucking you?" he demands.

"Charming phraseology, but yes," I say, resisting the urge to lean over and swat that hat off his head.

He turns to openly look me over, head to toe. "They're right about you," he says. "You're a cool one. Hot in bed, with a cool, cool head." He laughs, turning his tape recorder back on.

"Actually," I say, leaning slightly toward him, "I'm more of a hothead," and I swat his baseball hat off into the back seat.

Ha. Knew it. He's bald.

Roderick doesn't react right away. Then he says, "Fuck you," abruptly flips off his seat belt and turns around in his seat to find his hat.

He's got a problematic derriere, too, I notice.

Aren't we the ideal couple on this sunny winter day.

After demonstrating to Roderick that I am capable of physical violence, I seek to make peace by asking him if he would like something to eat or drink. He does. So we stop in Litchfield to order a lunch to go (he wants two grilled cheese sandwiches with bacon, French fries and herbal tea), and then I continue driving while he continues eating and asking me questions. Then he has to stop at a gas station to use the bathroom. Then he tells me I have to slow down on these back roads because I'm making him carsick. I tell him to stop looking at the map, repeat for the third time that I am *not* lost and that this *is* the way to Hillstone Falls.

We finally reach Hillstone Falls at twenty-five to one and it takes another five minutes to find the town hall. I park in the lot and leave Roderick in the car.

Inside the town clerk's office a lady slides a registration form over the counter for me to fill out. It takes me about fifteen seconds, but then I have to wait while she explains to other people in line the ABC's of applying for a handicapped-parking sticker; how to obtain a permit for brush burning from the county fire marshal; and explain, yes, ice-fishing licenses are available here. By the time she returns her attention to me, I am fretting because the office is supposed to close soon, but she assures me I will be allowed to stay until I find what I'm looking for.

Roderick appears just as the clerk is locking the outer door. She lets him in, relocks the door and pulls down the shade. "All right, let's see what we have here," she says, circling back around the counter and groping on her chest for the glasses that hang there on a delicate chain. She focuses on my registration form and asks for my driver's license.

I take it out of my wallet and slide it across the counter. Roderick cranes his neck to get a look at it. I'm sure he's checking the birth date. I'm at the stage in my career, he knows, when it is tempting to start changing such things before too much notice is taken. "You look like a tango instructor," he observes.

The clerk photocopies my license and returns it. Then she disappears into a back room. We wait. And we wait. Almost twenty minutes go by and Roderick has started sincerely irritating me by listing the many ways I am lacking in comparison to Alexandra Waring.

"How on earth am I to respond to this? It's not even a question."

"A lot of people are wondering how you got chosen, that's all."

Frowning, I turn to him, leaning on the counter. "I'm good and people will watch me to get their morning news. That's it."

He narrows his eyes slightly. "Yeah?"

"Yeah."

After a moment, he says, "So what ever happened to the cop?"

"What are you talking about?"

He's flipping through his notebook. "Paul Fitzwilliam. Your shining knight on a motorcycle?"

The clerk emerges from the back room and we turn to look at her. Her expression isn't promising. "I'm a bit confused," she admits, drawing up to the counter and placing the request form in front of me. "The name *is* Percival F. Harrington?"

"Yes," I confirm.

"I can't find any reference whatsoever to any variation of that name." She pulls out a handwritten list. "I have these Harringtons—Clyde, Cynthia, Mark, Lawrence, Timothy, Yolanda."

I shake my head. "No. If there was a George, it could be someone related to us, but I don't know any of those names."

"I don't either," Roderick says, being a jerk.

"But let's say he did inherit some land," I say, "would his name be on this database, or just the previous owner's name?"

"Oh, his name would surely be here. I even looked in the old card catalog. No reference to Percival Harrington whatsoever." She looks earnestly across the counter at me. "May I ask what has led you to believe he is a landholder in Hillstone Township?"

I show her a copy of the letter Uncle Percy received from Harold Durrant, which Roderick is trying to read upside down.

"Oh, Hal," the clerk says, nodding. "I knew him. He used to always be in here, looking things up." She looks at me. "He was an ardent environmentalist, you know. I think he was a retired engineer. Very successful, I understand." She slips her glasses off, letting them fall with the chain. "He's dead now."

"So I understand."

She holds up the letter. "May I borrow this? There is one more place I can look."

"Go ahead, take it," Roderick tells her, impatient to get out of here.

The clerk disappears into the back room again.

"I've got a list of people I need permission from you to talk to," he says. He reads from his notebook. He names my mother, my brother, my college roommate, my boyfriend in Los Angeles after college, my boss at *Boulevard,* Doug Wrentham, Spencer Hawes, and some colleagues at WSCT-TV in New Haven. "Waring and Cochran and Darenbrook, all those guys," he says, "are cool, Alec Aldridge says I can talk to anybody there. And I've already talked to your boss at the Castleford paper, Alfred Royce."

Inwardly I cringe. "You've talked to Al?"

"Even gave me a tour of Castleford yesterday."

"Really?" This is not good. "That was nice of him."

He lets out a gruff laugh. "I suppose. If you like seeing dumpy old factory towns."

I can't help it. I reach out and knock his hat off his head again.

"Damn it! Stop it!" he commands, swatting my arm pretty hard.

"No, *Al Royce Jr.* is a dumpy old cracker clown," I whisper, furious. "I'll show you Castleford. Because there is no way you're even going to get remotely close to who I am, Roderick, unless you see my hometown through my eyes."

"*Je*sus," he says, yanking his hat into place, looking at the clerk coming out.

"I'm so sorry, Ms. Harrington, but this is going to take a little while. Could you perhaps come back during the week?"

"I'm sorry but I really can't," I say.

"And we just have to know if that land is mine or not," Roderick says, slumping against the counter. "I have a sick mother."

This guy is the biggest jackass I've ever met in my life.

"Oh," the clerk says, somewhat startled. No doubt Roderick is not how she pictured Percival F. Harrington. "Well, in that case, perhaps you could go across the street and have lunch. I have to check this by hand and it is labor intensive."

"Can I help?" I ask.

"I'm afraid not, the rules don't allow it."

I want to say she just told me Harold Durrant used to go through the records here, but decide to keep it friendly. "We already ate, so I think we'll go over to that charming library across the street."

"Oh, it is quite charming," she assures us. "Why don't you come back at—" She looks up at the big clock on the wall. "One-thirty?"

"Thank you *so* much," I tell her as she comes back around the counter to unlock the door.

Roderick and I cross the street to the small stone-and-stucco library. It's got to be at least two hundred years old. Inside there are only three rooms, crowded with books in wooden shelving and I bet the small back room was where, in the library's earliest days, the librarian lived. "Feels haunted," Roderick says, floorboards creaking under his weight.

I approach the librarian at the desk, asking if their collection has any old tax registers. "Yes, it does, but I believe they're only for 1930 through 1936," she says, leading me toward the back of the big room. "The rest are across the street at the town hall."

"And how were they organized?"

"Alphabetically," she says, scanning the shelves and then suddenly stooping. She pulls out a book that was lying on its side, a large, slim, leather-bound ledger about the size of a world atlas. She pulls out an empty shelf from a mahogany map cabinet and carefully places the register on it. When she opens the book, I make a quiet exclamation at the freshness of the paper.

"It's acid free," she explains. "We have eighteenth-century letters that are in far better shape than some books that were published twenty years ago. What are you looking for?"

"Anything under the name Harrington," I say.

She flips to H. We both scan the carefully handwritten list of names and taxes paid on specific properties and I can see at a glance there is no Harrington at all. "I don't see anything," she says. "Is there another name?"

"I don't know," I say honestly.

After a few more minutes of her time, it's clear the librarian cannot help me further. I look around for Roderick. I can't see him. Finally I find him in the back of the little room.

"I'm through," I tell him, startling him.

He jerks around and a small book falls to the floor. I pick it up. It is a beautiful little copy of Shakespeare's sonnets, with a hand-tooled binding and gold stamping. When I look at Roderick's flushed face, I have the sudden suspicion he might have been trying to pocket this. Heaven knows, there is no security system in this quaint place. "Where does it go?" I ask him.

He snatches the book from me and slams it back on a shelf. "So are you done or what?" he asks, turning around.

What kind of grown man steals a book from a public library?

We walk back over to the town hall in silence. He knows I know what he was about to do and I'm trying to think of a way I can use it to my advantage. "Hopefully we'll be out of here soon," I tell him cheerfully. He perks up a little at my tone, and at the top of the stairs even holds the door open for me.

I knock on the town clerk's office door and wait. And wait. And then I knock again, checking my watch: 1:31.

Nothing.

"Where is she?" Roderick says.

This time I use my car keys to loudly rap on the glass. "Hello!" I call.

"That's weird," Roderick says, banging on the door with his fist. "Come on, lady, we've got work to do and places to go!"

A figure emerges from an office next door. "They're closed," the man tells us. We stop banging to look at him. He is dressed rather nattily in a well-fitting dark gray suit, maroon tie and black tasseled loafers. As I walk toward him, I see the placard hanging over his door: Legal.

"The nice lady clerk told us to come back at one-thirty."

"I'm sorry, but she's left for the day," he tells me.

I look at Roderick. "She did say one-thirty, right?"

He nods. "She was very specific about it."

"I'm sorry," the man says, "I don't know what to tell you. Except that she left."

"But she has something of mine," I say. "A very important document and I need it back."

"I guess you'll have to come back on Monday then," the man says.

I'm getting angry. "You wouldn't happen to be the township's attorney, would you?"

He smiles slightly. "No."

"But you do work in legal?"

He pauses a moment and then says, "May I ask who you are?"

"You're the one who's being paid with the taxpayers' money," Roderick says, "so maybe you should be telling us who *you* are."

"Andrew Palmer," he says, turning to Roderick, "esquire. I periodically assist the township in legal matters as the need arises." His eyebrows rise. "And you are?"

"Percival F. Harrington," Roderick tells him.

Attorney Palmer doesn't even look at me now. "Mrs. Blake

won't be back until Monday at nine, Mr. Harrington. I suggest you call her or come back at that time."

"But as town counsel," Roderick counters, "you must have access to the records office and that's where we need to go. That's where she took our document."

"Unfortunately I don't have the keys to the records room with me," Palmer says. "I didn't expect to be in the office today. I just stopped by to pick up something."

Dressed like this, I wonder where he's been, wedding or funeral.

I sense that Roderick is going to say something pretty bad, so I take his arm, say, "Thank you," to Palmer and pull him down the hall.

"He's such a fucking liar," Roderick growls.

"Yeah, I know," I tell him. "But I'll deal with it."

CHAPTER FOURTEEN

I start Roderick's tour of Castleford by taking him to my childhood home. I called Mother's and got no answer, but sometimes she plays bridge on Saturdays at the country club. I leave Roderick in the Jeep while I go inside to check what shape the house is in, and to let the dogs out. Moments later I hear furious barking. I run to the front door and see Scotty barking and gnarling his teeth to keep Roderick in the Jeep and Roderick is standing by the open door, holding a pistol with two hands in front of him. The gun is aimed at Scotty.

"Don't!" I cry, rushing off the front step.

With a snarl, Scotty charges and retreats, maneuvering sideways to stand between Roderick and me; all the while Roderick keeps the gun trained on him.

"Scotty, *come!*"

Scotty gives one more warning bark and then shuts up, turning around and trotting over to me, tail wagging. Abigail nervously appears from the side of the house, and I kneel down to pet both of them, glaring over their heads at Roderick.

"He was coming at me," he says, slowly putting the gun away in the breast pocket of his overcoat. "See my scar?" He draws a finger under his chin. "German shepherd when I was a kid. Tore my face."

I let the dogs do their business and put them back in the house. Then I get back into the Jeep.

"I wouldn't have shot him. Unless—"

"Let's just forget about it," I say, backing out and slamming the car into Drive the way you're not supposed to do.

"What do you keep looking at?" he asks me.

"What do you mean?"

"You keep looking around for something."

I stop the Jeep and look at him.

"You just did it again," he says.

"Oh, yeah, that," I say, realizing what he is talking about. I *am* looking around. "We had a stalker here last weekend. I guess I'm just making sure he's not around."

"Oh yeah?" He's making a note. "So the dogs have a purpose. That's good."

"Yes," I say. Best that any would-be stalkers think they'll get torn up if they come to see me.

After I turn onto the road, Roderick glances up from his notebook. "I'd like to see where your father was killed."

"Sure," I tell him.

On the way, Roderick continues to ask questions regarding my physical safety, which I pretty much dismiss.

"Haven't you had any fallout from the trial?" he asks. "With the mafia or anything?"

"No."

"That reminds me," he says, writing, "I'd like to talk to Lilliana Martin."

I first met the famous actress at a publishing party in Hollywood. We've since experienced the "Mafia Boss Murder" trial together. "I can arrange that," I say, pulling into the parking lot behind Castleford High School. I point to the gymnasium. "That's the new gym. My father was killed in the old one. But that's where it was, the near corner." I turn to him. "Why do you carry a gun?"

"Because I can. So this is it?" he says, pointing.

"This is it." Pause. I notice the gas gauge is nearly empty, so when we leave I head for a station on West Main. "So what in Castleford did Al Royce show you yesterday?"

"Some brown fields, boarded-up buildings, that hideous railroad station and some kind of abandoned construction project."

"Lovely." We pull up to the pumps at the gas station and I hop out to insert my credit card and fill the tank while Roderick goes inside to investigate snacks. While he's gone, I slide back in the car to skim his notes. I read and write shorthand, but Roderick's handwriting is beyond horrendous. Still, I can make out enough to understand that his working title of the piece is "The Selling of Sexy Sally."

I drop the notebook back in the seat and climb out to hang up the hose and refit the gas cap. I walk inside to find Roderick. He's debating between Drakes Cakes and Twinkies. "Want any?" he asks politely.

"No thanks," I say, walking over to pour myself a cup of coffee. "Get milk or something, if you want. I'm going to take you somewhere in town where there are no stores."

"Okay," he says, pawing packages of both junk foods out of the rack and moving over to the refrigerated cases. He chooses Diet Snapple.

An older neighbor of Mother's walks into the store and says hi. I say hi back. I don't introduce Roderick, but explain that he's a journalist and we're doing an interview. The neighbor smiles and tweaks my nose. "Now you know what it was like having you following us around as a kid."

I look to see if Roderick has absorbed this exchange, for this is what Castleford is: a town where people you've known for years tweak your nose because you'll always be Dodge and Belle's little girl, even at thirty-three.

But no, his big behind is waddling out the door and Roderick's tearing the Twinkies open with his teeth.

The road winding up to Castle Kerry is almost two miles long. The castle is actually a turn-of-the-century stone tower built on the highest point in central Connecticut. While Roderick finishes his cupcakes (the Twinkies are long gone) and guzzles his Diet Snapple (what is the *point?*) in the car, I explain what it is he is about to see. It's going to be cold up in the tower and I might as well keep him warm now. The wind is blowing the flag the Castleford Lions' Club put up here very hard; it is a cold, whipping wind from the north.

We will see Long Island Sound in New Haven to the south, I explain, and we will see Hartford to the north. We will look over the two thousand magnificent acres of Castleford parkland; he will see reservoirs and traprock ridges; in the city he will be able to see our one-hundred-year-old former city library—domed in copper, built with white marble, skylights and soaring windows—that has been renovated into a cultural center; he will see our new state-of-the-art hospital, rated one of America's finest; he will see the ball fields and magnet schools and other city parks; and he will then, I tell him, see the housing projects in true context. "People come to Castleford when they need help, but we are, by nature, a generous community. Always have been."

"Yeah-yeah-yeah," Roderick says, tossing his sticky wrappers and napkins behind him on the floor of the back seat. "You're going to make me climb that thing?"

"Yes," I tell him, getting out. Whoooo boy, it is cold and I turn up the collar of my coat, jam my hands in my pockets and start walking. I take a quick look back to make sure Roderick is following me and then walk up to the stone wall that marks the edge of the landing to wait for him.

Golly it's beautiful, even in this naked time of the year. While we climb the circular stairs up to the top of the tower, I tell him about the festival of lights we have in the park from Thanksgiving through New Year's. I hear him puffing ahead and I back off a little, allowing him to slow down if he wants. He makes it, though, kind of pulling himself up the railing at the end, hand over hand.

What he sees at the top makes him involuntarily straighten to attention. And then smile slightly. Huffing and puffing still, he takes a few steps out, rests his hands on the stone wall and squints into the horizon, first looking south—"New Haven?" I nod, yes—then north, to Hartford, the state capital.

"Jesus, I wouldn't have believed it," he says, looking west and east, marveling at the cliffs and peaks and endless acres of woods and streams and reservoirs that stretch from Middletown to Middlefield to Castleford to Southington (although the latter has desecrated their peaks with a mess of transmission towers just around the corner). "This is really beautiful."

I smile. Maybe he will be kind to my town after all. I start telling him about how Castleford is regenerating and reinventing itself, of the progress and plans, and of the slow and steady improvement. I tell him about the Friends of the Library bookstore that has a bakery in it; I tell him about the YMCA, Girls, Inc. and The Boys and Girls Club; I tell him about the senior center, the community theater, the block associations, the Rosa Ponselle museum; I tell him about Rotary, Kiwanis, the Masons, the Elks—

"Yeah—yeah, okay," he says without taking a note and heading for the stairs, "but I gotta take a piss."

I sigh, rubbing my eyes. Then I take one last look out, take a deep breath of clean fresh air, and follow him down the stairs, reminding myself why this article will be important. What the point of this whole nightmare of a day is. "There's no bathroom up here, Roderick, I'll take you down to—"

"No, I gotta go *now*," he informs me, reaching the bottom of the stairs. "Wait for me in the car."

I stop on the last step. "You can't do it in here," I tell him, horrified.

"Why not?" He's already got his hands on his zipper.

"Because this isn't skid row." I grab his arm and push him toward the doorway. "Go piss on the view."

"It's cold out there."

"So help me God, Roderick," I tell him, shoving him outside, "if one molecule of you lands on this tower, I will throw you off it myself."

"All right, all right," he says, turning away. "Just go away and let me do my business."

I stomp back to the car, calling back, "I'm going to check, you know!"

I climb into the Jeep and start the engine. I turn on the radio, scanning stations for a weather report, find one, and glance back across the parking lot, wondering what to do with this idiot now.

After a minute, I look around for him again.

Where is he? He's got to be freezing in that wind.

After another minute goes by, I start to worry that he's sick or something. Maybe he has the trots. Heaven knows, with what he's eaten today that could be a possibility. That or sugar shock.

I decide to wait a little longer.

This is ridiculous, I think after two minutes, grabbing some

Kleenex out of the glove compartment and climbing out of the car. I walk tentatively toward the tower. "Roderick?" I call. Nothing. "Roderick? Are you okay? I've got some Kleenex if you need it."

Nothing. Well, the wind is blowing, maybe he can't hear me. I step next to the tower and yell, "Roderick? Are you okay? Can I hand you some Kleenex? Or help you?"

Now I have a queasy feeling. Something is wrong. I can't stand the guy, and I don't want to embarrass him, but—

I walk into the tower. And through to the other side. "Roderick?"

All I hear is the wind, and the flag rope banging against the aluminum pole. I look around. No sign of him.

I walk all the way around the tower calling his name. Now I'm getting scared. He couldn't have—

I try to look over the stone wall, but I can't see over the cliff. "Roderick!" I call.

I run up the stairs to the top of the tower. He's not here, either.

I run over to the south side and look down. Rocks, shale, bushes, traprock. Where *is* he? I scan the horizon, noticing the clouds that have rolled in, and that my breath is coming out in puffs of frost, quickly taken by the wind.

Dear God, where is he? I think, looking. Looking. No movement but the flag waving wildly, no sound but the wind in my ears and the flag rope banging.

And then I see something. Way down.

It's a leg. I can't see anything more. Not from here. Except that the leg is not moving.

I call 911 on my cell phone while I fly down the tower stairs, telling the operator where we are and what has happened, but then while I'm scrambling over the wall, trying to get over the upright rocks that are there to prevent you from doing so, my fingers are so cold I drop the damn thing and the cell phone slides over the cliff. I skirt the edge of the cliff, working my way over to the slope, leap over to it, fall on one knee and then slide my way down over the mountain shale. By the time all of Roderick has come into view, my heart is in my throat because the way his body is lying is not good. It's not natural. Something, or many things, are broken.

I fall down on the last part and crawl over the rocks and frozen dirt to reach him. His Yankee hat and glasses are gone, there's a bloody gash on the side of his head, and his lips are turning blue.

I know I'm silently crying as I try to figure out if he's dead and I wonder what I have to lose by moving him a little at this point, because I know by now he isn't breathing and there is only one way left to help him. So I pull his body a little straighter, turning him over on his back, forcing his mouth open and holding his nose as I start CPR. *Please come back, please come back,* I think, mechanically going through the motions, over and over, filling his lungs and pushing the air out, filling his lungs and pushing the air out, *Please don't, Roderick, come back, come back.*

I can hear the sirens screaming up the mountain.

CHAPTER FIFTEEN

"**L**et's go over this one more time," Buddy D'Amico says in a quiet voice, pushing a piece of paper back across the table to me.

I look dully over at the female officer and then pull my chair closer to the table. "The car was here," I say, pointing to the box drawn on the schematic around Castle Kerry. "He walked out in front of the tower."

Buddy shakes his head. "But why would he have climbed over the wall?"

"I think he might have stood on the wall," I say. "Because I yelled at him, because he was going to take a whiz at the bottom of the stairwell." My eyes start blurring with tears. "I said something like, 'Piss on the view,' because if he left anything on the castle I would—" I clap my right hand on my forehead and press my palm hard against it. Then I drop it, looking miserably across the table at Buddy. "If he did, I told him I'd throw him off myself," I finish, voice breaking on the last.

Buddy's eyes are sympathetic and his hand starts to reach across the table, but he stops himself. He looks over at the female officer who meets his look with no expression.

I take a sip of water from the disposable cup in front of me.

"And you didn't see anything from the car?"

I shake my head. "No."

Pause. "You didn't see anybody else up there?"

"No."

"No other cars, no sign of anyone?"

I shake my head. "No."

"So if you had to guess, you would say he stood up on the wall to relieve himself and the wind made him lose his balance."

I look up at Buddy and shake my head. "No. I don't."

He waits for me to elaborate.

"You know how that wall is constructed," I say, pointing to it on the schematic. "It's designed to keep people off of it. It has those rocks that are set upright, so you can't sit on it and you can't even really climb up onto it. I had a hard time getting over it—I'm not sure I could stand on it."

"So what are you saying?" Buddy asks.

"I'm saying I don't think he could have climbed up to stand on the wall in the first place."

"So how did he fall over the cliff?" Buddy looks at me. "Are you saying he climbed over the wall to jump off the cliff on purpose?"

I shake my head. "No."

"But, Sally—"

"I know, Buddy!" I wail, running both of my hands through my hair and then holding them against my head as if it might help me keep my thoughts together.

Buddy turns to the officer. "See if someone can scare up a cup of coffee for Sally. With sugar. And milk."

When the door to the room closes, Buddy says, "We're going over every inch of the area, Sally, but the ground's frozen and I'm not sure how much we're going to find that can help to tell us what happened." He sighs. "And who knows if he'll ever be able to tell us."

"But he is still alive." I sound childlike.

"He is still alive," he confirms. "Head wound, heart attack, broken bones. But you saved his life."

"Yeah, right," I say, covering my face. While hiding there, I say, "He's brain-dead, isn't he?" I drop my hands. "I was too long getting down there, wasn't I?"

"No," he insists. "You brought him back, Sally, and they got him to MidState. He's in a coma, but they're airlifting him up to Hartford Hospital for surgery."

"What kind?"

"Brain," he admits.

I fall back in my chair.

"He's still got a chance, Sal."

I nod, trying to believe it. I keep seeing Roderick's expression when I knocked off his hat in Hillstone Town Hall. I push it from my mind. "I saw somebody from the *Hartford Courant* at the castle."

"He picked the call up on a scanner," Buddy explains. "He came up behind Emergency Rescue before we closed the access road."

"So the news is out."

"Not until the morning," he says. "The *Courant*'s the only one who has pictures. It was dark by the time News 3 got their helicopter there to look."

I still have enough loyalty to the *Herald-American* to bristle a little.

The officer returns, sliding a cup of coffee across the table to me, along with a pack of sugar, two little buckets of cream and a black plastic swizzle stick. I pick up the latter, examining the upper end of it, wondering if I have truly lost my mind or does this have a plastic torso of a naked lady on it. "Oh, I'm sorry," she says, embarrassed. "That must be left over from the raid on The Chalet." The Chalet, a dodgy-looking joint on the edge of town, was busted recently for a live-sex show. (If you ask me, the live-sex shows are outside in the parking lot.)

"Let me—" she begins, reaching for it.

"No, it's fine," I tell her. I put in the sugar and cream and use the swizzle stick to stir it. Lacking a napkin, I have to lick the bottom of the stick before putting it down on the table.

The officer is whispering something to Buddy. "Your mother's arrived," Buddy informs me. To the officer, "Tell Mrs. Harrington it will only be about five minutes more and then she can take Sally home."

"I can drive, Buddy," I say wearily, raising my coffee cup toward my mouth.

"But I can't release the Jeep."

The coffee cup freezes on my lip.

"We have to go over it, Sally."

I take a sip of coffee. It is good. Then I put the cup down on the table, holding it with two hands in front of me.

"You said you expected the magazine article to be unflattering," Buddy prods.

"Yes. Verity Rhodes assigned him to write it."

"Not the woman who—"

I nod. "Yes. The one and same."

"And you went along with this?" Buddy asks in disbelief. "Knowing what she might do?"

"DBS wanted publicity for the newscast," I explain.

"Yeah, well," Buddy says, looking a little startled, "they'll certainly be getting that, won't they?" He frowns and writes something down.

I'm starting to feel sick. I'm thinking about what Roderick wrote about "The Selling of Sexy Sally." At the time I understood what he was trying to do, how he wanted to package the story to sell, but only now is what he was really driving at hitting home. Roderick might be a sleaze, but he isn't entirely wrong. I have become a notorious figure in the news but though a publicist's dream, my story is not anchorwoman material. In case of an emergency, people are to look to a news anchor as a calming, trustworthy source of information and procedure. Why would anyone look to someone like me, someone so—so…?

God, *I* wouldn't watch me. *DBS News America This Morning with Calamity Jane?*

I bite down on my lip to keep from smiling. I can't help it.

"Did you remember something?" Buddy asks me.

"No," I say, bringing my coffee up with both hands to sip.

After watching me a moment, Buddy pushes his chair back and stands up. "Okay, Sally, go home with your mother. Get some rest."

I stand up, taking my coffee with me. "You want me to stay in town, I imagine."

"I wish you would. But if you have to go anywhere, just let me know, okay?"

Mother takes me to her house, where instinctively I go through the front door and head straight upstairs to my old bedroom. I throw myself on the twin bed nearest the window and curl up on my side, Scotty jumping after me and forcing a space between my back and the edge of the bed. I am looking out the window for several moments before I realize I am looking at Castle Kerry.

When I awaken, the room is dark and Mother is sitting on the edge of the bed behind me instead of Scotty. Her hand is on my shoulder. "Darling, it's eight-thirty. I think you should come down and have something to eat. And then maybe have a hot bath."

I turn over in her direction, crunching up the pillow under my head. "The phone's been ringing," I tell her.

"Yes."

She rubs my arm and then pushes back strands of my hair. "It wasn't your fault, darling."

"I know."

I hear breathing. Panting. I push myself up on one arm and look past Mother to see in the light from the hall that Scotty and Abigail are sitting there, tongues hanging, eyes bright. "Hi, guys," I say and Mother says, "Oh, no," as the dogs bound over her onto the bed, making it very crowded indeed. Then they make it worse by starting to play with each other, whacking tails in our faces and stepping all over us.

How can I help but laugh a little. Mother looks relieved.

"Doug called to find out if he could do anything," Mother says halfway through our chicken soup. Mother has a freezer full of things like homemade chicken soup.

"That was nice of him," I say. Since we're in New Haven County, any suspicious "accident" swings through the D.A.'s office; my former boyfriend, Doug Wrentham, must be on call this weekend.

"And Paul called." She sips some soup and then takes a small bite of bread. She carefully chews and swallows, placing her spoon on the plate under her soup bowl before speaking again. "He didn't know, of course, and when he called your cell phone tonight he got somebody at the police station. So I filled him in." She pats her mouth with her napkin. "He wanted to come over but I asked him to wait until you called."

I nod, reaching for my glass of water. I pull Mother's robe around me a little tighter because I feel cold. I took a hot bath before dinner, and only then, when I was undressing, did I notice that my pants were torn and dirty and that I had dried blood on one knee and on the sleeve of my sweater. The police have my coat. What was creepy was how, after my bath, I found my clothes downstairs in a garbage bag, and when I told Mother that we should just throw them out, she told me that Buddy had asked for them.

"Some fellow named Hugh called from the DBS newsroom," Mother continues at the kitchen table, "and then Alexandra called. And then a lot of other papers and TV reporters. I had to unplug the phone."

I eat some more soup.

"I think I may have annoyed Alexandra," Mother adds, picking up her spoon.

I look up.

"Before she could say anything, I told her I would appreciate it if she would keep the wolves at bay at least until morning—and that included DBS News."

I smile into my soup. "So what did she say?"

"To please make sure I let you know she called tonight and then she left a number where she can be reached."

I drop my spoon in the bowl with a clatter to genuinely laugh. "I bet she did."

"Yes," Mother confirms, smiling. "I'm afraid she is *very* annoyed with me, so maybe you should call her. If you feel up to it."

I take the cordless telephone into the living room and within a minute Alexandra is asking me how I am. I tell her the truth, "Numb, and when I'm lucid, freaked out."

"Was it an accident?"

"I don't think so," I say. "There doesn't seem to be any other explanation, though."

"He didn't jump?"

"No way," I say. "Listen— Mark Rodino of the *Hartford Courant* got there before they closed off the road. You should be able to cut a deal."

"R-o-d-i-n-o?"

"Yes."

"Just a few yes or no's, Sally?"

"Sure."

"Did you call 911?"

"Yes."

"Did you reach him first?"

"Yes."

"Was he conscious?"

"He wasn't breathing," I say quietly. "I gave him CPR until the ambulance got there."

"Oh, boy," the anchorwoman murmurs. "And Joe says you were up half the night last night with an accident on the Hutch." A sigh. "We've got a line into the hospital, so I can find out Reynolds's condition. They flew him up to Hartford Hospital, by the way. He's having surgery to drain the blood in his skull and relieve the pressure on the brain. His chances are fifty-fifty, though. He could make it in one piece."

I don't say anything.

"Where were you when he fell?"

"In the Jeep."

"What was he doing?"

"He was supposed to be taking a whiz. These are not yes-or-no questions, Alexandra." Mother is making a motion for me to hang up. I turn away from her, protecting the phone.

"Were you physically harmed in any way?"

"No."

"Who has Reynolds's notebook?"

"The police. And his tape recorder. And the tapes. It was all in his bag, which was in my car, which they've also impounded."

Silence. "They suspect *you?*"

"Buddy's just trying to find out what happened. And nobody else was there."

"That you know about." Alexandra checks to verify Buddy's home telephone number. "Listen, Sally, I'm going to respect your mother's wishes—*tonight*—but Haydn Cooke will be out there with a crew first thing in the morning and I expect you to talk to him. On camera. Doesn't have to be long, but give us something."

"Okay." I'm beginning to feel like this is an out-of-body experience.

"And listen, take the week. And if anything breaks—"

"It goes without saying," I tell her.

After hanging up, I have to grab the phone back from Mother to call Paul. He picks up on his cell phone after the first ring. "I'm so glad you called! I've been climbing the walls. Jack's here and we're sitting on our hands trying not to interfere, because your mom said—"

"I'm fine, Paul, really." He's been drinking. "I'll tell you everything tomorrow." I try to sound cheerful. "What I really want to know is, how is the move going? Did Jack really get the U-Haul there? And say hi to him for me."

"Sally's okay and she says hi," Paul says.

"Sally *RULES!*" Jack cries. He's bombed.

Paul furiously whispers something to shut him up. Then he comes back on, apologizing, and I ask him again about the move and he tells me about the couch not fitting through the door and how they had to take the door off, how cool the bedroom is turning out and that he can hardly wait for me to see it. I hear Jack yelling again in the background and I tell Paul to go on, I'll call him tomorrow.

"Love you," I think he says as I hang up.

I wander into the kitchen and surrender the phone to my mother. "Do you have any wine?" She gives me that Do-you-think-this-is-a-good-idea-at-a-time-like-this? look while she unplugs the phone station again, but says to look in the door of the fridge. I find an open bottle of Chardonnay and pour some into a glass. Then Mother comes over to say that she'll have some, too.

We clink glasses and drink.

CHAPTER SIXTEEN

It is all over the papers the next morning, but as Buddy said, the *Hartford Courant* is the only paper to have photos of the scene from yesterday. Everybody else was using file photos—of Castle Kerry, of me, and of Roderick Reynolds, aka Rick Robertson, Roger Rossiter, Rory Ross, Ross Regan, Reginald Ralston, Robert Rinaldi and Rupert Reid of tabloid fame. (*What, no Rabbit Redux?*)

Mother thoughtfully kept the phone off the hook last night and went out early to buy newspapers other than the *New York Times* and the Castleford *Herald-American*, which are delivered to the house each day. The headlines all took a different slant:

MAN PLUNGES FROM CASTLE KERRY
CELEB WRITER NEAR DEAD
LOCAL SAVES WRITER'S LIFE

It's interesting, the photographs the different papers have chosen to run of me. Most are wire-service photos from the trial in California. It's strange to read the accounts about yesterday; few have all the circumstances, many have them wrong, and with one I feel almost as though I'm reading about my own death.

There are no charges currently pending against Ms. Harrington, authorities say.

Roderick was originally from Bayonne, New Jersey, I learn. His real name is Roderick Harold Reynolds Jr. and he wrote under several different names for such diverse publications as the *National Enquirer, TV Guide, People, Us, Style, Tiger Beat, Parade* and *Screw Magazine* (!?!). He was freelancing for *Expectations*, working on a profile of Sally Harrington of DBS News, who, network executives say, will be coanchoring a morning newscast for them late this spring.

He was twice divorced, no children.

I plug the phone in and call Hartford Hospital, explaining to the nursing staff who I am and why I am calling. They can tell me little except that Roderick came out of surgery at three this morning and is in ICU. I thank them, unplug the phone and rejoin Mother in the living room, where she has a fire going. Just as I'm thinking how weird it is no one has come to the door yet this morning, the doorbell rings, which launched the dogs into a barking frenzy.

I peer out the window. Outside is the unmarked van of DBS News. (As if anyone wouldn't notice the transmitter on top.)

I take a breath, tell the dogs to please shut up, and open the door to Haydn Cooke. "Believe it or not," I tell him, "you're the first news group to show up this morning."

"That's only because DBS sealed off your mom's entire property," Haydn explains. "There's got to be twenty security guys around here, to say nothing of your local police."

"Oh, I forgot to tell you, dear," Mother calls from her wingback chair by the fire. "Wendy Mitchell from DBS Security coordinated it with Buddy. I saw Buddy at the end of the driveway this morning as I was leaving to get the papers."

I stare at the back of Mother's head. "You forgot?"

"We brought Cleo with us to pull you together," Haydn says, looking down at my pajamas. "It's a new ball game,

Alexandra said to tell you, what with the morning newscast. We can't just shoot you au naturel anymore."

Oh, right. I'm a face of DBS News now. I look past him to the truck. "Who's interviewing me?"

"Max was supposed to, but there's a story breaking in Stamford, so I dropped him off with Eric."

Eric's a field cameraman. "What's going on in Stamford?"

"FBI arrested the chairman of the Weer Group this morning."

"Busy Sunday," I comment, seeing Cleo picking her way carefully up the walk with an armful of clothes and her traveling cosmetics suitcase. She's wearing a full-length mink coat, black sweater and tights and stiletto heels. Her hair is in some kind of polka-dot wrap and, of course, she has on her Lina Wertmuller butterfly glasses. I keep telling Alexandra we should use her on the air for something.

"I'll make some coffee," Mother says, going into the kitchen. "I've got some scones in the freezer."

"I'm going to ask you questions off camera and you just look into the camera and say whatever it is you can say," Haydn instructs me. "Unless you can give us something major the *Courant* hasn't already, Alexandra doesn't much care what you say, just as long as we are the only ones to have you on camera today."

"Fine," I say, stepping back to let the gang in.

"Hey, Sally," Cleo says, tottering, and dumping the clothes in my arms. "Alexandra sent these out." She kisses me on the cheek leaving, no doubt, a big red lipstick mark. "Glad you're okay, kid," she adds, patting my arm. "Go and try these on. I have accessories in the truck if you need them."

"No, my mother's got loads of stuff, thank you." I go upstairs to change while the crew sets up downstairs. In a few minutes Cleo wanders up to find me standing in front of the full-length mirror in Mother's room. She approves of the short blue skirt and blazer and silk blouse I've chosen and starts setting up her stuff at Mother's dressing table. "They want to shoot by the fire," she tells me, pushing her glasses up on her nose and brushing imaginary lint off her shoulder.

How it is Cleo can choose to look like this and yet always manage to whip all of us into basic Ralph Lauren is beyond me.

"We shot some pictures of that stone tower," she tells me, spraying my hair liberally with water and something else that smells like watermelon.

"Castle Kerry."

"Yeah. The cop let us up. Everybody and their uncle was bitching and screaming at the bottom of the mountain."

I make a sound of acknowledgment, looking at the circles under my eyes.

"I thought that was bad till we got here," she continues, hands moving quickly. "It's Grand Central out there. The cops are handing out parking tickets."

She prattles on while revitalizing my hair and reconstructing my face. When we come downstairs into the living room, I certainly look better than I feel. I hear the rattle of china in the dining room and assume Mother is playing hostess. "Where do you want me?" I ask Haydn.

"Let's try on that footstool by the fire."

I walk over and sit down, Cleo starting to pluck at my clothes so they fall correctly. "Thank you, Mrs. Harrington," I hear a deep male voice say.

I turn to look. It's David Waring coming in with a mug of coffee in one hand, Mother right behind him.

"You certainly look like your sister," Mother tells him.

David laughs. "Since she's my little sister, I still like to think she looks like me." He sees that I've spotted him and seems to hesitate.

"It's hard to imagine Alexandra being a little anything," Mother laughs and the cameraman cracks, "A little bitchy sometimes," and everyone laughs.

"I hope you don't mind," David says to me. "They said I could ride along."

"'They' meaning his sister," the cameraman translates while taking a light reading.

Oddly, I'm starting to relax. It's good to have these guys here; the world doesn't feel so weird; it's just another wacky workday. Truth is, I feel exhilarated that David's here.

"I don't think it's going to work," the cameraman announces. "It's not the fire, it's the glare from those windows. I can cover them, but then the fireplace is going to look disembodied."

"Where do you suggest?" Haydn says.

"I like the kitchen. Put her at the table. I can get the castle in over her shoulder. I'll open on that, zoom out and then down and focus on Sally."

"All right, let's try it."

So we all shift to the kitchen where they place me in front of the sliding glass doors so that the castle can been seen over my shoulder on top of the mountain. Haydn suggests letting the dogs stay in the shot, but I nix that. They'll be too meek and mild-looking and that is not what I want strangers to think.

So we shoot the morbid but effective opening and then Haydn asks me a bunch of questions that I don't know the answers to, but I do explain that Roderick had been out here to write a story about me, and why. And as I'm outlining our day together, I realize tears are welling up in my eyes and I'm struggling to blink them back. Finally, I throw my hand at the camera, wanting them to turn it off. "Please," I say.

"Fabulous!" Hadyn announces a moment later when the camera shuts off. "Perfect in one take."

"Oh, shut up," I tell him, getting out of the chair, walking briskly out of the kitchen and up the stairs to my room, slamming the door behind me.

A little while later, there is a quiet knock and the door opens. "They're ready to leave, Sally," my mother says. "I think Haydn would like the chance to apologize."

"He won't mean it," I tell her, looking out the window. "He's thrilled I broke down on camera. He's thrilled Roderick's half-dead, they all are."

I hear Mother sigh a bit. I hazard a look back at her. She's crossed her arms over her chest. "You know better than that," she says quietly. "They're worried about you. Alexandra sent her brother."

I don't bother to tell her I'm sure Alexandra has very little to do with why David's here, and that he's married and his intentions are anything but honorable.

And that I am thrilled to see him.

What the hell is the matter with me?

Wordlessly I roll off the bed and walk back downstairs where Haydn apologizes, saying he knows it's been a tough twenty-four hours. I tell him not to worry about it, everything's fine, and walk him out to the van to say goodbye to everybody. The sliding cargo door is still open and I see that David looks as though he is dying a thousand deaths for having come. Well, he should be.

"Drive carefully, guys," I tell them.

As they drive out, Buddy D'Amico pulls in. I bring him inside where he reports to Mother and me that our stalker, Luke

Jervis, was seen in Castleford yesterday. "The question is, Sally," Buddy says, "could he have been up there yesterday at Castle Kerry? Could he have followed you two?"

I tell him I don't have the slightest idea. And I don't.

CHAPTER SEVENTEEN

"**I**'m surprised Buddy D'Amico let you leave Castleford," Alexandra says Monday afternoon, breezing into my office at DBS.

"I didn't ask him to," I say without looking up from my work.

In my peripheral vision I can see that the anchorwoman is still wearing her overcoat (a long, navy blue, capelike affair with hood, à la *The French Lieutenant's Woman*) and is still carrying her purse and briefcase, which implies a certain eagerness to see me. She dumps her purse and briefcase on my couch, unbuttons her coat and pulls up a chair to the other side of my desk. She slips her coat off and starts tugging at her leather gloves. "Ah," she says, reading upside down, "Tad's draft for the economic forecast. Good. But why aren't you doing it on the computer?"

"Mother says if you want a student to do better," I say, "you've got to give them something to refer back to when they try the same exercise again." I straighten up, twirl the papers around in her direction and push them over to her. "I didn't grade it, but I think he'll get the point."

"He flunked all right," Alexandra murmurs, scanning the copy that has red ink lines and slashes and comments scribbled all over it.

"Who is he related to again?" I ask, sitting back in my chair.

"He's Cordelia Payne's nephew—Jackson Darenbrook's sister," she answers, turning a page.

"And this kid supposedly went to the University of North Carolina?"

"That's what they tell me. But I don't think he'll be here long." She pushes the papers back toward me. "He told Will he's waiting to hear if he can work in Dale Earnhardt Jr.'s pit crew." She smiles. "Thanks for doing that, by the way."

"You're welcome." I scoot my chair closer to my desk and fold my hands neatly in front of me. "And what may I do for you this fine afternoon?"

She sits back in her chair, pushing her dark hair up with both hands and holding it there a moment. It looks good that way. She wore her hair like that to last year's Emmys and for a second, people didn't recognize her. Her shoulder-length hair, as well as the blue-gray eyes, has become her trademark.

"I'm just very surprised and very happy to see you here." She drops her hair and leans forward to rest her arms on my desk. "And I'm very, very sorry about what happened." Pause. "How are you?"

"The whole thing was very weird," I tell her. "I'm still in a little bit of shock." I take a breath. "I went up last night to Hartford Hospital. I saw Roderick in ICU. He's in a coma."

"So I heard," she says quietly. "Any new leads?"

"Not to publicize."

She gives her head a little shake, as if to separate this Alexandra Waring from Alexandra Waring, news-hungry anchorwoman. I know better than to completely buy this distinction.

"Off the record," I say. "That stalker guy, Luke Jervis? He was seen in Castleford on Saturday. Buddy's trying to link him with what happened."

Alexandra squints a little. "But you would have seen him, right? I was under the impression there was no way anyone else could have been up there."

"Oh, there's a way," I say, nodding. "Down the road—it's maybe four hundred yards down the access road from the castle. Well, here, let me show you." I pull out some schematics I drew yesterday and show her the one that spans a quarter-mile radius around Castle Kerry. "See, this is the access road that splits off from the Castle Kerry road to reach the transmission towers in Southington. It's possible somebody could have parked on that road, cut through here, and then come up the ravine side of the castle. I certainly did it as a kid. There's an egress there." I gnaw on my thumb a second and then sit back in my chair. "The timing's weird though and that guy, Jervis, looked malnourished to me, weak—you know?"

Alexandra nods.

"So it's hard for me to believe he could think and act that quickly and be physically capable of doing anyone harm." I bite my lower lip and raise my eyebrows. "But that's what Buddy's looking at." I shrug. "And I'm at a loss to explain what happened otherwise."

"Did you drive in last night?"

"No, Joe picked me up early this morning. Buddy impounded my Jeep, thank you."

"You're not a suspect," she assures me. She lowers her eyes for a moment and then says, "I might as well tell you that *Expectations* has already filed a lawsuit against us today and legal says there's probably one in the works against you personally."

I blink.

"And I talked to Verity yesterday. She's her usual horrid self, determined to bring us all down." A small smile. "I'm not convinced it's Roderick Reynolds that she's upset about—

I think it's the fact that the whole wide world knows she hired a writer that used to write for *Screw*."

At this, we both laugh heartily.

"So does she think I pushed him?" I ask.

"No." Alexandra absently touches one of her diamond studs. "It's liability issues for them, I'm sure. Sue us before he sues them."

"I hope he does sue them," I say quietly. "Because it would mean he was going to live. Without brain damage."

Alexandra meets my eyes. "I sense in some way you feel responsible."

"You sense that I feel guilty," I tell her. "If you knew the thoughts I had about him on Saturday—I mean, Alexandra, I wanted to physically *hurt* this man—"

"Come on," she interrupts. "If anything, you should be livid with us, with me. We made you do the interview, Sally. We told you everything was going to be fine when we knew it would probably be a hatchet job, but we needed the exposure."

"Roderick said something to me on Saturday that made sense to me." I try not to look as upset about what I am about to say as I am. "He kept asking me what kind of credible newscast would want to have a loose woman as its representative."

"Who said you were a loose woman?"

"During the trial, just about every media outlet in the country," I suggest.

She looks sad. "Sally, if DBS News was vulnerable to what was said or written about me, we would have folded years ago. Or at least DBS would have yanked me off the air." She shrugs, raising her hand to gesture. "People are either going to give you their time and attention and eventually their trust, or they won't. It's as simple as that. And we're betting that your viewers will be younger and hipper. You know, they watch *Survivor,* buy their clothes at the mall, their children have 'play dates,' they lease cars."

Maybe.

"And it's not as if your behavior has been—" She searches for a word. *"Excessive,"* she decides upon. "It's just that speculations about your personal life have been...rather well publicized, shall we say."

I think of Paul and me coupling like animals the other night in the driveway and look away. "The second I'm on the air, you know that tape of me and Spencer will surface."

"I'm not so sure about that."

"It's going to be like that Rob Lowe tape at the Democratic convention," I say, feeling my throat tightening. "That thing's *still* floating around after all these years."

"It's not your job to worry about it," Alexandra finally says, standing up. She turns around to pick up her coat and sling it over her arm. "It's your job to show up, be smart, write well, read well, react well, get the facts straight and report the news in a way people can fully understand."

True.

"And after twenty years in the business, I do know a thing or two," she adds, walking over to retrieve her purse and briefcase. "And I'd bet my career on you." She turns around. "Understood?"

"Excuse me," a tentative voice says at the door. It is Edith, our researcher. Today's piece of yarn is pastel blue, which of course matches the cardigan. "I wouldn't interrupt, Ms. Waring," Edith says, moving forward in a two-steps-forward-one-step-back fashion, "but Sally asked that I—"

"It's all right, Edith," Alexandra assures her, moving toward the door, "I was just leaving."

Edith's eyes nervously dart about and then sneak over again

to look at Alexandra as she walks out. Her face has flushed red. She is hopelessly in love with Alexandra, we've all decided, but is devoted to me for delivering her from the Darenbrook Communications general research pool.

"So what's up? Have a seat."

"I'm afraid I still don't have much to report," Edith says. "It's most frustrating."

"I don't want you spending a whole lot of time on this, Edith. It's not work related, as I explained to you. It's a personal favor."

Edith sits down in the seat recently vacated by Alexandra. "I don't officially begin work until two," she reminds me. "Two until ten, with a half hour for lunch and a coffee break," she recites. She leans forward slightly. "I've finally located someone in Sharon, Connecticut, who may be able to help us, but he's not home right now." She looks down at her pad. "His name is James Mather. He's the current president of a regional historical society, and he is reputed to have been a close friend of Harold Durrant."

"The man who wrote to Uncle Percy."

"Yes."

"So where is this James Mather?" I ask, writing his name down on a sticky.

"He's traveling, but he is soon to return and I have left several messages for him to please contact us."

"Good. What about the Hillstone Town Hall?"

"They're sending the copy of the letter back to you. They still insist there is no record of your great-uncle anywhere in their files or database."

I make a sound of skepticism. "What about the attorney guy? Did you find out anything about him?"

"Received his law degree from Syracuse and is in private practice. I'm waiting to hear what kind of practice it is."

"I told you he said he worked part-time for the township, didn't I?"

"Yes, but it hasn't been verified yet." She absently fingers the neck of her cardigan. "I'm attempting to circumvent Hillstone Township by making inquiries through the state system."

Ah. Good. She's getting one of the Nerd Brigade to do a little more unobtrusive hacking.

"I've also written down some information regarding the major land transactions in the area for the last twenty years." She stretches to hand me a sheet of neatly printed names, dates and locations.

I scan it. "Are these housing developments?"

"Not all. Two are wealthy people who took over the larger part of farms to use as country retreats."

"The Hudson Cement Project," I read. "What's that?"

"It's huge, if nothing else. Nothing's been built yet, but it's some kind of proposed factory site. As you can see, it's a lot of land, stretching from Hillstone Falls into Claverack."

"I see." But I don't. I don't know what any of this could mean. "Thank you very much, Edith," I tell her. "But remember, none of this is to be on company time, and I expect an accounting from you of any services that DBS needs reimbursement for."

"Be rest assured," she says, rising.

After Edith departs, I call down to the newsroom to see if Cordelia Payne's nephew, Tad, has rolled in yet. The answer is no. I look at my watch. He's forty-eight minutes late. We get a hundred good applicants for every entry-level job here and we have to pay this jerk.

I tackle my in-box, into which Alexandra's office habitually dumps the problems that were dumped on her. On top is a memo about an alcoholic news executive at the Houston affiliate. I reach for the telephone to call human resources and think about how wonderful it will be, in the near future, not to have to deal with this stuff anymore.

I plow straight through my tasks until just after two when my second line rings. "Sally, it's Mother."

By the sound of her voice I already know something is wrong.

"I just got the strangest call from Margaret Kennerly at the Gregory Home about Uncle Percy." I can hear people in the background and realize Mother is still at school.

"She said a man showed up about a half hour ago and asked to see Percy. The receptionist at the front desk was suspicious—she had never seen or heard of him before—and went in to tell Margaret. She came out and the man told her he was Percy's cousin, John Harrington, and to buy a little time so that she could check this man out, Margaret said she was sorry, but Percy wasn't there, he was out."

"Who is he?"

"I have no idea. I've never heard of a John Harrington, except your cousin that died. And Margaret said he just didn't look quite the ticket, that he didn't speak the way she would have expected and that there was something not right about his eyes. He made her very nervous."

I frown. "That's so weird. And was Uncle Percy there?"

"Yes. And she apologized profusely for putting this man off, in case he is a relative, but then when she went upstairs to ask Percy if he knew a John Harrington, Percy said no. Except for your cousin who died."

"Mother, call Buddy. Unless you want me to. I'm going to grab my stuff, right now, and come home. Ask Buddy to send somebody over to the Gregory Home, or ask him if he can go himself."

"Do you really think that's necessary?" She is unsettled by

my reaction, I can tell, but too many strange things are happening to spare her nerves.

"It may very well be that stalker guy, Mother, the Jervis guy. And in light of what happened on Saturday, I think it's best to err on the side of caution. So please call Buddy."

"I will," Mother says faintly.

"And I don't want you to go home until I get there. Or I send somebody over to meet you." I look at my watch.

"I don't think—"

"Mother, swear to me you won't leave school until I tell you it's okay."

Pause. "All right."

"And I'm calling Buddy myself right now. I'll see you in a couple hours."

I disconnect the phone, flip open my Rolodex and call the Castleford Police Station. When I explain who it is and why I'm calling, they patch me through to Buddy at another location.

"Where the hell are you?" he wants to know. "And don't say *home*, because I've already been to your cottage and I'm standing here now at your mother's."

I skip the question and tell him about Mother's call, about the man at the Gregory Home. Buddy says he'll get somebody over there immediately. I also tell him I've instructed Mother to stay at school until I get there. "Where *are* you, Sally? I can't protect you and your family unless we know where all of you are."

"I know, I know," I tell him. "But just get someone over to the Gregory Home, will you?"

"And get your ass out here, understand?"

I switch lines and buzz Benjamin, asking him to find a DBS car that can get me out to Castleford ASAP, and see if Haydn can come up here to take over on this economic forecast/Nephew Tad fiasco. Then I throw some stuff into my briefcase, wishing I could swing by my apartment, but knowing I don't have the time.

Benjamin appears in the doorway. "Alexandra's brother's going to drive you," he announces. "He'll meet you downstairs in ten minutes."

"Call one of the rental agencies if there isn't a DBS car available," I tell him, going for my coat.

"David was going out to Wallingford today to see his daughter anyway," Alexandra says, appearing next to Benjamin.

"So why didn't he see her yesterday while he was out there?" I snap, irritated. This is all I need.

Alexandra murmurs something to Benjamin and he leaves. She closes the door. "I would prefer that he takes you." She cocks her head to the side, crossing her arms. "What's going on?"

"Look, I don't want to offend you, Alexandra," I tell her. "He's your brother—"

"And he's ganging up on me with Georgiana and I want him out of my hair," she finishes. "So he's taking you, all right? He was supposed to leave and he's staying another week and he's driving me absolutely up the wall."

I glare at her. "As it happens, it's *not* all right. You'll have to find another solution to your domestic *challenges*."

She holds out her hand. "So where's the brat's economic forecast?"

I sigh heavily, walk back to my desk to swoop it up and march back over to slap it into her hand. "Haydn's coming up for it."

"I'll take care of it myself," she says.

"Fine, whatever," I say, grabbing my briefcase, "but I'm not going out with your brother. Pun intended." I try to walk around her but she grabs my arm with surprising strength and pulls me back in front of her. There's a knock at my door and she drops her hand.

The door opens. "What am I supposed to tell people about Sally?" Benjamin wants to know. "We just got through telling everyone she was here and I've a stack of stuff that just came up from the newsroom. Will's not here again, he's not coming in—"

"Sally's on temporary leave," Alexandra announces without turning around. "As of this moment. Forward all of her calls and e-mails to Haydn. We might as well see what he's made of."

"Oh, criminy," Benjamin sighs, "can't we ever get anyone else to come in every day except the two of us?" He pulls the door closed a little harder than necessary.

Alexandra turns to face me. "Here's where we are, Sally." She starts ticking off items on her fingers: "I want somebody to call me and tell me what's going on out there in Castleford and I know it's not going to be you. Two, my brother has to get the hell out of here before I wring his neck. Three, he needs to see his daughter and he didn't see her yesterday because his daughter refused to see him. She's mad at him. And, finally, four." Her voice softens a little. "My brother's wife is absolute poison and I would like him to spend a little time with a woman who might make him wake up to that fact—particularly since he's separated." She turns for the door, takes hold of the doorknob and turns back to look at me again. "My brother is a gentleman and would never do anything out of line. At the very worst, he might ask you for your advice. At least, dear God, I hope so."

And with that, she leaves me.

CHAPTER EIGHTEEN

I imagined that David would be driving the navy blue MG Alexandra keeps in the city, but he arrives in the West End driveway in a vehicle I don't recognize, an all-wheel-drive silver Mercedes station wagon.

"That car couldn't climb over a snowball," David says about Alexandra's MG as we drive out the gates to Twelfth Avenue, "and we're supposed to get snow."

I look at the sky. It is vaguely gray, but the air doesn't seem heavy to me, the way it should before it snows.

"I didn't think so either," he says. "But the weather guy said there's a front blowing in from the east." (Great, the brother reads minds, too.)

"Isn't that what you were thinking?" he asks me a little while later as he accelerates to join the outbound traffic on the West Side Highway. "That it doesn't look like snow?"

"Yes," I admit. "I should remember you're from a farming family, that you'd think the same way."

He smiles. "That's what I figured about you."

This has got to win the award for strangest conversation in quite some time.

"It's not a good sign in New England," I remark, looking

out my window at the trees of Riverside Park racing by, "when the wind blows in from the Atlantic. We could get walloped." After a minute, I say, "My family hasn't farmed in a hundred years."

"Doesn't matter," he says. "I've seen where your parents built their house. It's in your blood."

I smile slightly. I must admit, the weather has always seemed to have inordinate amount of importance in my family.

"The MG used to be mine, you know, that's how I know how it handles in the snow. I used to slide off the road in it all the time."

"And then it got passed on to your sister?"

He nods, putting on his signal to change into the left-hand lane, and then looking back over his shoulder before he does so. "I don't know where she gets the parts for it these days."

"She has another one in the barn at the farm," I tell him. "It looks cannibalized."

He looks at me in surprise. "Huh. I didn't know that." He focuses on his driving now, verifying which way he should take. He is wearing corduroy slacks, a sweater, shirt and fleece-lined leather coat. He smells good. I don't recognize the aftershave.

I excuse myself to check in with Buddy, who complains he has so many telephone numbers for me he never knows where or how to find me. "I have seven numbers!" he cries. I notice how David has the same shaped knuckles and nails as his sister, but that his fingers are proportionally shorter, thicker. *Good working hands,* Daddy would say.

Funny that Paul's hands are more refined. The cop has refined hands; the congressman's son's hands are workmanlike. Interesting.

"Your home number in Castleford, your mother's, your apartment in New York, your office, your cell phone—which is at the station, I find—the newsroom and what the hell is this number?" he rants, rattling off a New York number I've never heard of. "It's Spencer Hawes's apartment, I bet," he mutters. "Okay, so here's where we are, Sal— Where are you, by the way?"

"White Plains. About an hour and fifteen minutes away."

"You're speeding then," he tells me.

I flinch, being reminded of a recent insurance notice I received that after my third speeding ticket within two years they're canceling my policy. I have yet to scour the world for another. "No," I tell him, craning my neck to check the speedometer, "a friend's speeding for me."

Buddy says he has a plainclothes officer inside the Gregory Home, roaming the vast network of community rooms and hallways under the guise of a health inspector. Another officer is parked down the street in an unmarked car. When I say how grateful I am, he says, "Yeah, well, let's hold off on that until we take care of this."

The hair on the back of my neck goes up. "What do you mean?"

"Right after this guy left the Gregory Home, he went downtown to the senior center and was asking around about your uncle."

I frown.

"He's definitely *not* your stalker," he tells me. "Whoever this guy is, he weighs about a hundred pounds more than Luke Jervis and he drives a Lexus, not the heap Jervis had. So we're waiting for him to return to the GH to find out what the story is."

I ask Buddy to hold on for a second and bury my phone in my coat. "I need to get something straight, David. Can I, or can I not, trust you to keep a confidence from your sister?"

"Give me a dollar and we'll consider it lawyer-client privilege," he says without batting an eye, taking the left-hand exit off the Cross County Parkway.

I wrestle a dollar out of my pocket and hand it to him. "Okay, Buddy, so listen," I say. "I think I might know what it could be about." And I explain to him about the possibility of Percy owning land in New York, and how I had been making inquiries about it in Hillstone Falls on Saturday and how I was stonewalled. "The whole thing smells to high heaven and I wouldn't be surprised if someone slipped over to see how much Uncle Percy knows about that land. It's got that 'somebody-in-the-family-screwed-us feel,' if you know what I mean."

"Maybe," Buddy says, considering this. There is noise on his end. "What?" Buddy says to someone. He lets out an expletive. "Get a car over there and I'm on my way. Tell them to put her somewhere that doesn't have windows. Sally?" he says, coming back. "Now we've got some guy at your mother's school asking to see her. By name."

My stomach churns.

"And this *does* sound like Jervis."

"What is going on?" I murmur, trying to think.

"Look, I want everybody out of here," Buddy says. "Your mother—I don't care where she goes, Sally, but get her out of town for a few days."

"Done. I was planning to send her to Mack's tonight anyway."

"And I think you should get Percy away from the Gregory Home," he continues. "We've got over seventy senior citizens over there, including my aunt Rosalie, so the last thing I want is for us to be running around there playing cops and robbers and scaring everybody."

"I'll pick him up," I promise. "But I need the Jeep back. Can I pick it up?"

Another expletive. Buddy's upset all right; he almost never uses profanity. At least not around me.

Buddy is talking to someone else again. "No, go ahead, you drive." Another muttered expletive. Then a sigh. To me, "Why do I have to be the one who has to ask you this?"

"Ask me what?"

"It's about the Jeep. The preliminary lab report says there are recent stains on the driver's seat."

I squint. "What kind of stain?"

"Semen stains. On the driver's seat. And they're very recent."

Oh, God.

"The blood work on Reynolds isn't in yet," Buddy says, "so I need to ask you now if there's anything else you need to tell me about your relationship with Roderick Reynolds?"

He thinks the semen stains belong to Roderick Reynolds. He needs to clarify our relationship because it might imply a motive for me to push him off the cliff.

I take a deep breath, trying to get my stomach to settle. "They won't match up with Roderick. They were from about two o'clock in the morning."

The silence is truly awful.

"Paul?"

"Paul," I confirm.

"Okay, good," Buddy finally murmurs and I imagine he is making a note. "I'm sorry, but I had to ask you about it."

When I get off the phone, I simply sit there, watching the road. David glances over, but has the good sense not to say anything.

In a minute I call Mother's cell phone and reach her message center. "Mother, please call me about what's going on there. Buddy's on his way over and I'm about an hour away. Please call. Note the new number I'm calling from. The police have my old cell phone. I love you. And I'm worried—so please call."

"I could use some gas," David says. "Maybe you would like some air."

I must look as nauseous as I feel.

"Two minutes, that's it," he says without waiting for a response, taking the exit for the Mobil rest area. "Maybe you should go in and get something to drink."

I get out of the car. The cold air feels good. As I head toward the mart, my cell phone rings.

"We're having a little bit of excitement here," Mother says.

"Did they get him?"

"Not yet. He's in the woods behind the football field somewhere."

"And it's the same guy?"

"It sounds like him. I didn't actually see him. He walked in the front doors of the school and went into the office and said to Mrs. Otavi, 'I'm here to see Sally Harrington's mother.' Gloria said if he hadn't looked so strange—he was wearing some kind of Beatles sweatshirt—she would have thought something had happened to you. But she quickly caught on, God bless her."

"For a stalker who supposedly doesn't know what he's doing," I say, taking a few steps to stand by the air pump, "he seems to know an awful lot about our lives, doesn't he? Listen, Mother, Buddy wants to make sure you go to Mack's for a couple of nights until this is cleared up."

Silence.

"Did you hear me, Mother? Didn't Mack get home?"

"Yes, but I'm not wild about the idea."

"I know it's a long commute, but—"

"It's not the commute," Mother says. "It's the appearance of it."

Leave it to Mother. "There's no one within a mile of Mack's

house to even see that you're there," I say. "Besides, you've spent the night there before and you didn't seem to care then."

"Oh, I cared," she assures me. "Now, what about the dogs? I can't take them both."

Good, she is shaken up, and she is really going to go. Hallelujah.

"I'll take them," I say. "DBS has security all set up for me," I lie.

"Then why can't I stay with you?"

"Don't shoot the messenger, Mother, I'm just telling you what Buddy asked me to do. He wants you out of town for a couple of days. Call him if you don't believe me." I look at my watch. "We've just crossed into Connecticut. Don't leave school until four, okay? And then I'll meet you at the house. Okay? I'll pack you a bag and see you off."

There is the squawk of a walkie-talkie. A man is talking to Mother. "No," I hear her say. "I'm going to stay in my classroom until four." He says something. "Why?" she asks. He says something. "All right," she says, sounding tired. "They haven't found him yet, Sally, and they want me to go into the teachers' lounge."

When I hang up with Mother, I hold my forehead in my hand a minute. I feel something on my hand and look up. It's starting to snow.

Where can I take Uncle Percy? And not make him suspect that something's wrong?

I know someone who works in the New Haven Courthouse, who has a hideaway Doug's used as a safe house for key witnesses in capital murder and drug cases before. But to use the safe house would pull Doug into this, I think wearily, and that's all I need. I've got enough lawyers and would-be lawyers around me to last a lifetime. Besides, how would I take care of Uncle Percy in such a place?

I jump at the touch on my shoulder.

"I'm sorry, I didn't mean to startle you," David says. "But unless you need to use the ladies' room, we're ready to go." He holds out a can of Coke to me that has a paper cup upside down over the top. "I thought this might taste good to you."

Brother like sister, the Warings are always holding Coca-Cola Classics out to people they think are going to faint.

I thank him, accepting it, and walk back to the car.

"If I can be of any help—" he says, hurrying around the car to open the door for me.

"I might," I say. And then I stop suddenly, bringing a hand up to my mouth.

David releases the door and quickly moves to my side. "Are you going to be sick?"

"No, I'm fine," I say, not meaning to sound so irritated. "It's just that I think I'm beginning to get what's going on." I dive for the car. "Come on, we need to put the pedal to the metal."

I make calls all the way to Castleford.

III

Allies & Enemies

CHAPTER NINETEEN

To make sure Mother will go to Mack's house in Middletown, I make David put on my sunglasses and park the station wagon on the side of Mother's driveway. I tell him to sit there as if he is a guard waiting for an assault. Mother packs for a week and leaves the dogs in my care.

Once I know that Mother is really and truly gone, I walk back outside and cross the driveway to David's car. He rolls his window down and I ask him for a ride to the local car rental place. We get into an argument. "This is the part where you go see your daughter in Wallingford, remember?"

"I've been listening to you make these calls all the way from New York. There's no way I'm clearing out yet. You shouldn't be on your own."

I rest my hand on the roof of the car. "I told you before, I have a police officer in my life."

"Fifteen miles away in New Haven," he says. "Going to school at night, working seven to three-thirty during the day." He narrows his eyes slightly. "You're going to have to do better than that."

After a moment, I straighten up. "You are most obnoxiously like your sister right now."

He looks at his watch. "Come on, we better get going on your uncle Percy."

"Fine," I tell him, opening his door, "but I'm driving."

That settled, David hauls himself out of the car and walks around to the passenger side.

He's taller than I remember. I like that leather jacket. Corduroys fit well, too.

Sometimes I amaze myself with how my mind works.

I take off for downtown Castleford. The Mercedes wagon handles beautifully, although I miss being higher up in the Jeep. I get on 691 to zip across town and then exit on the east side. Within a minute I am parking in a spot near the double doors of a relatively new three-story office building whose sign proudly proclaims: O'Hearn Construction.

"I do this by myself, thank you," I tell David, getting out of the car.

In the lobby the receptionist looks both ready and vaguely scared to see me. "Miss Harrington," she says, making three people in the corner of the lobby stop talking and turn around to look. I recognize one of the men—an electrician—and say hello, and he nods, evidently fascinated by my presence there.

Of course he is. This is the company that employed the man who killed my father. "Hi," I say, walking up to the reception desk. "I think Mr. O'Hearn is expecting me."

"Yes, he is," she says. "Just let me call."

While she does, I walk around to look at the artistic renderings of some of the O'Hearn construction projects. School. Train station. Office building. Condominiums. Highway overpass. Waterside mall. On a sign that reads, Building in 31 States, added in thick Magic Marker is written, & 6 Countries! (It's not really corrected by hand, though; on closer inspection I see that it is a printed graphic.)

"He will be right down," the receptionist announces.

Moments later Phillip O'Hearn is coming down the open staircase, smiling. "Sally," he says loudly, holding out both hands to me in a gesture I know is being theatrically offered for the benefit of our audience. News of our meeting will spread quickly through Castleford.

I play along, smiling, extending my hand for him to shake with both of his, and then he leads the way back up the stairs to his office.

It's some office. Wood paneling, leather chairs studded with brass tacks, maple bookcases, a wall of glass looking across the horizon to the Hanging Hills. He seats me on the leather love seat in the corner, pulls up a chair and sits as if he's a coach, leaning forward to rest his elbows on his knees and clasping his hands, tie hanging between his legs. He smiles. "Tell me for what I deserve this honor."

I know I am supposed to still hate this balding sixty-something tycoon, but I have witnessed some of the recent torment he's been through. His wife of forty years was stricken last year with a virulent form of cancer, of which she died in November. The thing is, before she died, she pleaded to see me so that she could tell me about a lie she had told her husband twenty-three years before, a lie that had prompted O'Hearn to have my father killed. Afterward, O'Hearn begged me to tell him what she had said, and so I did. And now he has to live with the knowledge that my father—formerly his best friend and mentor—was killed for absolutely no reason.

So do I still hate him, I wonder.

No, I don't feel much of anything, really, sitting here. It could be my heart has simply shut down altogether at this point in the matter of how and why my father died, or maybe

I am merely intensely focused on the matter at hand, which is to obtain O'Hearn's help.

"I've got a favor to ask of you," I tell him.

"Anything," he tells me.

And I believe he means it. Forgiveness is his only chance now and, judging by the weight he has lost and the circles under his eyes, O'Hearn knows that if he is ever able to forgive himself, the key will lie with my family. "My uncle Percy," I begin, "has suddenly become of enormous interest to a shady-looking guy, and given the turmoil Mother and I are in at the moment—"

"I heard about the accident at Castle Kerry," he concedes.

"But you haven't heard about our stalker," I tell him. "Anyway, the situation is, for the sake of the other residents in the Gregory Home, Buddy D'Amico wants me to send Uncle Percy somewhere for a little while."

"This is Percy Harrington? Dodge's uncle?"

I nod. "Yes. Grandfather's youngest brother. The thing is, I'm not in a position to be able to care for him and I need him taken somewhere—" I look at my watch. "Like thirty minutes ago."

O'Hearn straightens up, absently scratching the side of his face. "What about Belle?" He mentions Mother's name softly, in a voice full of emotion.

"Mother's already left town."

"What on earth—" he begins, frowning. "All right. Tell me what you want me to do."

"I want you to take Uncle Percy. I'm pretty sure I can get him out of the Gregory Home without being seen, but I don't want him to know that anything's wrong. He's eighty-four, he wasn't feeling so hot over the weekend, and I'd like him to stay in good shape."

O'Hearn's eyebrows knit together. He used to wear glasses, but recently, I heard, had laser surgery. He looked better with the glasses, I decide, but with his kind of money I don't suppose it matters anymore what he looks like.

"Do you want to bring him to my house?"

Given the extensive security around O'Hearn's nouveau riche mansion, this wouldn't be such a bad idea. But there's no way Uncle Percy is going be the guest of the guy he thinks is responsible for the murder of his nephew, regardless of whether that guy feels bad about it now or not.

"I know it's a lot to ask, but I was wondering if you could get someone to take him somewhere warm. Then I can tell him I won a trip, but that I can't go, and he has to go in my place." Now I lean forward. "And I'd like Uncle Percy to be accompanied by one of your really, really strong guys, if you know what I mean."

"I'm not sure that I do," O'Hearn says.

"Like the guy who drives you around sometimes?"

"Ah," he says, getting it. "A bodyguard."

The irony is, O'Hearn originally got the bodyguard and his extensive security system because of me.

"I'll do it, Sally. I'll do it for you. But I would like to know a little bit more about what you think this might be about."

"Sure," I tell him, falling back against the couch and crossing my legs. "Except I don't really know what's going on. Except that Buddy arrested a stalker on my mother's property last weekend and he showed up again today, at Mother's school, a magazine writer who was interviewing me on Saturday was nearly killed, and Buddy's beginning to think it wasn't an accident. And today, some big, creepy guy is trying to get into the Gregory Home to see Uncle Percy, but it's not the stalker guy."

O'Hearn frowns again. "Is this all related?"

"Could be," I say, throwing up my hands. "All I know for sure is, anyone I can't personally protect I want away from here, and I need someone to take good care of Uncle Percy. I can't do it."

"And you have no idea who it was that came to the Gregory Home."

I sigh, shaking my head. "The man claimed to be Percy's cousin—who we've never heard of—and he was so strange, and so intimidating, Margaret Kennerly put him off until she could check him out. Right after that, a man—we think the same one—went downtown to the senior center to ask about Uncle Percy. Buddy's had the Gregory Home under watch since then, but the guy hasn't come back yet."

"And whose stalker is it? Is he yours or your mother's?"

"Mine. He can't find me, though, but he has found Mother. Today he showed up at school, asking to see Sally Harrington's mother. Then he got nervous and ran off, and they haven't found him yet, either." I sigh. "So Mother's staying elsewhere for a while."

"That's wise." He's thinking. And then, "Do you have any idea what this business about Percy could be about? So I can plan better for your uncle? Like where to send him and for how long?"

I consider this and think, *Why not? Maybe he'll see something we missed.* "I think that the guy might have gone to the Gregory Home because of this," I say, extracting papers from my blazer pocket. I unfold them and hand O'Hearn a copy of the letter from Harold Durrant to Uncle Percy about the possibility of the trust purchasing his land.

He quickly reads the letter and looks up. "I didn't think there was anything left in either the Harrington estate or the old family trust."

"Nor did we," I say. And then I explain about going up to Hillstone Township Saturday morning and getting the runaround, the dead ends Edith found and how strange it all was.

"It wouldn't be strange at all not to have any records," O'Hearn says, "if this guy Durrant scammed Percy's land."

"Durrant's dead, though," I tell him.

"But I bet his fellow environmentalists aren't," he says, returning the letter to me.

I try to think. The clerk in Hillstone Town Hall had said something about how Harold Durrant used to be in the records office all the time. Is it possible that when he didn't get a response from Uncle Percy, he simply "acquired" the property for the land trust by altering records in some way?

O'Hearn smiles knowingly at me. "Just because they're environmentalists doesn't mean they're honest in their means to get what they want."

As a developer, I should think of course O'Hearn would suspect this, but I also have little doubt about the variety of methods O'Hearn Construction employed in its quest for success.

I hand him my second sheet of paper. "Do any of these names ring a bell? They're the major land deals in and around Hillstone Township for the last twenty years."

He accepts the paper and scans the list, his eyes coming back to one. "Two of these are housing developments I'm familiar with. But this one—" He turns the paper toward me and taps his finger on the Hudson Cement Project.

"I noticed that one, too."

"It's not one," he says, pointing, "it's these four as well. They're all subsidiaries of World Sound Industries out of Canada." He looks at the paper again and nods. "Yeah. Hillstone Falls, bordering Claverack, I know what this is." He presses his lips into a line and shakes his head. "Not good, Sally. If this has anything to do with these guys, it's not good."

"Why, who are they?" I'm getting that creepy feeling again in the back of my neck.

"It's who works for them that's the problem. But listen, let's just focus on getting Percy safely out of here first," he says, standing up. "I'll be right back." He walks outside of his office. After about ten minutes, he pokes his head back in. "How about Florida? I can fly him down on the corporate jet. It's at Bradley."

"That's a great deal more than what I was hoping for," I tell him. "Thank you. That would be great."

About two minutes later, O'Hearn comes back in to discuss logistics. I am to slip Uncle Percy out of the Gregory Home and meet a man named Louie DeMateo, in the parking lot of Castle Bank. Louie will then take Uncle Percy to Bradley and then on to Florida. "Bal Harbor?" he asks. "I've got a great location there." I nod in agreement.

I call the Gregory Home and tell Margaret Kennerly of my plan to take Uncle Percy away. She would particularly welcome such a plan right now, she says, since one of the residents recognized the unmarked police car outside the entrance—because the officer sitting in it is her best friend's grandson—and the resident has been running around raising the alarm that the Gregory Home is surrounded by cops.

Then I call Uncle Percy and tell him the great news: I won a trip to Florida but I can't go! Would he like to go in my stead? In like forty-five minutes? No, I'm sorry, I tell him, he can't take Mrs. Milner.

O'Hearn is waving at me, so I cover the phone. "Go ahead, let him bring a friend," he says. "There's plenty of room. And in ways, it'll be a lot easier." I nod and start to tell Uncle Percy this, but then O'Hearn starts waving at me again.

"What?" I whisper to O'Hearn.

"I know Shirley Milner," he whispers back. "So you better

tell Percy there will be a chaperon at all times, and it will all be quite proper, not to worry."

I can't help but chuckle a little; O'Hearn smiles.

I tell Uncle Percy the good news, that the company has agreed that Mrs. Milner can go, too, but there must be a chaperon at all times. Yes, I'll be right over to handle all the paperwork with Margaret Kennerly. Yes, I tell him, we'll have the number where Mrs. Milner's family can reach her. Yes, he needs to get packing. Now.

I hang up and look at O'Hearn. "Go get your great-uncle," he tells me, "and let's see him off, safe and sound, for a Florida vacation. But I'm going to make some calls on this Hillstone land, Sally, and I'll get back to you later tonight. Where can I find you?"

"Try Mother's first and if I don't pick up, then try my house." I scribble both numbers down on his telephone pad and hand it to him.

"Is that a good idea?" he says, frowning. "To go to your mother's? Isn't that where the stalker first showed up?"

"To be honest? I sort of hope he does come," I say in a low voice, thinking of my grandfather's Parker shotgun in the gun safe.

O'Hearn studies my face a minute, but doesn't pursue the subject. "Well, on this end," he says, walking me to the door, "I can promise you, Sally, no one is going to get near your uncle Percy. Not while he's on his vacation." He opens the door for me and hesitates.

I take a breath and hold out my hand to him.

And we shake.

It's the first time I've voluntarily touched Phillip O'Hearn since I slugged him at the country club.

CHAPTER TWENTY

When I finally reach the Gregory Home, Margaret Kennerly is clearly relieved to see me. "I didn't mean to imply that Percy couldn't stay here," she begins, "because this *is* his home—"

"No, I understand," I interrupt, explaining that Mother is spending a few days out of town, too.

"Really?" Margaret says. "And is this related to Percy?"

"Actually, no," I reluctantly admit. "We have another problem. A stalker."

"And it's not the same man?"

I shake my head. "Not unless he was wearing a Beatles sweatshirt and looked half-starved."

"No," she acknowledges. "This man was *very* well fed. And big. Six-four at least. The problem is, that accident Saturday on Castle Kerry already had the residents talking and they've been grilling Percy about it." I get the message. *The faster you're out of here, Sally, the better.*

We go over the paperwork involved with Uncle Percy and Shirley Milner going on a trip and I give Margaret the number O'Hearn's secretary gave me, begging her to keep it confidential.

Margaret then comes upstairs with me to the second floor. Uncle Percy's door is open and he's dozing in his armchair. His suitcase lies closed on the bed. I knock on the door frame.

His eyes flutter open. "Come in!" he calls, his face growing bright.

"You're all packed and ready to go, aren't you, Percy?" Margaret says. "You've got everything you'll need to do Florida up right?"

Uncle Percy stiffly pushes himself up out of his chair and I walk over to kiss him. "Margaret wants to come with us in the worst way," he confides to me.

"Margaret has to work, Percy," Margaret laughs. "And frankly I don't think it is wise for both you and me to be absent from the Gregory Home at the same time. Who would keep people in line?" Then she excuses herself to see how Mrs. Milner is getting on.

"My, my, my, young lady," Uncle Percy says, giving my arm a poke. "You win a contest and you can't go because the police think you threw that man off Castle Kerry?"

"Kind of," I say.

"I'm sorry for you, but not for me, kiddo," he says, poking my arm again. "So where are we off to?"

"Palm Beach, I think," I lie in case he tells people on the way out. I grab his suitcase. Since he hasn't traveled very much in years, Uncle Percy's big suitcase is of the older variety, rugged and heavy and without wheels.

"Hot damn, Palm Beach," he says happily. "Hang on, sweetheart, I need my blue blazer in the closet." I wait as he retrieves it, puts it on, pats his sleeves and checks himself in the mirror. He plucks a little at the handkerchief in the breast pocket. "Ah," he says, going back to the closet, "I think Margaret found my... Voila!" He pulls out a straw hat, sort of tropical Stetson I guess.

"Very dapper, Uncle," I tell him.

"It was in my storage space, waiting for summer," he says, admiring himself further. Satisfied, he takes the hat off and carries it carefully in hand as we walk down the hall to Mrs. Milner's. She, too, is packed and ready to go, dressed in a pretty, gray suit and pearls. Margaret takes her suitcase, which, like Percy's, does not have any modern conveniences attached to it.

I check my watch and am anxious to get going, but Uncle Percy and Mrs. Milner have evidently decided to play this up for all it's worth. On the first floor they look into each room as we walk by, hoping to accidentally find people they can hastily relate their sudden good fortune to. After we hit the computer room, the Gregory Room, and one of the community rooms, their enthusiasm is somewhat quashed by the lady in the library who ignores Mrs. Milner's good news to peer over at me and say, "What are you doing, young lady, involved with all this unpleasantness? What does your mother say about it? What were you doing up at the castle alone with a man?"

"Sorry, gotta go," I tell her.

"God's *sake!*" the lady mutters.

"She's always a stick-in-the-mud," Uncle Percy tells me.

We finally reach reception, where Mr. and Mrs. Happy Vacation sign out. David appears and I introduce him as a friend and we all climb into the station wagon. Uncle Percy sits up front as I drive.

"I'm sorry you can't take the trip with Sally," I hear Mrs. Milner say to David in the back seat.

"Me, too," David says.

"Is he the policeman Belle told me about?" Uncle Percy whispers so that everyone in the car can hear.

"No," I explain. "David is Alexandra Waring's brother."

"Oh!" Mrs. Milner says, impressed.

"His daughter goes to Choate and he's out here to visit her," I continue.

It is only half a mile to Castle Bank and when we swing into the parking lot I am relieved to see a gleaming black Lincoln Continental limousine parked there. "This is the beginning of the prize, Uncle Percy," I say as I park the car. "A limousine to your private plane at the airport."

"Mercy, I had no idea," Mrs. Milner says.

"She's always saying that, *Mercy, Percy*," my uncle says to himself, laughing, struggling a little with the unfamiliar door handle. David is quickly at his door, opening it for him, and then steps back to open Mrs. Milner's door and assist her out.

A large, heavyset young man climbs out of the passenger side of the limo, dressed in a blue blazer, white shirt and gray pants. The blazer cannot hide his tremendous forearms. "I'm Louie DeMateo," he says, offering me his hand. A little louder, he adds, "I'm one of the representatives from Vacation Florida who will be accompanying your uncle and his guest."

He smiles across the roof of the Mercedes wagon at Uncle Percy, who in return gives him a little wave. "Mr. Harrington?" Louie calls, walking around the car.

"Yes, yes, I'm Percy Harrington," my great-uncle greets him.

The limo driver has climbed out now, and he walks around to the back of the station wagon to get the bags. While Louie is chatting with his new charges, I commend the driver for getting here so quickly. He glances over, smiling a bit, hefting both suitcases out with ease. "We're always around," he says cryptically.

"Ah," I say.

"There's one other passenger coming with us," he says.

"Miss Banford. Do you know her? She used to be Mrs. O'Hearn's private nurse."

I remember her and say so.

We walk over to the trunk of the Lincoln. "She's going, too," the driver says. "I guess Louie's probably tellin' 'em that. Mr. O'Hearn wanted to make sure there was a lady, you know, somebody who could keep an eye on their medications and stuff." He gently closes the trunk, the car finalizing the closure and sealing it.

"I have a list from the Gregory Home of their medications," I tell him.

"Give it to Louie. We're picking Miss Banford up at her place." Louie and David have escorted the couple over to the limousine. We exchange kisses and hugs and we get Uncle Percy and Mrs. Milner settled in the back seat. Then Louie and I talk a few moments and I hand over the list of their medications and the telephone numbers of everybody who is anybody to these two.

"We'll take good care of them," Louie promises. "Don't worry."

"Please do," I tell him.

He leans to whisper in my ear, "What better place to hide them than greater Miami? They're *old*, they'll blend in."

We wave goodbye as the limousine pulls out and then David follows me back to the station wagon as I climb behind the wheel.

"Now what?" he asks, closing his door.

"We're going to stop at home to let the dogs out," I say, backing out. "Then you'll drop me off at the car place on your way to Choate." We drive out of the parking lot, turning onto Main Street. I'm feeling much better about things already.

After a while, David says, "I think I should hang around for a while."

I glance in the rearview mirror at a car behind me. I'm still a little paranoid and am looking for strange men. "Thank you, but that won't be necessary. You should go see your daughter."

"So you're just going to sit there, all by yourself, while some weirdo's stalking you and maybe a would-be killer is running around?"

"I have the dogs." Pause. "I also have a Parker shotgun." I look over. "Do you know what that is?"

"One to a hundred thousand dollars," he replies.

I smile. "They were all made here, you know." We're heading west and since it's just past five, the traffic is not the greatest.

"I can't thank you enough for what you've done," I say a few minutes later.

"And if I told you I would like to stay for a while because I'd like to get to know you better?" David says, looking out his window as though he hasn't just asked what he has.

I feel a small thump of alarm. "I need to talk to someone tonight. And I'm not quite sure when it will happen."

"I thought he had law school."

I was speaking of Phillip O'Hearn, but realize perhaps it's better that I leave David with his own conclusion.

After another moment, he says, "I'm sorry, Sally. It's none of my business."

I don't have to tell him that he's right.

He looks at his watch. "I guess I should call my daughter." I concentrate on driving while David searches for a number. Finally he finds it and dials. "Hi, it's your dad. I wondered if I could buy you a burger tonight. It's five-thirty. Call me when you get in." He disconnects his phone and slips it in the breast pocket of his coat. "Not answering."

"So I gathered."

His cell phone rings and he answers it while I stop at the

end of Mother's driveway and climb out to get her mail. "Oh. I didn't know," I hear him say. "Well, okay. All right. I'll call you in the morning. Oh, wait—why don't you call me when you get up? Great. Be careful, okay? Bye."

"She's night-skiing in Massachusetts," he reports when I get back in. Pause. "I could use a cup of coffee."

I look at him.

It seems awfully intimate in here suddenly.

"Sally," he says quietly, "I'm not trying to force myself on you."

I swallow. "Then what are you doing?"

If I had reached out and slapped him, I couldn't have surprised him more. My annoyance is increasing, though. He is a married man, father of two, I don't understand what it is we're doing.

"I see," he says, pulling back and turning to face front again.

"You were a hero today, David," I tell him, throwing the car into Drive to head to the house, "and I can't tell you how grateful I am to you." Mother's outdoor lights are on and I quickly scan the yard. "But I've got an awful lot on my plate at the moment and I can't afford another distraction."

He's looking out his window.

I park the car and hesitate whether I should leave the car running and thus encourage him to leave right away. I sort of feel bad, but I'm also feeling cornered.

I turn off the ignition and turn toward him, waiting for him to look at me again before I speak. "You're married, David. And you have children." Blink. "In other words, I would never dream of disrupting the life of anybody's family. Life is hard enough."

He is sort of squinting at me as if I am very far away. Then he sighs, looking down a moment. "Yeah," he murmurs. Then he opens his door to get out and I get out on my side. I hear the dogs barking in the house. I look up and see them on the second floor, piled up in the window seat.

"Can I just tell you—" David says, suddenly coming purposely around the car toward me.

I'm trying to be patient, but it's hard. I'm tired, I'm hungry, I've got a lot to do and he's married. I guess my expression says it all, because he looks as though I've hit him again and he backs away. "Okay," he says quietly. "You're right, it would be best if I just leave."

Normally I would have given him a big hug of thanks, but I don't think it's wise to touch him. I thank him again for all he has done this day and he just nods, clearing his throat, hand on the car door—you know, that kind of sequence that is to say, *Okay, back to business, I'm in control again*—and then he climbs into the driver's seat and starts the car.

I walk up to the front door and unlock it and wait for him to drive away before I let the dogs out. He doesn't wave; he simply drives away.

"Hi, guys," I tell the dogs as they come tumbling out on the front step. I receive one lick on my hand from each dog and then they're off. I smile wearily, going inside. I hang up my coat, turn the living-room lights on and notice that the wood has been laid for a fire. That's the ticket. Then I continue to the kitchen to scavenge for food.

I need a car, I realize. Or I'm stuck here. I call around to car rental agencies, asking for a four-wheel-drive vehicle because of the pending snow. I finally find one at an agency next door to the GM dealership and the guy is willing to pick me up. No wonder. He rents me a huge black Cadillac truck thing for a kazillion dollars. The Escapade? Escalade? Something. Man, is it big.

When I return to the house, I turn my cell phone on and find new messages.

Paul left a message, "How are you, *where* are you?"

Edith from research. She's still working on, "Our special project. In fact, I will remain here tonight until I hear from you."

Mother. "Please don't forget to put the drops in Abigail's ears. The medicine is on the windowsill and there is cotton up where the first-aid kit is."

Alexandra. "Where are you? Let me know."

Paul again. He'll be in class from seven to nine tonight. Hopes he'll get to talk to me. Hopes everything is all right. Hopes everything is better than all right and is great.

I dial Edith's number on Mother's telephone. Conversations on cell phones can be hazardous, I know, since I myself have one of the older portable scanners that can tune into people's cell phone calls.

"I found our Mr. Mather!" Edith triumphantly announces.

"And how *is* our Mr. Mather?" I say, pouring myself a large glass of wine from a new bottle of Pinot Grigio—which I know I shouldn't, but am doing anyway.

"He's just returned from Thailand, he's fine," Edith says. "It took a little bit of doing to convince him I was who I said I was—working on behalf of the Harrington family—but he finally believed me." Pause. "I think he might be older."

"So what did he say?"

"He said, *yes,* absolutely Percival Harrington, once be-lieved to live in Castleford, inherited some land. Five acres to be exact, in Hillstone Falls."

"Does he know when Uncle Percy inherited it?"

"He's not really sure, but he thinks it could have been as long as six or seven years ago."

"And how does *he* know this, when nobody else does? When there doesn't seem to be any records?"

"He had some very definite ideas about that, Sally."

The doorbell rings. *Some watchdogs,* I think. Whoever it is reached the front door without a single bark. I ask Edith to hang on a sec, and hurry out to the living room to open the door. There stands Phillip O'Hearn with the dogs—traitors to the core—standing happily on either side of him, tails wagging.

"Come in," I tell him. "I'm on the phone. Come back to the kitchen with me." He follows me and I pick up the telephone. "Go ahead," I tell Edith. I point to the kitchen table and make a motion to take his overcoat. He slips the black coat off and as I hold the phone between my ear and shoulder, I take it from him. It's soft and smells very nice. Armani. Of course. I drape the coat carefully over the back of the chair the dogs are least likely to brush up against.

"The land did not come down through the Harrington family," Edith tells me.

"Then where did it come from?"

"Mr. Mather said it came from one of the old farming families around Hillstone Falls, the Kindricksons."

"Never heard of them," I say. I cover the phone to ask O'Hearn if he would like a drink.

"What you have would be fine," he whispers, nodding to my wineglass on the counter.

I pour him a glass while Edith continues. (Never in my wildest dreams could I have ever imagined this scene, pouring a drink for Phillip O'Hearn in my mother's kitchen.)

"The Kindricksons settled in Hillstone Falls in 1792," Edith says as I hand O'Hearn his wine and move on to feed the dogs. "They were the original farming family in the area. By now, we're into—let's see—the seventh generation. In the last two generations, five and six, the primary heir sold parcels of land to raise the money to buy out his siblings. And while the size of the farm somewhat decreased, a Kindrickson son was able to keep it and farm it. They kept dairy cows, grew apples and vegetables. For a while they had a pumpkin stand."

I wait impatiently for something that has to do with something, and in the meantime, mix the wet dog food in thoroughly with the dry food, just the way the dogs like it, and put their bowls on the floor where they are waiting.

"Mr. Mather said when the last farming Kindrickson—the sixth-generation primary heir and farmer—died seven years ago, the land was resurveyed and it was discovered that the sale of one parcel of land from thirty years before had never been completed."

"How much land are we talking about?"

"Twenty acres."

"Out of how much land?"

Silence. I can visualize Edith poring over her notes. "I think the farm was down to about three hundred acres at that point."

I am jotting down notes.

"When it was discovered the transaction for the parcel had never taken place, and that the sixth-generation siblings had never received their money from it, the siblings sued the estate of the *last* farmer Kindrickson to get the twenty acres back."

"So they could sell it and get the money."

"Right. The problem was," Edith continues, "one of the dead farmer's siblings, a sister, had died before the farmer and her estate, at that time seven years ago, was tied up in litigation. Her two sons were suing each other over elements in her will. There were three heirs, two sons and a daughter, and the two sons were trying to get everything."

"Nice family," I observe. "So how many Kindrickson brothers and sisters are we talking about? The ones who had claim to the twenty acres that was never sold?"

"Four. So each wanted twenty-five percent of whatever the

land could bring, which, as it happens, was a lot, because that particular parcel runs along a large stream that feeds into the Hudson."

"Big enough to float a boat on?" I ask.

"I don't know," Edith says. "You'll have to ask Mr. Mather. I told him you would no doubt be calling him tonight, by the way. He said he would be home."

"Good," I say. "So what's the upshot?"

"Mr. Mather says that because the dead sister's estate was tied up, her share of the land could not be sold until her estate was settled. So the others went ahead and sold their fifteen acres of the parcel and shared the money three ways."

I bring my pad and pen with me across the kitchen and pull out a chair across the table from O'Hearn.

"When a new survey of the properties was done two years ago, because the heirs of the last dead farmer Kindrickson were going to sell the entire farm, this man, Harold Durrant, found out that the five-acre parcel was still being held in a trust."

"Because the two sons were still suing each other?"

"No, because the judge ruled, in his settlement of the estate, that the five-acre parcel was part of the daughter's inheritance. And that is where I believe our connection may lay."

"Who was the daughter?" I ask.

"Her name was Martha Hollins."

"Martha Hollins *Harrington*," I say, excited, "Uncle Percy's wife, my great-aunt Martha. She died eight or nine years ago."

"Before the twenty-acre parcel was even discovered," Edith says.

I'm quickly writing all this down.

"Evidently her brothers did their best to tie up the land so it did not go to their sister's widower, Percival Harrington."

"So it's just been sitting there?"

"Until Harold Durrant stumbled across it. The trust the judge set up was paying the taxes each year until either the rightful heir showed up, or the trust ran out of money, at which time the brothers would have the option of filing claim to the property and paying the back taxes on it. The trust had not run out of money and Mr. Mather remembers his friend being terribly excited about his discovery, that there was this five-acre parcel that the legal heir had never claimed, and he traced it to Percy. That's why Mr. Mather remembers Harold Durrant writing to Percy Harrington. Their little group—this Western Connecticut Land Trust—thought maybe they could buy this land from Percival Harrington, because with it they could thwart the development of the area for industrial use."

I look at Phillip O'Hearn while I say, "Tell me, Edith, did Mr. Mather happen to mention anything about the Hudson Cement Project or World Sound Industries?"

"Yes, he did," she says, sounding surprised. "He said that the five-acre parcel was in the middle of massive land acquisitions by subsidiaries of something called World Sound Industries for a proposed plant of some kind."

Edith gives me Mr. Mather's phone number and I get up and cross the kitchen to hang up the phone. Slowly I turn around. "One hundred points, A-plus for you," I tell O'Hearn. "You were exactly on the money."

Instead of looking pleased, O'Hearn looks gravely concerned. "Percy owns the land?"

"It looks like it."

"Near the Hudson Cement Project?"

"It could be in the middle of it," I say, walking over to the counter to take a large swallow of my wine. I put the glass down and look at him.

O'Hearn grimaces a little. "Then consider yourself hitting

head to head with organized crime again, Sally. Just how familiar are you with the Gambinos?"

"*That's* who's behind the Hudson Cement Project?"

"No," he answers. "They're just one of the groups that work for them."

CHAPTER TWENTY-ONE

"I'm going to tell you a little story about this group," Phillip O'Hearn begins, leaning on the table after I sit down. "They nearly dragged me and O'Hearn Construction into bankruptcy over the Windsor Hills project."

I had forgotten about that. Of course, before I had known that O'Hearn had anything to do with my father's death so many years ago, I didn't pay too much attention to O'Hearn Construction, except to notice how very wealthy Phillip and his wife had become. (When I was a little girl, you see, they lived in a tiny three-bedroom cape with four children.) When I returned to Castleford in the late '90s, when my mother was so ill, the newspaper was still making references to Windsor Hills, New York, as the one tremendous failure of O'Hearn Construction.

In the 1980s, as I recall, O'Hearn had proposed building a luxury second-home community in upstate New York. After it was begun, something happened—I can't remember what—but everything ground to a halt, there were a bunch of lawsuits and, in the end, O'Hearn Construction withdrew from the project.

"I had no idea it was that bad," I say. "Bankruptcy?"

"It was that bad," he assures me. "It took us four years to get the clearances we needed in the first place. And we had everybody on board—or so we thought—with signed contracts. We broke ground, and then—" He gives a wave with his hand. "There they were. They just appeared one day."

"Who?"

"You name a troublemaker and he or she was there causing problems. An environmental group sued us, the truckers' union showed up to protest our use of our regular drivers from Connecticut. The township sued us, another union started picketing the site, although we were using a lot of New York union members. The state started making noises about rescinding our zoning permits, some watershed group filed suit to stop us from tapping into the water supply, a United States senator even made a speech in the house about dishonest Connecticut builders crossing state lines."

"But why?" I ask, resisting the urge to ask how many of these actions might have been the correct ones to take if O'Hearn Construction *had* been doing something wrong.

"Well," he says, frowning, swallowing some wine, "at first it was because we were bringing in cement from our usual suppliers."

"From Connecticut?"

"From right here in Castleford. The company had a distribution center up in Litchfield. Looking back, I guess it was kind of stupid to think the mob was going to let us bring in good cement from sources they didn't control. And we had contracted for tons and tons of the stuff from this one firm." He runs a hand over what hair he has left. His is a large, well-manicured hand, although it has seen a great deal of work. There are small scars all over it. "The cement our friends in New York wanted us to buy cost roughly twelve percent more."

Everyone's heard of the mob tax in the tristate area. I just didn't know it reached so far north.

"What did you do?"

"If I broke my contract with my usual cement supplier, I still had to pay him regardless of whether I used his cement or not." He shrugs. "And that was fair. He had cleared the decks for us. He had to turn other business away." He lets out a heavy sigh as he remembers. "So if we wanted to get on with the development, then that's what we had to do. And that is what we did— we bought ourselves out of the contract. He was sympathetic and gave us the best break he could." He looks at me. "We're talking about enough cement to build concrete foundations and sidewalks for two *hundred* houses and sixty condominiums." He drains his glass. "And the pool areas... Oh hell." Agitated, he looks at me. "Do you have something not so sweet?"

"Sure," I say, rising from my chair. I go into the pantry and report what there is to choose from. He opts for Johnny Walker Red on the rocks. I fill a highball glass with ice, place it in front of him, pour maybe three ounces in his glass, put the bottle down on the table, and sit down.

He sips, swallows, nodding his head in approval. "Thank you."

"So you bought the mob concrete," I say.

"Cement," he says. "Cement's wet, dries into concrete."

"Oh." I never knew that.

"Yeah, so, the minute we signed on the dotted line for their damn cement, the unions magically disappeared, the state backed off, the senator shut up, and all was well." Pause. "Well, the environmentalists were still around, but the judges suddenly didn't seem to agree with their viewpoint anymore." A sip. "So we broke ground, poured cement, things were going great. And then the carpenters' union started to protest, and the electricians began picketing us, and then there was the matter of where we were buying our lumber from."

I sip my wine, frowning.

"This was a little easier to cope with. We didn't have a large outstanding contract on the lumber and so we just had to pay the nine percent markup on the lumber from their chosen yards. And after we were fleeced on that, it was Sheetrock. When we balked, the state started in on us again through the state senate, so we ended up having to buy their damn Sheetrock." He polishes off the scotch. "And we used their damn Sheetrockers. The Sheetrockers were from Queens and Brooklyn, Sally. I don't think there was a local in the entire group."

"Please," I say, gesturing to the scotch.

He pours himself another. "Finally, when the homes started to sell on spec, our liaisons demanded outright payments to insure there was no trouble." He leans back in his chair and sticks his hands in his pants pockets to nervously jingle the change in them.

"Couldn't you have called the FBI? Or a federal prosecutor?"

He smirks a little, withdrawing his hands to sit forward again at the table. "If you were one of the largest employers in your hometown, a town economically hard hit since the 1970s, and you found yourself in a make-or-break project and someone was threatening to destroy you if you didn't pay up, what would you do?"

"If I were desperate, I suppose I would lay people off."

"And if you were determined not to lay anyone off? Because there were no other jobs to be had?"

I consider this. "I suppose I might try to cut a deal with the thugs."

"Exactly," he mutters into his glass. He puts it down. "And suppose in the process of cutting these deals to stay alive, you realized that if the Feds ever did investigate, the only people who would go to jail were at O'Hearn Construction."

I wonder what they did.

"It was a very bad time," he continues. "As soon as things were looking up—" He shakes his head. "Then something like a fifty-foot crane would just disappear." He snaps his fingers. "Vanish overnight. The whole thing was a nightmare."

"So what happened?"

"It was one setup after another, and there seemed no way out."

He looks longingly at the bottle, but does not touch it. "We were bleeding to death and they knew it." He pauses. "I thought Windsor Hills was going to be my calling card to the world, Sally." He snorts. "Talk about a lesson in humility." He folds his hands in front of him. "And it was my arrogance that brought it on us."

He reaches out to shake the ice in his glace. "Every single person who was supposedly helping the Windsor Hills project lied to us, cheated us, stole from us, and left a knife in our backs. I'm talking state senators, state reps, judges, town counselors, zoning officials, building inspectors, the power company—you name it, they were on board. They lured me in with flattery and I bought it hook, line and sinker."

He falls back in his chair and thrusts his arms up as though he's weight lifting. "The whole point was to lure us into the project and then slowly but surely wear us down, suck our blood and, in the end, force us to sell out for pennies on the dollar. Before they pulled us under entirely."

He drinks what he can from the glass, making the ice loudly clink again.

"And what is the connection with the Hudson Cement Project?"

"Well, for one, in order to make cement in New York, you have to work with whoever controls the cement-making now. Understand?"

I try to think. "And that would be the mafia?"

"That would be the mafia, yes." He leans forward again. "Let me tell you about this cement factory, Sally. The parent company is supposedly Canadian, but there are almost no Canadians in it. It's simply a funnel into the country to move money from sources the U.S. otherwise might not allow in."

"It sounds like money laundering."

He shrugs slightly, as if I am to come to my own conclusions. "They own quite a few industrial enterprises in the States. But what they do, you see, is they pick a hard-hit economic back-woods and start buying everything in sight." He blinks. "Do you know how big this cement factory is they want to build?"

I shake my head.

"Two and half square miles." He lets that sink in. "Two and a half square miles filled with a coal-burning, cement-making plant. They're going to dump their solid waste in the Catskills, their fluid waste into the Hudson and send their poisonous air into Connecticut and Massachusetts."

I am stupefied. "But I've never heard of this. Why doesn't anyone know about it?"

"Around Hillstone Falls they sure do. They're being promised a lot of new jobs, new taxes, you know, the usual package used with hurting locals to push the project through. The politicians aren't much good because they can't go up against the machine and the machine is up to its neck in this. Eventually people will hear about it, but only because the Connecticut attorney general is filing suit to stop the air hazard."

I scratch my forehead. "But, Phil," I say, realizing I have blurted a term of friendly familiarity. He realizes it, too. "I don't understand why, in this day and age, and with the kind of wealthy people who have vacation retreats on the Hudson, people aren't rioting in the streets over this."

"Some people are trying to stop it. But look at what happened to me. I can't imagine what they do to people of little means."

"And what about the media?"

"You *are* the media, Sally, you tell me."

He's right. And I find it very strange I've never heard about this coal-burning cement plant before. I think I might have read an editorial in the *New York Times* at one point, about pollution in upstate New York, but I don't remember where.

Two and half square miles?

"So people may have in some way been intimidated," I say, getting up to let the dogs out through the sliding glass door. "It's begun to snow," I announce.

"They said it would." He sounds almost morose now.

"Will you wait while I call this guy from Litchfield that my researcher talked to? He remembers Harold Durrant writing Uncle Percy about the land two years ago."

"Sure," he says, helping himself to a little more scotch.

I use Mother's telephone again to dial James Mather. When he answers, I realize Edith is right, he is much older. I take care in introducing myself and in explaining how much information was relayed to me from Edith. "If this turns out to be correct, Mr. Mather, that my uncle Percy is the legal owner of these five acres, what is it you would wish he would do with it? Sell it to the land trust?"

"I don't think he should do anything with it," he says.

"I'm sorry, I don't quite understand. I thought the Western Connecticut Land Trust wanted to acquire that land."

"This will sound a little pathetic, I know," Mr. Mather says, "but at our age, Miss Harrington, I don't think anyone is willing to take the risk anymore. We'll have to trust that the young people will one day wake up. Before it's too late."

I'm jotting this down. "No one is willing to take what risk, Mr. Mather?"

"When Harry Durrant was alive, we felt bolder. After he died, after the way he died—we just seemed to lose heart."

"How did Mr. Durrant die?"

"He was a great hiking enthusiast. In love with the land." Pause. "They say he fell."

"They say he fell while hiking," I repeat the statement for O'Hearn's benefit. "That's interesting," I tell Mr. Mather. "We just had someone fall off a cliff at Castle Kerry."

"I heard about that. Was he someone you know? Oh, of course he is," he answers himself. "Because you were with him, Miss Harrington, weren't you?"

"Yes."

"But you didn't see what happened?"

"No."

"That's what happened to Harold. His son was up ahead on the trail and went back to see what was keeping his father. He found him with a broken neck in a ravine. It was very unlike Harold to be clumsy, to say nothing of being so clumsy as to trip for twenty feet across the trail and then jump."

I feel as though the wind has been knocked out of me.

"Your fellow was luckier than Harold, I understand. He is alive?"

"Yes, but in a coma."

"Pity." Pause. "Perhaps he wasn't a big fan of World Sound Industries either."

"That's really what you think, Mr. Mather? That Mr. Durrant was murdered?"

"I believe his efforts to stop the building of a colossal coal-burning cement factory didn't enhance his health."

Could this really be true? "Mr. Mather, on the morning the

man fell from Castle Kerry, we had been at the Hillstone Town Hall, inquiring about the possibility of Percival Harrington owning land near there. They claimed there was no record of him; no records were available to us to examine and the clerk even told us to come back at a specific time later, and when we did, she had cleared out. And then I talked to an attorney who claimed he did part-time work for the township. I found him rather alienating as well."

"I bet you did. Andrew Palermo. Smooth as silk, that one."

"He said his name was Andrew Palmer," I say.

"His father was Palermo," Mr. Mather says. "The son went to Colgate, much to the discredit of my alma mater." Pause. "The father went to the university of the state penitentiary, I believe."

Blink. "Really. For what?"

"I think it was racketeering or something to do with trafficking in stolen goods. Something like that."

I write this down. "Mr. Mather, if I were to tell you that the man who fell off Castle Kerry had introduced himself to the clerk and Attorney Palmer that morning as my uncle, Percival Harrington, what might you assume?"

"That I really do not want my name mixed up in this."

"But why?"

"Miss Harrington, either you are trying to bait me or you are indeed very dense."

I wait.

"My wife is not well. We are older and we are vulnerable." Pause. "Suffice it to say, someone obviously wishes very much to prevent your uncle from making a claim on that land. And when you find out who that is, then I would imagine you will find out what happened to your friend at Castle Kerry."

After I hang up, I have to stand there a minute, fully absorbing what Mr. Mather said. Then I cross the kitchen, sit down at the table, and drain what's left in my wineglass. I look at O'Hearn. "From the bottom of my heart, thank you for getting Uncle Percy away from here."

He looks at his watch. "They should be landing soon. Oh, and before I forget—" He takes out a slim pocket organizer from the inside pocket of his blazer, opens it, and takes out a card to hand to me. "That's where they will be. I imagine you can reach them in about an hour."

"Good, thank you. I'll call this into the Gregory Home." I tap the card on the table, nervous. "There's something else you want to tell me. What is it?"

He meets my eyes. "Give them what they want."

I hesitate. "But Uncle Percy is entitled to something."

"And maybe it is to be left alone in peace," O'Hearn says. He pushes his chair back to stand up and reaches for his coat.

I walk O'Hearn to the door and open it. The snow is coming down heavily now. As if we are merely friendly neighbors, we say good-night and he hurries out to his car.

I stand there, watching, and lean against the door frame until Scotty and Abigail come bounding over to play.

CHAPTER TWENTY-TWO

The snow is flying in earnest now, in large wet flakes that are the bane of every shoveler. While picking up in the kitchen, I return Paul's call—I look at the clock; he's at school—and leave a message. I pack Abigail's eardrops, let the dogs out, activate the alarm, close up Mother's house, and make a mental note that I will need to come back tomorrow to do her walks. Mother gets her driveway plowed, but she claims she enjoys shoveling snow, rather reveling in her ability to do it after once being so ill.

Looking at Mother today, it is hard to believe she was ever ashen and rail thin. She's not voluptuous, exactly. No, I take that back. Mother *is* voluptuous, but she's my mother, so I simply think of her as beautiful. I have a paler version of her large blue eyes and I do have her nose and long neck. But where her mouth is generously full, mine is thinner, more like Daddy's.

Men have been falling in love with Mother all of her life. Her combination of gentleness and beauty make them goofy. They look at me in a very different way. I think the expression is, "There are women you date [moi], and there are women you marry [Mother]."

I'm obviously still smarting from David Waring. It's one

thing for a married man to express casual interest in me, but it's quite another to feel pursued, and suspect that some encouragement may have been given to him from his sister. Yes, that's what I'm beginning to suspect, that Alexandra pushed him my way because he has suffered some kind of confidence failure she thinks I can remedy.

I call the dogs. I have no idea where they are in this snow.

Someday, if I become very famous, I'm going to write my autobiography so I can explain what happened in my romantic life. I will explain how, for years and years, I channeled my energies into other things, and was satisfied with sleepwalking through my sex life with my two longtime boyfriends. I will explain how that worked as long as I knew of nothing else, but I think I should have suspected that there had to be far more to sexual passion if so many people were obsessed with it.

First there was Bill, in Los Angeles, the blond Adonis who was an aspiring actor (working as a bartender), whose fragile ego I did not want to hurt by confessing that I found our sexual experiences so complicated and orchestrated (he liked costumes) as to turn me off completely. As it turned out, he was only in love with the idea of me helping his career through my job at *Expectations* magazine anyway. And when Mother got ill, I had an excuse to get out of it by moving back to Castleford.

And then there was Doug, of course, whose sexual tendencies, I discovered on our second time around, had not changed since high school—it was still that kind of tentative, horribly restrained 1-2-3 that always left me feeling like a freak for wanting something more. What happened then, you see, was I met Spencer Hawes and did something I had never done before. I slept with him practically the night I met him and I found myself giving over to a kind of abandonment I had never experienced before—or felt free to have before. And what happened was, because I didn't know him well, I think, because I had nothing invested in him, the incident became a sheer sexual epiphany for me. And I pursued it. Explored it. And gave way to it—over and over and over again—and for that, I will always be grateful to Spencer. He literally brought a part of me to life.

Does it make sense to you, then, if I say that after that, the development of a deep emotional relationship feels suspiciously like an early death to me? And that beyond the sudden, cataclysmic surge of desire I can feel in an initial encounter, the fear starts in and I begin to feel, and to think, and that's when everything seems to break down?

I wish I could get over the feeling of panic that comes when I am asked to settle down. I feel as though I am on the verge of something in my life right now, of breaking free of something, and when I feel cornered, that quiet panic comes back.

Doug Wrentham has begged me for years to see a therapist and I used to use the excuse that I didn't have the money. It has not been a case of money for a while now and I know I don't want to go to a therapist because I don't want to change. The highs of my life still outweigh the lows, I guess. I suppose someday I will become a person who wants to share her life fully with someone else—and who knows? it could be Paul—but right now it feels like a race to live as much as possible, to feel as much as possible, before I die.

In the back of my mind, you see, lurks the magic age of thirty-seven. That's how old Daddy was when he died, and as irrational as it may seem, I've never been able to visualize myself living beyond it. So you can imagine how I feel about having children when I maintain this irrational certainty that they will lose their mother when they are very young and therefore I would be condemning them to the same loneliness, the same hole in their little hearts, that I carry to this day.

This big black Cadillac thing (you can turn it into a pickup truck?!?) I am driving is a lot bigger than my Jeep. Scotty and Abigail balk a little when I open the hatch and tell them to get in. Scotty finally goes first, not jumping high enough, scrambling frantically with his front paws, but then sliding back down. Showing off, Abigail simply bounds neatly from her spot inside. (It isn't fair, really. As a mutt, Scotty's parts don't add up well for certain situations. His slender collie legs can't launch his large German shepherd frame very well, whereas all of sleek little Abigail seems to operate as one singularly smooth athletic entity.)

"It's higher, boy," I tell him, patting the carpeted floor of the cavernous cargo space. He backs up, a little nervous, and gallops forward to give it his best shot. This time I catch his rear end on the fly and boost him in. The dogs circle each other happily a few times and then abruptly collapse, eyes shining. "Love you dogs," I tell them, closing the hatch.

I drive to Super Stop 'N Shop, changing over from the four-wheel drive I used on the back roads to two-wheel drive on the major roads, which are still only wet. It's going to be a hell of a night for driving, though. The snow is falling wet, but the temperature is supposed to drop into the twenties, making perfect conditions for black ice. The New Englanders do all right, but in downtown Castleford we always have a number of new-comers from Mexico and Puerto Rico, and they almost always make for dramatic drivers their first time out in weather like this.

Already on East Main there is an accident. I pass the whirling red and white lights of the patrol car and the dogs, I see in the rearview mirror, are pressing against the glass to look. The grocery store parking lot is mobbed with the antic-ipation of a lasting snowfall. I park way out in nowhere, leaving two windows open a little, and trek into the market. On the way I watch an older Toyota slide through the slush into the back of a pickup. No one is hurt, but everybody is upset.

I find the store bright and festive as I wheel my cart around—apples, grapefruit, lettuce, tomatoes, green beans, onions, carrots, potatoes, peanuts in the shell, smoked Gouda, ham, Swiss cheese, some chicken, a filet, canned tuna, coffee, cheapo seltzer (after eight, can't get beer), pasta, granola bars, dog food, Milk-Bone, toilet paper, paper towels, yogurt, milk, white bread, calcium chloride and fat wood fire starters—and I see several people I know. We don't stop and chat as we otherwise might, as we are anxious to get home.

At the checkout I am suddenly exhausted, my body struggling to carry out commands. Everything feels heavy; it's as though someone has been sandbagging me over the head.

It's the letdown. It's been a very long run on adrenaline today.

And I'm hungry, I realize, wheeling the cart outside. Starving. I rip open the box of granola bars to get one and I think of Roderick and his Twinkies. I need to call and see how he is. Maybe I'll run up to see him in the morning.

Thank God Uncle Percy got out before the storm.

My cell phone starts ringing and I retrieve it from my pocket.

"Hi, it's Phil. I just wanted to let you know the gang landed safely and just reached the condo. After a light supper, the contest winners are going to bed."

I thank him for letting me know and continue pushing the cart through the swirling snow. Weird how he called just as I was thinking about Uncle Percy.

My cottage looks very pretty in the snow, but it also looks forlorn. My road is a long, bumpy, curving journey and in the clearing, where the cottage is, I find it impossible to distinguish the driveway from the front yard. The big rock is already covered. The trees are blanketed and look gorgeous. The cottage itself is covered with pristine snow and sort of looks like one of those glass globes you shake.

The motion-detector light at the front door comes on. The only real definition of the house against the snow in this light are the shutters and the interior of the porch.

The dogs bound gleefully out of the big black Caddie thing (what *is* it called?) and tear around after each other, messing up the tranquillity. I carry the bags of groceries to the porch and put them down to unlock the front door. Then I turn around, watching the dogs. It is so beautiful out here. So quiet, so beautiful.

I wonder if Paul would come over if I invited him.

But in the next moment I realize that perhaps it's not Paul that I would most like to see.

I am asleep on my couch in the living room when the telephone rings. I didn't have the energy to make a proper dinner, but ate a bowl of Cap'n Crunch cereal, the empty bowl of which I see is still on the coffee table. It takes me a minute to figure out where I am and which telephone is ringing.

Ah, land phone. Right there. When I reach for it, I realize I have one dog curled between my feet and there is another squished along my side against the couch. That one's Abigail, determined to hang on to her space by playing dead; Scotty, at my feet, raises his head a moment to look at me and then drops it again, closing his eyes.

"Did I call too late?" Paul says quietly. "I'm sorry, I woke you up, didn't I?"

"No. I was just dozing on the couch," I say, propping myself up on one elbow and clearing my throat. "I have to get up anyway if I'm to go to bed. What time is it?"

"A little after eleven."

Eleven. "So how was your first night of school?"

"The whole day was crazy, but good," he says, and then he tells me about arresting some guy who was off his medication and had broken into his childhood home in East New Haven; he tells me about racing over to school and being a little late; and then about how everything in law is Greek to him and he doesn't think he'll ever be able to understand it all.

"Everyone feels that way in the beginning," I assure him, yawning. "That's why it's called the 'practice' of law." Then I ask him if he talked to any of his classmates; did he see a possible study partner.

"I don't think any of us ever looked up from our notebooks," he laughs. "Nobody knew what the professor was talking about, so we were all writing down every single thing he said."

We talk a bit more. His apartment is chaos, he says, he hasn't put anything away. Jack's still in town, but where, he has no idea. Last time Paul saw him was last night, when Jack left the Anchor Bar with a girl from Yale.

I don't ask if he had a good time at the Anchor Bar. There are always many pretty girls there, but rarely *older*, professional women like me.

It is clear that Paul is not hoping I will invite him over tonight and I think I'm upset. He has some studying to do and has to be up at six, but I can't help but think that if he were really into me, he'd be on his way over. Things like sleep don't get in the way of sex for a twenty-five-year-old. (Unless, of course, it had been me at that age.)

What the hell is the matter with me? I don't want to see him, but I'm mad I'm not going to see him. I'm so tired at this point I don't know what I want.

When we get off the phone, I get up to prepare for bed. The dogs, on the other hand, won't move.

I walk into the kitchen and make a list of what I need to do tomorrow. Then I call the dogs and I can hear them reluctantly stirring from the couch. While I'm waiting for them, I open the back door to look at the snow, and I'm just about to flick on the outside light when I see them.

When I see the footprints in the snow. At the back door and moving around the side of the house.

CHAPTER TWENTY-THREE

After it sinks in that if these are footprints, then someone must have made them, I say loudly, "Okay, dogs, you missed your chance," and close the door. Walking back into the kitchen, I'm not exactly sure what to do. Somebody's outside.

I'm in no mood to see my stalker, Luke Jervis. So I walk into the living room and pick up the telephone in my study to dial 911. "It's Sally Harrington," I tell the dispatcher, snapping my fingers for the dogs to sit, "at the cottage on Brackleton Farm, just off Forth Road. Detective D'Amico told me to call if there was anything suspicious and someone is creeping around my house as we speak."

"Could it be a neighbor?"

"No one lives within a quarter mile of me," I tell her.

Suddenly the dogs' ears prick up and they tear off to the kitchen, barking their heads off. In a panic I try to remember if I locked the door. I must have. I call the dogs back but they refuse to come. I hang up the telephone and move to the kitchen doorway. The dogs are in the mudroom, furiously barking at the back door. The panes of glass in it are unbreakable, so I know the dogs can't crash through it. Or that someone outside can get in at them.

The house is pretty secure. I'm not really worried, but I do hope the police get here quickly. *But look at the snow,* I think. *My driveway will be impossible in anything less than four-wheel, and how many CPD squad cars have it?*

Maybe I should let the dogs out to chase him away.

No. That would be like sending my children out to protect me. "Scotty, Abigail," I command. *"Come!"*

With one last bark, Abigail trots back toward me, tail waving high, while Scotty lingers at the door, still growling and tail twitching. *"Scott!"* I yell. Finally he backs out of the mudroom and slowly walks toward me, head down. I turn off the kitchen light and pull the swinging door from its latch so that it swings closed. I herd the dogs into my bedroom and close the door on them. Then I go back into the living room and peek out the front window. No cars other than the black Cadillac thing in sight, not that I can see very well, the snow is so thick.

But since it seems unlikely that somebody just happened to get lost for a quarter mile through the woods and farmland to pass by my back door tonight, it's best I operate on the premise that someone is out there.

It's gotta be the crazy guy, Jervis. He's probably been waiting for me to show up.

I turn off the living-room lights and return to the bedroom, pretending that I'm retiring. The only other person I can think of that it could be is poor Crazy Pete—Peter Sabatino—Castleford's resident conspiracy theorist, who might have gone "off" again and be skulking around in paranoia. He often comes here when troubled.

But Crazy Pete wouldn't hang around for long without letting me know he's here. He'd tap on the window or something.

I'm starting to get the willies. I know Jervis hasn't shown any tendency toward violence yet, but I don't want him near me.

I herd the dogs into my bedroom closet and turn off the bedroom light. We're not coming out, I decide, until the police get here. I push some shoes around to make room for the dogs to lie down, which, in a hushed command, I tell them to do.

My telephone starts ringing.

Darn it, it's probably the police. I tell the dogs to stay, and crawl out of the closet, closing the door behind me. But by now my answering machine has come on, and I hear my voice cheerfully saying, "Hi, it's Sally, please leave your name, number, time and date of your call, and I'll get back to you as soon as I can."

"This is the Castleford Police Department," a man's voice says.

I pick up the phone and whisper, "I'm here. Where are you guys? I've got somebody outside."

"We're on our way," he says, but not sounding very sure about it. "The roads have iced over. They're putting the chains on and we will be right there."

"Please hurry," I say, hanging up and crawling back toward the closet. So now what? Just wait, I guess.

Scotty scratches once at the closet door. "No!" I whisper. He doesn't do it again and I crawl back inside with them.

I don't want the outside porch light to come on with the motion detector and chase Jervis away; I want the police to get this guy. (Defense or offense, on which line am I?) I stand up to push back my clothes to reveal the circuit-breaker box. I open it, look at the dogs and whisper, "Don't worry, guys," and flip the master breaker. The overhead light goes off. Then I sit down with the dogs to wait.

Nothing. No sound but the dogs' breathing. I sit there, blinking in the dark.

After five minutes I can't stand it anymore.

I crawl out of the closet and close the door. Then I crawl

out of the bedroom to the living room and over to the front window. I straighten up slowly. I can't see anything. I crawl across the living-room floor and pause at the swinging door. Then I push it, slipping into the kitchen.

Silence.

The ticking of the clock.

And then I hear something at the back door. A muffled scraping sound.

I freeze, the hair going up the back of my neck.

The double-paned glass is shatter resistant, I remind myself, and the locks on the door are new. He's not going to get in that way.

There's a muffled bang.

He just tried to break a pane in the door.

There's another bang.

Silence. He's figured it out; it's not going to break.

Where are the police? For a crazy stalker, he seems rather adept at this.

Try to think. Okay. Jervis wants me, so if I run out the front door to the car, then he'll go after me. Then I'll drive until I meet the police and lead them back here.

It's still silent. Slowly I stand up to see if I can see anything out the back door. There is an explosion of glass in the dark and I cry out, my head getting whacked on the side with something big and heavy. I fall backward on the floor. Holding my head in one hand, I try to brush particles of glass away from my eyes with the other. I open my eyes, trying to focus, seeing nothing until a flashlight is turned on and I realize someone is climbing in through what used to be my big bay window.

I scramble backward through the swinging door—he's heard me and the flashlight moves in my direction, but I'm already on my feet and running across the living room. I grab the keys on the table and struggle to unbolt the front door. I hear chairs being overturned in the kitchen and then the swinging door is flung open, crashing against the wall, and the flashlight swings my way.

I throw open the front door and tear off the porch, jumping the three stairs, slipping and falling on the snow, but scrambling up and stumbling toward the car. I hear an oath behind me. My hand searches for the unfamiliar door handle and at first I think it's frozen, but then I think *damn it, it's locked,* and the guy's coming and I don't know this stupid key chain, so I have to start running again, slipping and sliding my way down the driveway.

He's running after me, but is slower than me. I cut off into the woods, carefully weaving my way through the trees, heading for the grove of Scotch pine. The flashlight is flickering through the trees behind me and I think I'm just out of its reach. And then I clobber myself by running smack into a tree trunk and I want to cry out but don't. I feel the blood spurting down my face, but I keep going. When I reach the pine grove, I search for the path I know is here somewhere, and find it. The limbs of the pines are high, heavy and thick, so there is still little or no snow on the bed of pine needles. I run up the path to the end of the grove, start footprints onward, then turn around to retrace my steps back into the grove, and run back to the other end to hide behind the largest tree.

I'm squatting there, hand on the frozen ground, panting. I pull my turtleneck over my mouth to stop the sound. The guy is coming, slowly, following my footprints in the snow with this flashlight. The light is bright and I close my eyes and tuck my head, not wanting to lose my night vision. I hear his steps. He's breathing heavily, too. As the path clears of snow, he starts jogging.

I count to five and then tear off again back toward the house. He hears me, but this time I am taking a shortcut over the field where I'm pretty confident I can gain a lead. By the time I've crossed it, I see the flashlight is only at the beginning and I slow down, taking my time through the trees to come out in my backyard.

I see headlights around the front of the house and thank God the police have arrived. But as I reach the back of my shed, something makes me wait. The headlights are moving slowly around the side of the house, and as they sweep over the backyard I duck behind the shed. Once they pass over, I peer around the side to see that it is not a police car but a small four-wheel-drive vehicle. It's a Wrangler.

No cops I know drive a Wrangler.

I look back and see the flashlight bobbing in the woods behind me.

I've got to decide.

As the Wrangler circles the far end of the house, I push the buttons on the key chain and see the Cadillac's lights flicker. Either I've unlocked it or locked it again. I run to the back of the house, following the tracks of the Wrangler, and hear the dogs barking inside. I race around the far side of the house and slip, falling hard on my shoulder. I've done something to it. But I've got to get around to the front yard to see where everybody is. I hurry around the corner and slow down as I pass my front door. I sneak to the edge of the house and look. The guy in the woods is waving his flashlight and the Wrangler jumps ahead to meet him at the edge of the yard. I run back across the front yard, duck down behind the Cadillac and feel for the handle. The door's open.

The dome light comes on as I climb inside and stays on while I struggle with the key—my hands are numb. I use my elbow to hit the lock on the door and hear all the locks snap down. The windshield is covered with snow and there is light playing over it, but I can't tell what the Wrangler is doing.

I drop the keys under the seat and curse. I can't see them, I can't feel anything, but then I hear the jingle of the keys and use my frozen fingers as a claw to pull them out. I try again to hold the key and get it in the ignition.

Suddenly they're on top of me, shining their brights. I hear a car door open. I bend under the dash to get the light out of my eyes and I get the key into the ignition and manage to turn it. The engine roars to life and the windshield wipers flail, flooding the interior with the light from the Wrangler.

Okay, now we're getting somewhere.

The Caddie's lights have come on automatically, but now I blare my brights back at the Wrangler and sit up to throw the car in Reverse. My window suddenly explodes and a hand roughly grabs at me, so I floor the accelerator, the wheels spinning and then catching, which yanks me forward, and the window frame knocks his arm off me. I keep reversing toward the driveway, but then I see the large man is slipping and sliding his way back into the Wrangler and I think, *Why not?* So I slam on the brakes and put the Caddie in Drive.

And floor it.

I head straight for them and they try to shoot to the side, but I smash them behind the driver's side and keep gunning the engine, pushing the Wrangler sideways up toward the house until I hear the satisfying crunch of it meeting the big rock.

I know what the safety ratings are on Wranglers.

I cough a little, then, and realize I'm spitting blood. I put the Caddie in Reverse again, spinning backward, and I'm getting ready to ram the Wrangler in the front end this time, but there is this dull *thunk* sound and I see the windshield spiderweb from the center out.

They're shooting.

I fly back into Reverse and wheel madly backward down the driveway—the passenger window suddenly spiderwebs this time—and when I reach the turnoff for the pine grove, I throw the truck back into Drive. I bounce onto the path—taking branches with me—all the way through the grove to the field. I can't see the Wrangler, but then I can't see much of anything, because to be able to see well I need to poke my head out the window and for obvious reasons I don't want to. So I power up the middle of the field to the top of the hill, shut off the engine so the lights will shut off, and put the truck into Neutral to roll down the other side without being seen. The Caddie bumps and swooshes through the snow until, finally, it comes to a stop.

I listen. I choke on the blood that is streaming down the back of my throat again and have to spit some more out. I lean out my window, straining to see. I don't see lights. Just whirling snow. There's no way they can follow me if they don't have their lights on, so I should be able to see them if they should come this way.

I hope the dogs are all right. They better be all right.

I shiver. Part of me says I should wait here until I'm sure the police have reached the house (*How am I going to know that?*) while the other part worries that without the engine on, I'm going to die out here of exposure. I shiver again. Damn these cars you can't turn the lights off.

I hang my head out the window, trying to see, trying to re-member how to reach the Brackleton Farm road from here.

Well, I've got to try.

I turn on the ignition and once again the Caddie roars to life, first giving me courage and then blessing me with blasting heat. I start driving slowly through the snow in what I think is the direction of the farm road, first holding one hand over the heating vent and then the other to warm them. I can't make out any landmarks, but I take my time, and eventually I find the stone wall, and I drive along that until I find the break in it for tractors. I know where I am now; I'm not far from the road, so I speed up, cushily bumping across the frozen field (nice ride in this) and then suddenly I feel the Caddie nose-diving and slamming to a stop, engine roaring and wheels spinning.

Where the hell am I?

I put on the brakes and look out my window. There is a horrible sound like a gunshot and I duck, but a few moments later, when I hear an awful groaning sound, I realize that it was not the sound of a gun but of breaking ice, and the right front end of the Caddie is listing downward. I put it in Reverse and coach myself, *Don't gun the engine; slow, slow, slowly back,* but the front wheels are turning on nothing and the back can't get a grip.

The snow is blowing in hard through where my window should be, but when I look down out of it, I think I see the whiteness below starting to darken.

Water.

Damn it, I'm in some sort of drainage pit of that ever-expanding quarry. I crawl out of my seat into the back and find the button to unlock the door. As I'm opening it, I feel the truck starting to move and I jump out. When I scramble up the bank there is another horrendous cracking sound and the truck lurches down two feet more, the entire front end now submerged in slushy water. The engine's still running, and the lights are still on. I stagger back a few steps, thinking of the *Titanic.*

I hear the roar of an engine and instinctively drop to my knees to hide. I cough more blood and cover my mouth with my frozen fist.

It's not a car engine, I don't think. No. It's louder.

A snowmobile. Somebody's snowmobiling across Brackleton Farm.

I am sick with cold, but know I have to get farther up the slope. I fall down, though, and I start to cry, because I know I can't get there, I have no feeling in my body, I think I might be freezing to death—

And then I think I might see something in the snow. Is it a light? The sound of the snowmobile has stopped. "Hello?" I hear a boy's voice call.

"Careful, Sam," a man calls.

"It's a truck!" the boy cries. "It's sinking or something! Dad!"

I stagger toward the direction of his voice. "Hello!" I call. "Hello! I need help!"

"Sam, where are you?" the man yells.

"Over here!" he yells back and suddenly there is a figure standing in front of me. "You have no coat," he says.

"I need help," I say weakly.

"Dad!" the boy yells. And then I feel hands on my head. And then I feel something being pulled over my head and I can't see. "There're holes to see through," the boy says. "You have to look through the holes."

I try to fix it, but I can't feel my hands and tell him so. Then I feel tugging on my arms and realize he is trying to put gloves on my hands.

"Oh, no," I hear the man say, arriving with the flashlight. He hands it off to the boy and kneels beside me. He adjusts the mask so I can see, and what I see is blood all over his hands. I hear the sound of a zipper and then I realize he is putting his coat around me. "Give me the flashlight and put your hands in your pockets, Sam."

"Do you think you can put your arm around me and around

my son?" the man says next. "So we can get you up to the snowmobile?"

"There's something screwed up with my left shoulder," I say.

"I'm shorter, so put that arm around me," the boy says.

And so we start up through the snow, the man and the boy half carrying me. I remember being helped onto the snowmobile, but after that, I don't remember anything.

CHAPTER TWENTY-FOUR

The first thing I become aware of is the throbbing pain in my head. The second is that I'm warm. I open my eyes and find a boy of about ten hanging over me, whose blue eyes are widening in delight. *"Mom,"* he whispers, "she's awake."

Immediately there is a movement somewhere behind me and then a pretty, blond woman's head drops down next to the boy's. She is smiling. "Everything is all right," she tells me gently, fussing slightly with the comforter that is over me.

I seem to be stretched out on a couch.

"You're safe and medical help is coming," she adds.

I squirm a little, realizing that I have several blankets on me, and I try to sit up but fail. I can see there is a roaring fire behind them, but that's about it.

I wince again at the pain in my head and draw a hand up to it. "I think your nose may be broken," the woman says. "And you've got a head wound."

"Mom wiped off most of the blood," the boy says. "You had it all over you. We couldn't even see what you looked like." Pause. "I'm not sure you look like you do now all the time, though."

His mother hushes him.

I try to smile. "I remember you. You gave me your hat."

He smiles back. "My mask." Pause. "It's kind of gross now."

I try to prop myself up again, but there's definitely something wrong with my shoulder. Since I seem so determined, the woman assists me into a sitting position. Her eyes move to something behind me and I hear the man's voice say, "Hunters Ambulance is sending someone over."

It's starting to come back to me. The men at my house. The dogs—*the dogs!* "I need to go to my house," I say. I sound like a frog.

The woman is offering me a steaming cup of something. "It's only a little beef broth. Can you sip some? You were awfully cold when Bob and Sam brought you in."

"How long have I been here?" I ask, trying to sip. It tastes wonderful and with a pang I realize how hungry I am. I also realize my upper lip is terribly swollen.

"A half hour," the man says softly, appearing behind the other two. "I'm Bob Laurencelle. This is my wife, Wanda, and our son, Sam." A smile. "Sam was the one who spotted your car."

I touch the side of my head and close my eyes. "Could I have a hundred aspirins, please?" Eyes still closed, I take another sip of this wonderful broth. I'm terribly thirsty, too.

"They said not to give you anything," Wanda says. "I'm afraid I'm pushing it with a few sips of broth as it is."

"Ah, the ambulance. They're coming, right," I say, trying to get my head together. I sip again and realize the broth is almost gone.

"I'm afraid that is all I'm allowed to give you," Wanda says.

"In case you have a concussion," young Sam adds.

I finish the soup and hand her the cup. "Thank you." I look to the man. "I need to call the police."

"They know you're here," Bob says. "When I called to say we found you, they seemed to know who you were before I even described you."

"Your car's probably at the bottom of that pond by now," Sam adds.

Bob turns his head slightly. "You are Sally Harrington, aren't you?"

I nod and immediately stop it because of the pain. I close my eyes again. "I'm worried about my dogs," I tell them. "I left them in my bedroom closet." I open my eyes to see the whole family looking rather startled. "There were prowlers," I say. "I didn't want them to hurt the dogs."

"Maybe next time you should let the dogs out to make sure *you* don't get hurt," Sam says seriously.

The ambulance arrives shortly and the medics troop in to look at me. "I'm going to take my truck and go over to your place," Bob tells me. "I'll check on the dogs and find out what's going on."

"Dad, I want to go with you," Sam says.

"Sam, you need to go to bed," Wanda says.

"No way the schools will open at all tomorrow," the medic taking my blood pressure says, letting the air run out.

"Dad, please?" Sam says.

"We'll all go then," Wanda says to her husband and he nods in agreement.

"Judging from the radio calls," the other medic says, "the police are over there big-time."

"Do you know if they caught anybody?"

"Don't know," the first medic says, ripping the blood pressure thing off me and pulling my sleeve back down.

I explain to the Laurencelles where they can find my spare key if they need it to get in. "Although I seem to remember,"

I say, "there's a huge hole now where the bay window in the kitchen used to be."

Bob is pulling the coffee table back to make room for the gurney. A few minutes later I'm rolling down the front walk through the snow toward the ambulance. I hear Sam call, "Don't worry, we'll take good care of your dogs!" The doors of the ambulance close.

And I awaken to the bright lights of the E.R.

"Hello, Sally," a kindly female face says, hanging over me. "Taking a little catnap?" A curtain is being pulled around us and then a man comes to stand next to the woman. "You've gotten a little banged up," the woman says, leaning close to examine my face. "See when Dr. Richards comes on, will you?" she says to the man.

"The plastic surgeon, Doctor?"

"Yes," she murmurs, looking, but not touching, the side of my head now.

I close my eyes, thinking woman doctor, male nurse, how far we've come.

"Sally—"

I open my eyes.

"We're going to have to take some X rays," the doctor says, "but I don't think this is quite as bad as it looks."

I close my eyes again. "That's good," I say, "but my head is killing me."

"Dr. Richards comes on at six," the nurse reports.

The doctor says something indistinguishable to the nurse.

"Tell Dr. Richards," I say, "that this is supposed to be the face of DBS News, so I would appreciate any help he can offer."

"I knew you worked for one of the networks," the doctor

says. "My son has your mother for English." Pause. "Open your eyes, please."

I do.

"She's a terrific teacher, your mother," she says. "Sally, look here, please." She shines a light into my eye. "Okay, good. And over here." She shines the light in my other eye. "Good," she pronounces. "Now I've just got to take a look in your nose. I'm going to try not to hurt you."

She does hurt me, but at this point it's kids' play. One nostril. Then the other. "Okay," she says under her breath, "looks like a simple break."

So that's why blood was running down the back of my throat.

The doctor clicks off the light and straightens up. "That's good. Where else are you having pain?"

"My head."

"Yes, well, you're going to need some stitches. I'm afraid we're going to have to shave a little bit of your scalp. Anywhere else?"

Broken nose, shaved head?

"My left shoulder," I say. "I don't know how you're going to get my turtleneck off."

"It's already off," she says, pulling the blanket and sheet down a little to look at my shoulder. "They cut it off while you were out."

She pushes a little here and there. "Ow!" I cry. "Right there. That's it."

"Hmm," she says, still poking. "Can you lift your arm?" I show her how far and she makes a kind of shorter *Hm* sound. "You've probably torn some ligaments in there."

I imagine the Hunchback of Notre Dame. God, my head is killing me.

The doctor is going over some numbers with the nurse and she breaks off suddenly to look over at something. "Hello."

I try to see who it is. "Oh, Buddy," I say, resting back down again. "How wonderful it is for you to visit. I'm afraid I'm fresh out of spinach and artichoke dip."

"Hey, Sally," he whispers, quickly rounding the far side of the bed to stand next to me. He looks across me to the doctor. "Detective D'Amico, Castleford PD," he explains. "How is she?"

"We're going to take some X rays to get a better picture of what's going on," she says. "She's broken her nose—"

"So I see," Buddy says in such a way it makes me cringe inside.

"She'll need stitches here, maybe ten or so."

I close my eyes.

"She's going to be extremely sore here, over her mouth, but the good news is, there doesn't seem to be any internal bleeding, her reflexes are good and her blood pressure's steady. She may possibly have a torn roto-cuff in her left shoulder and she has a lot of bruising on knees, right shin, and in the arch of her right foot."

I open one eye. "I do?"

The doctor nods. "The X rays will tell us more."

I move my legs. "Do I have *any* clothes on?"

She shakes her head.

"Oh," I say, wondering how long I was out. "My head," I begin.

"I'm giving you something right now," she says, dabbing my arm with alcohol. The nurse hands her a shot and she gives it to me. "You'll feel better in a minute," she says, giving my hand a pat. "I'll see you after X ray." She disappears around the curtain, and I hope she's going to go see whoever it is they've brought into the building who is screaming.

"So where were you guys?" I ask Buddy.

"There was a bad accident on 91. A tractor-trailer jack-

243 The Kill Fee

knifed and hit three cars before it was through. Two people were killed. The only cars left needed chains to move."

"So did you get them?"

"We've got them," he assures me. "And we've got the Wrangler. It was stolen in Poughkeepsie this afternoon." He squints at me. "How did it get so smashed up?"

"I hit it with this big Cadillac thing, this four-wheel-drive monster."

"And where is that? There's no sign of it."

I close my eyes, feeling the pounding in my head starting to lessen. "It's in a drainage pond near the quarry." I open my eyes. "Those creeps started mining up on the hill. They're not supposed to, you know. Why don't you arrest them?"

"How many men did you see, Sally?"

"Two. At first I thought there was only one prowling around the house. That's when I called 911. I don't know how he did it, but he smashed the bay window in the kitchen and came in after me. I ran out the front door and he chased me into the woods. I doubled back and saw the Wrangler driving round and round my house, looking for me. I made it to the Caddie and they were coming toward me and so I just let 'em have it. Pushed them up onto the rock." I close my eyes. "But they started shooting, so I drove out into the fields." I'm starting to feel better, but very sleepy. "I drove onto the ice and the car fell through, and this guy and his son..."

I'm so tired.

Buddy is giving my hand a little shake. "Do you know who they are?"

"Who?"

"Your assailants."

"No." I'm having trouble swallowing. I close my eyes. "Call Phil O'Hearn. I think he might know who they were."

"O'Hearn?"

I open one eye. "He didn't do anything. He's trying to help. I know it's weird, but he is. And he might know something."

"He's trying to help who, Sally?"

"Me and Uncle Percy." I close the eye. "Buddy, I am so tired."

"How did the dogs get into the closet?"

"I put them in there."

"The power's out at your house."

"I shut off the circuit breaker," I say, fading. "It's in the bedroom closet, in the back."

I drift away, hear murmuring, and feel myself being moved around. I want to sleep, but someone says not yet, we're going to X ray. "The Laurencelles are taking Scotty and your mom's dog to their house," I hear Buddy say. "They say not to worry, they have their food and leashes." Pause. "The boy, Sam, he's the one they say found you."

"It's a good thing he did," someone else says. "She was in the initial stages of hypothermia and the family did exactly the right thing."

I want to say something, but I can't seem to move my mouth.

CHAPTER TWENTY-FIVE

W hen I awaken, I find that I am in a private hospital room with an IV in my arm. The window blinds are open and I see that it is still dark outside. And still snowing. And blowing. Dancing under the halogen lights outside.

I find the call button and push it. In a few moments, a friendly face appears. "Ah-ha, she's awake," a nurse's aide says.

"And she's starving," I say. My words seem stilted and I realize it is because I can't move my upper lip. "And can we take this thing out?" I gesture to the IV.

"Let me get the nurse," she says, disappearing. In a very little while I am off the hydration IV, sipping ginger ale, watching CNN and tentatively touching the bandages on my face while waiting for soup and crackers. When the soup arrives, it is in the hands of Officer Paul Fitzwilliam, who is dressed in full uniform.

This is how I first met Paul. Dressed in the same sort of crisply ironed navy blue uniform with a shining badge, the same kind of black leather holster, and the same kind of hat smartly tucked under his arm. My young police officer. He is very handsome.

"Hey," he says softly.

"Hi," I say, clicking the TV off. "How on earth did you get here?"

"Buddy called me and sent someone down with your Jeep." He puts the soup down on the tray table, squeezes my hand in both of his and then stoops to kiss it.

"My face is that bad?"

"You'll be fine," he says, kissing my hand again and easing down onto the edge of the bed. He leans over me, carefully looking for something. He zeros in on my left temple—a kiss—and then the bottom part of my mouth. A kiss. Then he tosses his hat in the chair, draws the tray table over and takes the lid off the soup. "We need to call your mom right away. She's snowed in with her friend and is half out of her mind with worry. I told her I would call after I saw you with my own eyes."

"What time is it?"

He checks his watch. "Six." He gets a spoonful of soup, scrapes the excess off the bottom and, holding his other hand under it, steers the spoon toward me. I accept it as best I can. It's very good. (If you ever have to go into a hospital, make sure you go to Midstate Medical Center. Every room is private and the food is great, which in my book provides half the healing.)

"I can do it, thank you," I say, taking the spoon from him.

"Uh-oh, we spilled," he says, looking down the front of my hospital gown and blotting it gently with the napkin. He smiles, raising his eyes. "Same breasts, now I know it's you."

I don't know why this cheers me up but it does.

Paul calls my mother on his cell phone, and I examine a jagged cut on my forearm. Every part of me seems to have something wrong with it.

"It's Paul Fitzwilliam, Belle. She's awake and would like to say hi." He hands the phone to me.

"Hello, Mother," I say.

"Oh, Sally, thank God, are you all right?"

"I'm absolutely fine," I say with a brilliance I do not feel. "Banged up, certainly, but I'll be out of here in no time."

"Buddy said they put stitches in your head."

I feel the side of my head and instead of hair in one spot, I feel bandages. "Yes. And did he tell you I broke my nose?"

"Darling, as long as you're in one piece, who cares?"

"Could be that a couple million people will," I remind her. While Mother grills me about what happened, I reach toward the bedside table but a searing pain in my shoulder stops me. I grimace, pulling back and falling against the pillows.

"Torn ligament," Paul murmurs, circling the bed to reach the nightstand. "What do you want?"

"No, Mother," I'm saying into the phone, "Buddy's guys caught them both." I whisper, "Mirror." Paul opens the top drawer where there is a hospital kit. "No, it wasn't the Jervis guy." I look out the window at the storm. "Mother, please, don't *worry,* nobody's going anywhere in this storm. The bad guys are downtown and the stalker guy's probably frozen to death somewhere." Paul finds a handheld mirror and offers it to me.

"The dogs are fine, they're over at Bob and Wanda and Sam's house." I take the mirror. "Laurencelle." I notice the apprehension in Paul's face as I bring the mirror up.

Oh my God.

I've got purple rings of blood below both eyes. There's a huge X of adhesive tape over my nose. My left eye has no white in it; it's bloodred. And my upper lip looks like Homer Simpson's. "I'll tell Bob that Daddy knew his father. Anyway, they have the dogs." I bare my teeth in the mirror. Thank God all is well in there. "No, I don't think I remembered to tell them about the drops for Abigail's ears." I look at Paul, but he is at the window, looking outside at the storm. "I promise, Mother." I crane my neck a little to see the red marks on my neck in the mirror. It's where the guy grabbed me through the car window.

"Go back to bed and know that I'm absolutely fine." Paul has come back to sit on the edge of the bed again. He takes the mirror away from me and puts it in the drawer. "I promise, Mother. Yes. I love you, too. Very much. Give my love to Mack. Okay. Love you. Bye." I click the phone off and hand it back to Paul. He pushes the soup back in front of me.

"I don't know how you can even look at me," I sigh, reaching for the spoon.

"I've seen a lot worse," he tells me, watching me eat. "And you'll heal. I can tell."

He is adorable, this guy. I look down at his hands and think of David Waring's hands again and how much more refined Paul's are.

"I can get you something else to eat," he says, watching me. "But breakfast's coming shortly." He smiles at me.

It's so strange to see Paul like this. I feel entirely comforted.

"They had to take one of the suspects to another hospital, you know. Buddy didn't want him in the same E.R. as you. Guess he was scared you'd finish him off." He grins. "What the heck did you do to them, Sally? Buddy said something about running them down in a Cadillac."

"I pushed their Wrangler on the big rock in my front yard," I tell him. "I was driving one of those SUV truck things. It was huge. Did the job." Now that the vegetables in the soup are gone, I can simply raise the container to drink the remainder.

"An Esplanade," he says. "And now it's underwater?"

I wipe my mouth with a napkin, flinching when I press too hard.

"They're strip-mining on the farm."

"You mentioned that."

"Yes, well, unbeknownst to me, they expanded into the next field and I drove into a drainage ditch." I touch my stomach for a moment and look at Paul. "What on earth am I going to tell the rental car place?"

He shrugs. "What's a fifty-thousand-dollar vehicle? Just tell them two thugs attacked you and sunk it."

"Right," I say, sinking back into the pillows. I try to smile. "You need to get started to New Haven. Even in the Jeep, it's going to take a while."

"I don't want to take your car."

"Take it, please," I tell him. "You're so sweet to come. And talk to Mother."

When he looks into my eyes and then averts his, I am reminded how monstrous I look.

The nurse comes in with some medication for me to take, which I do. After she leaves, I say, "I hate having you see me like this."

"I'm psyched to see you like this," he says, taking my hand. "Because you're alive and well and on the road to recovery. Besides," he adds, bending to kiss my hand, "you'll always be gorgeous. It's in your nature."

I take my hand away from him and make a shooing motion with it. "Go. Protect us, Officer Fitzwilliam. Hit those streets. You're the new kid on the block and you shouldn't be late."

"It's going to take me a while in this snow," he admits. He suddenly bends to hang his head next to mine. "I love you," he whispers, kissing me softly on the ear.

After Paul leaves, I reach for the telephone, swearing under my breath because of the pain it sends through my shoulder, and start dialing numbers to use my phone card. "Newsroom," a male voice promptly answers.

"What are you doing in so early, Haydn?"

"Sally."

"I need a reporter and a crew in Connecticut."

"In the middle of the biggest snowstorm of the last ten years?"

"Yep."

"Right now, I'm afraid I'm a man without a crew. Everybody's out covering the storm." Pause. "The closest available crew is in Boston, and the storm's even worse there."

"Listen carefully, Haydn," I tell him. "I've got a smashed-up face, stitches in my head and torn ligaments from two thugs who came to see me. If what I suspect is true, about who they are and why they came, we're going to have ourselves a pretty big story. Think attempted murder, think bribery, think the mob, and think a host of New York state politicians and union leaders. All in the same bed."

"I'll see what I can do," he says. "Check back."

After I get off with him, I call Hartford Hospital to see how Roderick is doing. He's still on the critical list.

CHAPTER TWENTY-SIX

Breakfast arrives and the eggs taste great. So does the toast, although it does kind of hurt to eat it. But eat it I do, and I eat everything—the orange juice, the coffee, eggs, toast, sausage, fruit salad—and drink a cup of icy water. Very full and hopeful of recovery, I check the clock—seven-thirty—and decide I am going to have to wake up my boss.

Georgiana Hamilton-Ayres answers the telephone as if she has been waiting for my call for hours instead of being sound asleep.

"Good morning, Georgiana," I say, "and I feel very badly waking you guys up, but—"

"I know," she says, cutting me off, "something's happened and you need to talk to Alexandra." There is a muffled sound, then, "Darling, it's Sally."

A moment later Alexandra comes on the phone. "Sally?"

She sounds exhausted, but what am I going to do? "Sorry to bother you guys, but remember how you wanted a lot of publicity for the newscast?"

She doesn't answer.

"Well, I'm ready to go here. I've got a broken head, a broken nose, a screwed-up shoulder and I look like Homer Simpson, but as much as I hate to be seen like this, I think we're at the beginning of a great story—*if* we can find a crew in this storm. Think the mob, corrupt New York politicians, international money laundering, poisoning the land—the story could go in any or all of those directions."

"Ask Sally if she'd like to come to dinner this week," I hear Georgiana say.

"Where are you?" Alexandra wants to know.

There is a very well dressed, pleasant-looking man standing in the doorway holding a basket of flowers in one hand and a briefcase in the other. He's wearing a dark blue suit and red tie, dress shoes and a black overcoat, which I suspect is made of cashmere, it falls so beautifully. "Hold on a second," I tell Alexandra. "Can I help you?"

"I'll wait until you're off the telephone," he says.

"I think you may have the wrong room," I tell him.

His eyebrows go up. "Sally Harrington?"

"Yes. Okay, I'll be right with you." I suppose I could ask him to wait outside, but he looks important. "I'll call you right back," I tell Alexandra and hang up.

"These are for you," the man says respectfully, holding out the basket of spring flowers for me to admire.

"They're gorgeous," I say, deciding that he definitely must be an insurance guy. I bet I'm going to be talking to a lot of insurance guys before the day is out. "If you could just put them on the windowsill where I can see them, that would be lovely." I'm beginning to sound like Mother.

"My name is Stephen Smithfield, Ms. Harrington," he says, coming back to stand at the foot of my bed.

"You can sit down if you want," I tell him.

"Thank you, but that won't be necessary." He moves around the side of the bed to hand me a card.

Stephen Younger Smithfield, Esq.
Caswell, Norfolk & Dane
52 Broad Street
New York, NY 10001

A kitchen aide comes in to take my breakfast tray away.

"Your office is very near the World Trade Center," I say.

He nods once, a flicker of something passing over his face. They must have been in the middle of everything two years ago in September.

"And what brings you to lovely Castleford in the middle of the worst snowstorm in ten years?" I ask cheerfully, sipping some water. "Are you sure you don't want to sit?"

"Well," he reconsiders. "Thank you, perhaps I shall." He drags over a chair and sits down, although he still doesn't take off his coat. "I live down the road in Westport, so it wasn't too far to drive."

If he wants to consider driving fifty miles in the worst snowstorm in ten years "nothing," I'm game. But after looking him over again, I'm pretty sure someone must have driven him here.

"I'm here, Ms. Harrington, because my firm represents World Sound Industries."

I blink. That's the consortium behind building the colossal coal-burning cement plant in Hillstone Falls. "Ah," I finally say, watching as he places his briefcase carefully on his lap. "Don't tell me you actually know something about World Sound Industries, like who they really are." He doesn't even look up, but merely unlocks his briefcase and raises the lid, so I add, "And whether they have more of the Gambino crime family members working for them, or if it's more Genevese, or perhaps members of another crime family I haven't heard about yet."

"I'm here to open negotiations upon a small piece of land,"

he says, looking up, "which we believe belongs to your great-uncle, Percival F. Harrington." He pauses. "You hold power of attorney for him, do you not?"

"Yes." I am morbidly fascinated by this guy.

He pulls out a sheaf of papers and half stands to hand them to me. "The land is part of an inheritance that comes to Mr. Harrington through his deceased wife, Martha Hollins Harrington."

I look down, skimming the copy and flipping through pages. In reverse chronological order there are copies of rulings by the New York Supreme Court, and then going back to rulings in probate court. The lawyer half stands again to hand me copies of land surveys of the Kindrickson Farm in Hillstone Falls, New York, dated 2001, 1996, 1972 and 1824. Then he hands me a survey dated four days ago. The first page encompasses the lines of all the former surveys, with an arrow pointing to a tiny area. After that is page after page of details blown up of each area of the map. Finally I come to the land evidently in question, five acres on something labeled Barton's River.

Without looking up, I flick back through the pages and say, "Are you aware the township's land records for this piece of land are missing?"

"I wouldn't know about that," he says. "Our charge is merely to handle the negotiation and execute the transaction to purchase the land."

After thinking a moment, I decide I believe him. This highly polished law firm of repute has been engaged to cover decades of dirty dealings by others with an old-line WASP seal of approval. (The power of money is an interesting thing, is it not?)

"I understand your uncle is presently out of town."

"Yes."

"My client is anxious to settle this matter," he continues.

"I bet they are," I say, thinking of the two men they know were arrested last night. I'll say this for them, these guys move fast.

"My client is planning to build a manufacturing center that will hugely benefit the region," the lawyer explains. "It's a very hard-hit economic area, as you may know. This project is very important to the state."

"I bet it is," I say. "Just think of the benefits—a forty-story smokestack, particulate matter, sulfur dioxide, carbon monoxide, drainage into the Hudson River, it all sounds quite lovely and very beneficial to me."

The expression of the lawyer is one of patience. "The state of New York evidently disagrees with you, Ms. Harrington."

I save my breath. If this guy knows anything about who it is he's representing, he doesn't care. "So what are they offering?"

"My client wishes for your uncle to tell us—with your guidance, of course—what he thinks is a fair price. That survey packet includes a current market assessment, which I think he will find pleasing." He blinks. "This is something that could possibly change the quality of your uncle's life."

I turn to the assessment page. As a building lot on a stream, it carries a residential value of ninety-five thousand dollars. As a residential lot, however, located in the middle of a colossal coal-burning cement factory, it's worthless—except as the final acquisition for a billion-dollar project, in which case one would assume the sky is the limit.

It's an interesting position for Uncle Percy to be in. He has signed everything over to the Gregory Home in exchange for lifelong care. So does this mean all proceeds of the sale would go to the Gregory Home? I suppose the amount would determine how it's handled. I bet it's going to take yet another lawyer in my life to figure it out.

I look up, narrowing my eyes and cocking my head slightly

to the side. It hurts, but I want to get my point across. "Attorney Smithfield, do you have any idea why I'm in here? And why I look like this?"

"No. I was simply informed this morning that you were here and that my client wished me to give you these papers to consider."

I don't say anything for a minute. "If you were me, Attorney Smithfield," I finally say, choosing my words carefully because I am beginning to feel light-headed, "what would you think if a lawyer turned up to make an offer the morning after two unknown assailants broke into your home and nearly killed you?"

"I assure you, Ms. Harrington," he says, shaking his head, "I'm only here to open the negotiations on the land. I don't know anything about—" He searches for a word. "Anything other than these documents which I've given you."

"And I'm supposed to think the two events are unrelated?"

His face has blanched slightly and I know he is finally starting to wonder about this client of his. He looks down into his briefcase.

"At least on 9/11 we were on the same side, Attorney Smithfield," I say, "because we're certainly not on the same side now." *This is your one chance to get out before I drag you across the American airwaves with your client,* I say telepathically.

"Twenty-three Heron Road in Middletown," he says, reading from something in his briefcase.

I stare at him.

"Mountainside Lodge, Sunset Road, Aspen, Colorado," he reads before looking up. "I was asked to relay these addresses to you, although I don't know to what they refer. Other possible land purchases?"

Son of a bitch. The Middlesex address is Mack's, where Mother is staying now and Mountainside Lodge in Aspen is where my younger brother, Rob, lives.

"Could you write those addresses down for me, Attorney Smithfield?" I say, holding out his business card. "Write it on the back of this so I won't lose them."

Attorney Smithfield rises to take the card from me, and sits back down to carefully copy the addresses.

So he doesn't know what they mean, I surmise. Otherwise he would be reluctant to attach his handwriting to a threat that has been made against my family.

As soon as Attorney Smithfield departs I call Mack's house.

"Hello?"

"Hi, Mack. It's Sally."

"We were just about to pick up the phone to thank you," he says, "but your mother was concerned you needed rest."

I hesitate. "Oh?"

He laughs. "I was all set to get up and start plowing the drive again, but your guy was already there, clearing it away. He said he'll be back later in the day to do it again." I hear Mother in the background and then the phone is handed over.

"Darling, you were so sweet to think of us. You know how I worry about Mack taking that long driveway on. And now here you are, laid up—"

"I'm fine, Mother, and I'm glad the driveway got plowed." My eyes are closed; I'm fighting the urge to be sick. "I just wanted to check to make sure he got there."

"Oh, yes. And in such a nice big truck. He's in the waste disposal business I think he said. He said you went to a lot of trouble to make sure he could find Mack's house."

So that's that, I think, when I hang up with her. It wasn't an empty threat. They've already been there; they know where Mother is.

"Are you in pain?" the nurse asks a moment later, moving quickly to my side. "You're crying, aren't you?"

"Yeah," I say, "in frustration."

"But you can't," she says, "it will mess up your bandages."

God DAMN it! It's not fair to go after my family! No organized crime family I ever heard of did that; they should only be going after me.

But they are going after my family. Unless I—

I get rid of the nurse and call the DBS newsroom and get Hadyn on the line. "I found a crew!" he says victoriously.

"Cancel it," I tell him. "False alarm."

Silence. "You gotta be kidding. What happened to the big story?"

"It just fizzled."

Pause. "You're beaten up, in the hospital, suspects are arrested and the story has fizzled."

"Completely. Trust me," I say, nearly choking, "there is no story to be had."

"Alexandra is going to go nuts, you know. She ordered the crew off a breaking—"

"I don't care, just cancel it," I tell him forcefully. "And let them return to whatever they were working on."

"But—"

I hang up on Hadyn, feeling so angry and frustrated I could scream. But I can't. That's just the point. They've gagged me. There's nothing I can do but back off.

And find myself someone who can cut a deal.

I close my eyes to consider my options, but I know there is no other way out of this. People love their families, I know, but if one of your parents died when you were young, you would know how Mother, Rob and I clung to each other. The idea that anything— Well, forget it. It's over. I've got to cut bait.

I pick up the telephone and call Phillip O'Hearn.

IV

Exit Strategy

CHAPTER TWENTY-SEVEN

When I am released from the hospital the next day, I think the Enterprise Rent-A-Car guy must be the only person on the road. The snow let up for six hours yesterday, enough to get some serious plowing done, but it resumed last night and now, on Friday morning, the city has run out of places to put the snow. And it is still lightly snowing.

There's no need for this enterprising young man to know, I decide as I walk through the swirling snow and climb into the white Ford Explorer he has driven here, that I sank a Cadillac Esplanade on Wednesday night. His name is Ralph, he says cheerfully, and he does his best not to stare at the bandages on my nose and on my head, or the fact that in this freezing weather I am wearing a hospital gown tucked in operating-room pants, a button-down sweater from lost and found and hospital socks with slippers. Perhaps it is because he is trying so hard to appear unfazed that when I explain, about a quarter mile away from the hospital, that we need to drive to my house to pick up my wallet before we can go to the car place, he doesn't protest.

I can't begin to describe what Castleford looks like right now. After a parking ban on the streets and almost two feet of snow, this city of sixty thousand looks deserted. On the way to my house, we pass only two vehicles, a city snowplow and some other idiot like us in a Bronco. I have to talk Ralph through the negotiation of my driveway. Somebody must have plowed yesterday at one point, because there is a five-inch indentation in the snow that roughly matches the turns in my driveway.

When we arrived at the cottage, it is to find a crime scene blanketed in snow. The Wrangler is still there, hung up on the big rock (I smile to myself), but it is covered in plastic sheeting and yellow crime-scene tape. I limp though the knee-high snow in my slippers around the side of the house and see that someone has thoughtfully stapled plastic sheeting over my shattered bay window. I have to dig around in the snow for a while before I find my fake rock, and when I do I bless the Laurencelles for putting it back in the same place. I slip open the hatch on the bottom of the fake rock and extract my house key.

While poor enterprising Ralph is probably bemoaning the fact he ever took my call, I go into the cottage through the back door. In the kitchen I realize it is a toss-up between what looks worse, the kitchen or my face. The table and chairs are overturned, the hanging light is smashed and glass and shattered windowpane frames are everywhere. On the yellow crime-scene tape there is a note not to touch anything. There's also something covered in plastic on the floor. I walk over to look. It's a huge log from my woodpile.

Ah, so that's what hit me.

I tiptoe to the window over the sink to take Abigail's eardrops off the sill. Then I move on to my bedroom and go into the closet to sniff and look around, wondering if one of the dogs (Abigail) might have had an accident with all the commotion. No. I smile.

I change into some real underwear and clothes—minding

my nose and shoulder—and I put on some socks and boots. I pack some clothes in a duffel bag, retrieve my wallet and cell phone, get my laptop and from the front hall closet take out my full-length winter coat.

When I come back out to the Explorer, Ralph looks relieved. I have real clothes on and look like someone who will pay. He jumps out to help me with my bag and computer.

We slowly drive through the snow to Enterprise, windshield wipers working. Ralph has to unlock the door because no one else is there. We go inside and conduct our business; he hands the car keys to me and I hand him three of the five twenty-dollar bills I took from my emergency cache at home.

"I can't take that," he tells me.

"You really helped me out," I counter, pushing the money across the counter. "If you can't find a good use for it, I'm sure you must know someone who can."

He smiles shyly. At Enterprise they make them wear freshly starched white shirts and a tie, which makes his cheeks look rosier.

"Besides," I say, turning to go, "you didn't stare at me like the freak I am."

"You're not a freak," he calls after me. "You're famous. You're Sally Harrington."

"I never saw them in the light," I explain to Buddy and another detective in the police observation room. "Beyond his general build, I couldn't tell you what he looked like. The other one I have absolutely no idea about."

"I know, Sal, that's why we're not doing a lineup."

Inside the interrogation room, the suspect and his lawyer are whispering to each other while the captain is waiting.

"His right hand matches up with the marks on your neck,"

Buddy says. "And we're running tests on his gloves in hope of finding some trace of you."

In the interrogation room, the defense attorney says to the CPD captain, "Come off it. At the very worst you have a case of criminal mischief."

"And what about shooting to kill?" the captain asks.

"Self-defense, my client explained that. Harrington had rammed them once, trying to kill them, and was about to crush them. He had to shoot."

"Ah. Self-defense. I should write this down," the captain says, pretending to take a note. "Harrington was in her home when the suspect smashed a log through her kitchen window, hitting her in the head, then he chased her through the woods, broke her car window to strangle her and fired two shots into her car. And he is innocent, it's all her fault." He looks up. "Duly noted, Counselor."

I'm not feeling so hot. "Buddy, do I have to be here for this? I'm feeling like I should go home and lie down for a while. I'll be happy to come back if—"

"No, that's fine," Buddy says quickly, jumping up. "Let me get someone to drive you." He opens the door for me, and in the hallway guides me by the elbow.

"I've got a car," I tell him.

"You're driving yourself around like this? In the snow?"

"Yeah. It's fine, Buddy, really."

"No offense, Sal, but you look like hell. I don't think you should be—"

"How is our evidence, by the way?" I interrupt him. "Other than this glove test? You don't have the Cadillac out yet, do you?"

"We have to wait until it stops snowing," he concedes. "It's in a tricky spot. But I've seen the windshield. We'll get what we need. And the big thing is, we've got the gun and we got him while he was carrying it."

"What about the other guy?"

"Considering that we had to cut him out of the Wrangler with Mr. Innocent Bystander and his gun, we can prove he was an accomplice."

I try to kiss him on the cheek but can't do it very well. "Thank you for everything. I will sleep well tonight."

"We're going to need that complete statement, Sally," he says after me. "If you could come down in the morning, that would be great."

I wave okay and continue down the hall. I'm getting a little used to the jerk-and-stare reaction of everyone who crosses my path. Even here, in the corridors of law enforcement, officers are overtly startled by my bandages, my black-purple eyes (now turning green around the edges) and my Homer Simpson mouth.

Outside, unbelievably, the snow is still falling; at least another inch has accumulated while I was inside.

The plowing guy has come through Mother's driveway at least twice in this storm and the Explorer makes it in with ease. I park it in the empty garage. I have to make two trips into the house to bring my stuff in with my bad shoulder. I just dump it inside the door and go into the kitchen to call the Laurencelles to see how Scotty and Abigail are doing. "They're doing just fine," Wanda reports. "The question is, how are you? Where are you?"

I explain that I'm at my mother's, that I was released from the hospital, and am just going to take it easy. Would she mind keeping the dogs one more night since it's really bad out on the roads?

A half hour later, Bob and young Sam drive up in a shiny

pickup truck, the dogs tucked carefully in the seat between them. I fling open the door, not believing this, and the dogs come bounding through the snow to greet me.

The Laurencelles have come bearing presents: a crock of lobster bisque—one of Wanda's specialties, Bob tells me—homemade bread; a tossed salad; and six glazed doughnuts from Krispy Kreme. ("They're from yesterday," Sam confides, "but warm them up and they'll be good.") They also shovel the front walk and the back deck and stairs before they leave. Last but not least, Sam runs out to the truck and brings back his new snake skeleton and offers to loan it to me if I would like some company. I assure him that I don't, but thank him all the same.

I take a long hot bath and put on a flannel nightie and robe of Mother's. I am stretched out on the living-room couch with my eyes closed, the dogs on the floor beneath me, when I think I hear something and open my eyes to see headlights playing over the wall. I sit up and then get up to look out the window.

It's the silver Mercedes station wagon. It's David Waring.

CHAPTER TWENTY-EIGHT

David Waring is here.

I take a deep breath and walk to the front door. I catch sight of myself in the mirror on the way, think, *Well, this will take care of it,* and open the door.

His mouth parts in astonishment. "Sally," he finally says, stepping forward with his hand out, but then stopping, as if scared to touch me.

"Happy Halloween," I say. "Come in."

He kicks the worst of the snow off his shoes on the step and brushes down his pants and coat. Then he steps inside, slipping his loafers off and hanging his coat on the brass coatrack behind the door. "If it's possible for my sister to become hysterical," he tells me, following me into the living room and reflexively bending to pet the dogs hello, "she's almost there about you."

I sink into Mother's chair, drawing my legs up under me.

"You were supposed to call her back yesterday morning and you never did," he says, straightening up.

"I left a message for her on her office voice mail."

"And left her sitting there at home wondering what the hell happened to you."

I don't say anything.

"You called for a news crew, but no one knew where to send it, then you call in and say you don't need it anymore and hang up without telling anyone where you are. My sister calls me in a panic, so I drive through this storm from Wallingford to your house and find it roped off as a crime scene. I call the police and all they'll tell me is that you're okay. I come here and nobody's here, either. I've been to every hospital in this county, you won't answer any of your phones, your beeper, *nothing!*" The last is said with both hands rising high in the air.

"I'm sorry," I say quietly. I notice he hasn't shaved in a while.

"I don't know if sorry's going to be enough. I've never seen my sister like this."

"And how often have you ever seen anyone look like this?" I ask him, pointing to my face.

He backs down slightly. "I can see you've been through a lot." He looks around and decides to sit on the ottoman in front of me. "You need to call Alexandra."

"The phone's in the kitchen," I tell him. "You call her. And tell her as soon as I'm at liberty to tell her what happened, I will, and in the meantime, I'm okay, and she's not to worry."

"What do you mean at liberty? Why can't you tell her what's going on?"

I look at him for a moment and point to my face. "To cut to the chase, I don't want my mother looking like this. Or my brother."

His eyes narrow. "You've been threatened."

"Yes."

"Maybe we can help."

"I don't think so." I look out the window at the snow. I feel Scotty's nose nudging my hand, so I pet him behind the ears. I turn back to David. "I know someone who has come up against this same group. He's no angel himself, and he's scared for me, and scared for my family." I look down at Scotty. "You better call your sister."

"She's going to want to talk to you," he warns me, pulling a cell phone out of his pocket.

"Then go stand in the kitchen," I say wearily, "and I'll stay in here, so when she says she wants to talk to me, you say, 'She's not here.'"

He studies me a moment and I notice the bags under his eyes, the lines in his face. The eyes are still magnificent.

"You better call her," I tell him. He gets up and walks to the kitchen, and the dogs follow, no doubt hoping for some kind of accident involving food.

"Yes, I saw her," I hear David say a few moments later. "She's pretty banged up physically, otherwise she seems okay. She swore to me she'd talk to you when she was able." Pause. "Well, something's obviously happened and she's worried about the safety of her family."

I wince. Damn, I wish he hadn't said that. I sigh, haul myself out of the chair and drag myself into the kitchen, holding my hand out for the phone. "Hang on, she just came in."

"Hi," I say.

"Hi," Alexandra says, anger simmering. "I was just about to call Sky Preston and tell him something has happened to Sally that has to do with the mob, corrupt New York politicians, international money laundering, poisoning the land and whatever it is has stopped her from breaking a huge story."

Sky Preston is a special federal prosecutor.

"Please don't," I say in a small voice. I'm feeling small, vulnerable.

"Convince me."

"If I told you that Phillip O'Hearn is trying to help me,

would that convince you how serious the threat could be to my family?"

Pause. *"O'Hearn?"*

Alexandra knows O'Hearn's relationship with me rather well, since it was she who did a national exposé of him on TV a couple of years ago.

"How is he helping you?"

"I guess you would call it acting as my emissary. To the bad guys."

"I see."

"You do?"

"Yes." Pause. "I wondered if someday one of these stories would boomerang onto your family." Pause. "Though I thought there was supposed to be some honor among thieves."

"So did I."

"The mob doesn't normally go after people's families."

"I know."

"Okay," she says softly. "I'm putting you on medical leave."

"For at least a week, yes. I would appreciate that."

A sigh. "Be smart and take care. And stay in touch, even if it's just to let me know you're still among the land of the living."

I click the phone off and hand it back to David. "Okay, I made nice."

He's looking at the side of my head. "I think you're starting to bleed through."

"No, that's some stuff they put on it. I'm not supposed to take the bandage off until tomorrow morning. Then I'll be *really* attractive," I add, shuffling over to the refrigerator. "I'll have my bald spot with Frankenstein stitches in my head."

He starts to say something, but stops, rubs his eye and says, "Something smells really wonderful in here."

"It's lobster bisque."

"Lobster bisque?" he says longingly. "You've got to be kidding. Where did you get lobster bisque in this weather?"

"And I've got homemade bread," I say, opening Mother's bread box to show him. "And salad. The mother of the boy who found me—" I stop.

"What do you mean, 'found' you?" David says.

"Don't worry about it," I tell him. "Come on, I'm hungry, so if you are, too, we might as well enjoy a good meal. I can even offer you some wine or beer or—" I shrug, hurting myself. "Ow."

"Sit down," David says, walking over and taking the bread out of my hands. "If you buy, then I fly. I'll just have to ask you where a few things are."

"You're going to fix dinner?"

"I did help raise two kids, you know, and it wasn't all pancakes and peanut butter and jelly." He smiles. "Where do you want to eat? In here?"

"Sure."

"Then sit."

I sit down and watch him, and it is true, he does seem to know how to cook. He heats the bisque gently on the stove, not in the microwave. He carefully wraps the bread in aluminum foil and puts it in the oven. He finds balsamic vinegar and olive oil and sets about mixing in lemon juice, mustard (!), and a few other spices I can't see, and tossing the salad.

Next thing I know, he is seated across from me, eating salad and watching me try to chew mine. "I didn't think you got storms like this here much anymore," he says, looking out the sliding glass doors at the back deck.

"Can't tell me we haven't messed with the weather," I say, taking another forkful of this wonderful salad. Neither one of us is boozing it up (I can't; I'm on painkillers); we're both drinking ice water. "So tell me about your children."

He meets my eyes for a moment (what is left to see) and reaches around to extract his wallet. He pulls out a picture and hands it across the table. "Kyle, my son at Duke. Tory, the one at Choate-Rosemary Hall."

"Kyle certainly looks a lot like you."

"He's majoring in history. He might go into law. Or politics, God forbid. Of course, my father's encouraging that side."

I look up from the picture. "Was it difficult with your father being a congressman for so long?"

He nods. "Yeah, it was. It pulled our family all over the place. I think it was hardest on Alexandra, because they took the four of us to Washington, but by the time she came along, for whatever reason, they left her at the farm with my grandparents."

"Huh," I say. "I didn't know that." I look back down at the photo. "Tory is very pretty."

"She's a lot like their mother," he concedes, taking the photograph back and putting it away. Seemingly depressed now, he picks up his fork and starts spearing salad, and then playing with it.

Well, that was certainly a conversation killer.

"So what's going on with you two? You and your wife." I look down at my plate and continue eating salad.

"We're separated," he says.

I know that, bucko.

"We have, um—" He thinks a moment. "I guess you'd call it a lifestyle problem." He puts his fork down. "We were having some problems. Mary Ellen was drinking more than—well, than was good for her. Or for the children. And then she stopped."

"Did she go to AA?" I ask before sipping some water.

He shakes his head. "Are you through?"

"Yes."

He picks up our salad plates and brings them to the sink. "She didn't go to AA, she went to this church. One of those—I don't even know how to classify it. I guess it's Protestant, but a revivalist sect? It's Christian, anyway. You know, they're reborn and everything. Holy rollers for rich people."

He's ladling soup into bowls now. The smell is heaven.

"So Mary Ellen stopped drinking, but then she became obsessed with this church. And she just never stopped talking about it. And then she said—" He places one bowl down in front of me and one at his place. "Go ahead, Sally, I'm just going to get the bread."

I wait for him, and tell him where the butter is, so that, too, comes to the table. "You don't even like lobster," I tell Scotty, who is salivating at my side. Fed up with the dogs, I get up to open the sliding glass door and send them outside. Abigail just stands there, on the other side of the glass, looking in like Eeyore in *Winnie the Pooh*. Finally Scotty's barking and frolicking in the drifts lures her off the deck.

"What religion were you, or are you?" I ask.

"Presbyterian."

We taste the soup and both of us are momentarily overwhelmed by the rich taste of it. Heaven. I think Wanda may be my new best friend. A few moments later, I prompt David. "You were telling me about Mary Ellen, and what happened after she found this church."

"Well, to start with, in this church you only have sex to procreate. They don't believe in birth control." He gestures. "I love children, but we had ours. We raised two wonderful kids and at forty-four and forty-two years old, I don't think it's time to start all over again."

I carefully pat my mouth with my napkin. I may look like

a monster, but I am determined to be a monster with good manners. "So what did you do?"

He doesn't answer for a moment. And then, looking down at his soup, he says, "I was going to get a vasectomy and not tell her." Pause. "And as soon as I thought that, I knew our marriage was in shambles." He looks up. "We had been very close. And honest with each other. We didn't really hide things ever. Except for the drinking, that changed things."

I think to myself there's little likelihood that an attractive alcoholic woman in Santa Barbara does not have secrets, but decide not to share my conclusions with him.

"I tried going to her church, but it's just so—" Now he drops his spoon with a clatter and raises his hands. "I just don't get it. I believe in Jesus Christ as our savior, as the Son of God, but what they do there is so judgmental, so rigid, so—" He shakes his head. After a moment he reaches to tear off a piece of bread, but does not butter it. He looks up at me again. "Is there such a thing as journalist-client privilege?"

"Sure," I tell him.

He nods once, as if to consider this a promise and then decides to accept it. His eyes come back to mine. "Everything exploded over my sister and Georgiana. Mary Ellen refused to spend Christmas at my parents' if they were there, and she said she didn't want either one of our children to see Alexandra until she—" He sighs. "You know, sees the error of her ways. Mom said something to Alexandra and whatever it was, Lexy didn't come home. She and Georgiana went to Scotland to spend the holidays."

"I remember," I say softly.

He bites off a piece of bread and chews, though I doubt he is really tasting it. His anger is starting to fill the room.

I wonder if lobster bisque will keep. I'll have to ask Wanda,

I decide, putting my spoon down for what I know will be the last time. His story is giving me a stomachache. I hate marriage-unraveling stories, for I want so much to believe in it.

"And then I would come home and find her Bible study group," he continues. "Not once a week—it was almost every night, and it didn't take long for me to understand that this was an attempt to bring me into the fold. And there's this one guy—Aaron—who really, really gets to me. He's an evangelical preacher, they call it. But the thing is, this church doesn't believe in divorce, but this guy Aaron's divorced. I asked Mary Ellen what the problem had been, you know, was the wife sleeping around or had she abandoned the family, and then when she got really mad about my questions, I knew she felt something for this guy." He bites his lower lip, moving his water glass around on the table.

"So you think he's part of the problem," I say quietly.

After thinking a moment, he nods. "Yeah." He drains his water glass. "He's thirty-five, good-looking and obsessed with Mary Ellen. And she's *basking* in it."

"Why did he convert?" I ask. "Usually someone 'reborn' has experienced some kind of bottom. You know, like your wife and her drinking. For some people it's a financial mess or being abandoned—"

"Oh, yeah, he had a mess," David confirms. "I found out he got busted while getting a blow job from a guy in a public rest room at Fisherman's Wharf." He glances at me. "Needless to say, Mary Ellen didn't volunteer that information. Nor did she tell me that his wife left him because it wasn't the first time." He purses his lips a moment, thinking. Then he seemingly shakes off whatever it was and looks at me. "So, anyway, the story goes that Aaron came to this church and was reborn and so now he's straight again." He bites his lip. "The

Bible study group talks an awful lot about the damnation of practicing homosexuals, so it's a big deal to Mary Ellen. And since I know she's got a thing for this guy, it's a *really* big deal for her."

I nod, not knowing quite what to say. "How are your children with the situation?"

"Freaked out," he says. "They're glad their mother's not drinking anymore, but there are a lot of arguments when they come home about going to that church with her. They won't go."

There is an uncomfortable silence. "Well, it's all so new," I say, "everybody needs time to absorb these changes and settle down a bit. You know how gung-ho people always are in the beginning of something like this, David—the relief at feeling forgiven and accepted by a group." I'm thinking of Jessica Wright's description of her early days in AA. "I'm sure Mary Ellen will be more amenable in time. Certainly if she values her relationship with her children, she's going to have to develop some kind of acceptance about the way people choose to live their lives. Or risk losing them."

He stands up to clear the table. He puts the dishes in the sink and then rests his hands on the edge of it, looking out the window. "You want some wine?"

"No thanks, but please help yourself. There's an open bottle of white in the refrigerator and there's some red in the pantry."

He finds the bottle of Pinot Grigio and brings it back to the table, pouring a healthy amount into his empty water glass. He makes a motion to toast me and then takes a large swallow. Two swallows. He finishes off the glass and pours some more.

"So what was the final straw that made you guys separate? The Bible group or Aaron?"

"Oh, it was me," he freely admits, "and what I was doing. One night Mary Ellen just started in on Alexandra and went on and on and on—Aaron says this, Aaron says that, Aaron says to cut off all contact with her." He shrugs, taking yet another swallow of wine and putting the glass down. "I finally had just had it. I lost my temper and I told her what I was going to do." He sighs heavily.

After a moment, I say, "You mean, leave her?"

"No," he says, eyes coming back up. "Be the sperm donor so that Alexandra and Georgiana can have a child."

CHAPTER TWENTY-NINE

I think it may have been a full minute before I fully absorb David's revelation that he was going to father a child for his sister. In the meantime he continued clearing the table, asking where a Tupperware container might be to use for the leftover bisque.

The dogs suddenly come thunking up against the glass door, startling us both. They look like snow monsters, which makes me laugh. I spread a beach towel on the floor and let them in, brush the snow off each as best I can. "I knew Georgiana wanted a child," I begin.

"Lexy's always wanted children," he tells me. "But she felt she had to choose, though, between public life and, well, that."

"The suits at DBS don't know, do they?" I ask, trying to pick off the biggest snowballs out of the fur on Scotty's hind legs.

"I doubt it. They're just starting the conception process now."

I look over. "Is that why you're here?"

"I had to sign a lot of papers with them. Then we went to see the doctor and that's when they wanted me to—" He opens the dishwasher to load the dishes. "And then I had to go back a couple of times more. You know, to give them enough. It's hard to know how many times before it takes."

"I'm glad Alexandra decided to make the commitment," I say, releasing Scotty and standing up. "I was afraid she wouldn't."

"You knew?" he says, surprised.

I nod. "I stayed with Georgiana for a few days during the trial."

"Oh, that's right."

I walk over to lean on the counter and watch him clean up the sink with a sponge. "And I think you're probably the best brother in the whole wide world."

He smiles a little. "She's been a good kid sister."

He pushes the dishcloth through the handle of a cabinet and leans on the other side of the counter to face me. "So how will DBS react, do you think?"

"Well, she won't be carrying the child herself, so that's better. But there's going to be trouble from the board of directors. Jackson's family is a little, uh…"

"So Lexy tells me." He squints a little. "You didn't break your mouth or anything, did you?"

"Just banged it up here," I say, pointing with my finger.

He slides forward and kisses me gently on the lips, backs up a bit and then does it again. I don't move, I don't respond. But I don't pull away, either. Then he pulls back, stands up and clears his throat. "So, anyway, Mary Ellen is filing for divorce. And I'm relieved." He looks at me. "The last—"

The doorbell rings. We both are startled and I straighten up, brushing my hair back and cringing when I touch my head wound.

For a minute, I had forgotten what I look like.

And David kissed me.

Stop the butterflies, I think, walking to the front door with David following. I look out the window and see an O'Hearn Construction truck with a snowplow on the front. I open the front door and Phillip O'Hearn is stamping the snow off his boots. He does a double take when he sees me. "Good God, Sally."

"Nice wheels," I observe.

"Best way to get around in this," he says, eyes still on my face. He leans slightly to look over my shoulder at David. I make a quick introduction.

"Are you related to Alexandra Waring?" O'Hearn asks, pulling off his gloves and stuffing them in his coat pockets. Then he slips off his coat, which I hang next to David's on the rack.

"She's my sister," David says.

"Yes. I can see the resemblance." O'Hearn walks over to the fireplace and helps himself to Mother's tongs to poke at the fire to raise a sign of life before he throws three logs from the wood box on it. "I'm afraid I'm not one of your sister's favorite people."

David looks to me in confusion and I signal for him to dismiss the comment with a wave of my hand.

My eyes return to O'Hearn and I wonder what he is thinking, standing there, looking down into the fire. He helped my father build that fireplace some thirty years ago and every stone was from this property.

"Since you are here, David," I say, "I wonder if you could act as a consulting attorney for me."

O'Hearn turns around, his elbow resting on the mantel.

"Certainly," David says. "My fee is one dollar."

I look at O'Hearn. "Establishing attorney-client privilege."

"You better be awfully sure, Sally." His voice is so serious, I feel a chill. I walk over to Mother's chair and sit down. David moves next to me, continuing to stand, his eyes on O'Hearn.

"So what did they say?" I ask O'Hearn.

He looks down at the floor a minute before answering.

"You have to make a deal, Sally. They won't stop until they get what they want."

"Who are 'they'?" David asks.

"Take your pick, there's a crowd," O'Hearn says, removing his arm from the mantel to cross his arms across his chest. "Right now I'm dealing with Vito Sancione. He's the one I know personally." His eyes move over to me. "He was one of the principals that nearly bankrupted me on Windsor Hills."

I look up at David. "I believe he's connected to the Gambino crime family. And if it was just them, I wouldn't be so worried. But it's not. They're allied with some scum-sucking thugs that are threatening my family." I look at O'Hearn. "What did he say about that?"

"He basically said they're scum-sucking thugs, but they're all playing for the same piper."

"Right," I say, sighing. I look up at David. "My family should be free to live their lives without worrying that somebody's going to hurt them." And then I briefly outline the situation. I tell him that an international consortium thought they had acquired all the land they needed to build a two-and-half-square-mile coal-burning cement factory across the state line in Hillstone Falls, New York. That my great-uncle Percy owned a five-acre tract right smack in the middle of the factory site and that the consortium had been alerted to that fact when I made inquiries in Hillstone Falls. And finally I tell David that an attorney visited me at the hospital yesterday to let me know A, the consortium wished to buy the land and B, I should be aware they know exactly where my mother and brother are.

"This is an interstate crime," David says to O'Hearn. "We should bring in the FBI."

"And then what's Sally's family supposed to do? Go into hiding for the rest of their lives?" O'Hearn shakes his head.

"You don't know what this group is like. They're like cancer, they get into everything and they corrode every system that used to work. The kind of money these guys have is unreal and they simply employ the local cruds to do their handiwork to get their projects done."

"World Sound Industries has other plants like this?"

"Oh, yeah," I say, nodding. "The only question I have is if they're more interested in laundering money through them, or in the long run actually making some money."

"Do you know how much somebody would have to pay the cement mafia of New York to let you make cement?" O'Hearn says. "So much money that it's never happened before. And that's just part of their payroll. Vito's people are just one part of it. They've got a Russian gang working for them. Look at their handiwork on Sally's face."

I blink. *Russians?*

"They've got two mob families working for them, they own five state senators, a congressman, people in the governor's office and they've got people in seventeen other states. They've got lobbyists in Washington—I'm telling you, it's like a tumor with feelers that snake around," he sneers, "and sinks its roots to suck the life out of our country. Literally."

O'Hearn looks to me. "I also got the distinct impression from Vito that the Russians threw your writer friend off Castle Kerry."

"But why didn't they throw me off? I was the one causing the problems."

"Vito said they thought he was Percy Harrington."

I nod. "Because he was with me at Hillstone Town Hall." I look up at David again. "When we were trying to get somebody to help us, Roderick said he was Percy Harrington." I'm starting to get mad. "That smug son of a bitch at the town hall."

"Palermo," O'Hearn says. "I know him."

I look into the fire. "So what was the other night supposed to be about? At my house?"

"To scare you." O'Hearn smiles. "But according to Vito, it's unclear who scared who more."

I smile slightly, pleased at least with that.

"So they want to make the deal," O'Hearn says. "And part of it is that you have to drop the charges against the two in jail."

I give him a look. "Now how am I going to explain that to the police?"

"You're just going to have to do it." Pause. "Sally, I'm telling you, you want these guys out of your life. Out of your mother's life, for God's sake. Please, have your uncle sell."

I want to rub my face, but I can't. So I lower my head a minute, closing my eyes, trying to think.

"It's worth a lot to them," O'Hearn adds. "Without it, they can't move ahead."

"How much are they offering?" David asks.

"I think Percy could get as much as five hundred thousand," O'Hearn answers. "But, Sally, you have to drop the charges against the two in custody."

"Roderick Reynolds had to have brain surgery and is in a coma," I say, raising my head. "He could be dead tomorrow. And they expect to pay us off with five hundred thousand dollars for what they did to him?"

"Sally," O'Hearn says, sounding tired, "the cops have squat to convict anyone for what was done to Roderick Reynolds. Unless someone comes forward to confess, there's no case to be brought. There's no one to arrest. We don't even know if the two in jail were involved."

I mutter a very unladylike expletive.

"How do they propose to execute this deal?" David asks.

"My lawyers and their lawyers are working up the transaction papers as we speak. The plan is, if you agree, Sally," he says, turning to me, "we'll settle on a price, you'll drop the charges against the two in custody and we take the papers to your uncle to sign." He looks out the window. "This is supposed to stop in the next hour. I can fly you down to Florida in the morning to have Percy sign the papers."

I take a slow, deep breath and let it out as slowly. "When did you say you would get back to them?"

"Tonight."

"Tell your pal Vito baby I need to sleep on the offer, but in principle we have a deal." I stand up, feeling shaky.

"It's the right decision, Sally."

I walk O'Hearn to the door and we agree to a time to talk in the morning. I thank him. After he leaves, I close the door and lean back against it to look at David. "So what do you think?"

"You couldn't call the Presarios, could you? See if they can do anything?"

Rocky Presario is the don of a New Jersey "family"—of which some members have gone straight, while many others haven't quite yet—who happens to be very fond of me. "What, you mean like kill them all?"

"No, I mean the other Presarios, the ones allied with the Feds."

"It all comes back to the same thing, David," I sigh, pushing off the door. "And that is how would I protect my family? We can't even keep a stupid stalker away from my mother and it's not even hers." I walk past him to stand in front of the fire. I sense him coming up to stand behind me. Then I feel his arms gently encircle me, his hands resting on my forearms, which is about the only place I do not hurt. We stand like this for a while.

"I hate to send you back out in this storm," I finally say, "but it would be for the best. I have a great deal to think about and I need some rest."

"Of course," he says quietly. Then I feel him softly kiss the back of my head and move away.

The snow lets up as I watch David navigate the car through the snow and then I walk back to the fire.

I am scared.

I'm scared about my family. I'm scared about making the right decision. And I'm scared of how the police will react.

And I'm scared of how David Waring makes me feel.

CHAPTER THIRTY

I must admit, this is one of those scenes in my life I never even remotely imagined. I'm sitting across from Phillip O'Hearn, streaking across the eastern skies on his corporate Gulfstream jet. David Waring is sitting next to me, very close, and we are poring over the paperwork involved in selling Uncle Percy's land. About every fifteen minutes David calls somebody on the telephone and argues with whoever it is, writes stuff in the margins of the papers, crosses it out again and then writes something else. Then he gives a theatrical sigh, stealing a wink at me and mouthing "not to worry," hangs up and we go on to the next page.

O'Hearn, in the meantime, seems fully absorbed in a hardcover Tom Clancy novel.

My mind briefly veers to Buddy D'Amico. When I went into the station this morning to tell him that not only was I not going to finish my statement, but that I was dropping all charges against my two assailants, he was dumbstruck. Then he was furious and on the third take, demanded to know who had threatened me. (He is smart, my friend Buddy.) When I refused to answer, the captain came in to explain that I was not helping anyone by doing this and that I might be threatening the lives of other innocent people. When I still did not answer, in an infinitely cooler way, the police chief himself came in to tell me that I was a fool, to stop wasting their time, and to go out to the desk sergeant to sign the paperwork.

It wasn't pretty.

And so here we are, me, Phillip O'Hearn and Alexandra Waring's brother, making our way toward Miami International in hopes of some kind of closure. In O'Hearn's case, though, I think he might also be hoping for forgiveness.

I've always loved greater Miami. It's such a big, happening place with tons to do. It's got great food and music and clubs and hotels, and the city itself seems very kind to the public, making sure everyone has easy access to beautiful beaches, golf courses, tennis courts and fishing. And kite flying. I can't help but admire it.

We boarded the plane in Hartford in twenty-five-degree weather and with two feet of snow on the ground and land where it is brilliantly sunny and about seventy degrees. A car meets us at the airport, whisks us onto 836 and over the bridge into Bal Harbor. It is a quick jaunt down Collins Avenue and then over to the bay, where we are let out in front of a magnificent-looking ten-story condominium building. The sides and back have a series of interlocking gardens around two swimming pools—one saltwater, O'Hearn says, and one chlorine (he should know, he built the complex)—and the back of the building has a tremendous terrace and marina.

We stop into the management office to find the revised documents that were faxed from New York and then take the elevator up to the fourth floor. After I help Uncle Percy and Mrs. Milner recover from their shock and distress about what I look like ("I had a terrible fall"), I see that they have high tea on the terrace of their apartment. This is the real thing, with tiny cucumber sandwiches, tiny ham sandwiches, tiny cream cheese and pepper jelly sandwiches, to say nothing of open-faced salmon and capers on small triangles of toast. There are sliced tomatoes and mozzarella, fruit salad, croissants, cookies, petits fours and miniature éclairs. There are also, of course, two pots of tea, Earl Grey for him and Irish Breakfast for her.

Mrs. Milner excuses herself to take a short nap. (She knows I have something important to discuss with Uncle Percy and doesn't want to intrude.) After she leaves, I slowly and carefully explain to Uncle Percy that it turns out he does own some land in Hillstone Falls, New York, and that he inherited it through Aunt Martha. I also explain that the land was tied up in a trust for some time because Aunt Martha's brothers, years ago, had sued their mother's estate.

"Oh, yes," Uncle Percy says, nodding. "Those two." He looks at David. "I used to call them the Gruesome Twosome. Horrible people. Nothing like my wife. Couldn't believe they were related." He turns to me. "So they messed this all up?"

"Yes, they did." I take Uncle Percy's hand. "The thing is, Uncle Percy, the land is worth a great deal of money now. That's why we're here. I think you should sell it, but if you choose to do that, there are some other things we need to think about."

"Do whatever you think is right, Sally," he tells me.

His trustworthy eyes make my heart hurt. *May you never know from whom this money comes.*

"Uncle Percy, a company wants to buy your land for five hundred seventy-five thousand dollars."

When his expression doesn't change, I wonder if he's heard me. "Five hundred seventy-five thousand dollars," I repeat.

"I heard you the first time," he tells me. He looks at David again. "Does she think I'm deaf or something?"

"Of course not," I laugh. "It's just that you seem quite unfazed and it is a tremendous amount of money. It's a small fortune."

"And I'm sure you will do whatever you think is right with it," he tells me, patting my hand. "And I think you might start by considering a visit to a very good beauty parlor." And then he guffaws. "I'm sorry, dear Sally, but you do look like something that was shot in the field and left there a few days."

"I know I do," I say, trying to ignore David's laughter. "Anyway, Uncle Percy, as you might remember, when you chose to move into the Gregory Home, you signed over whatever assets you had."

"I remember." He looks at David. "Later I'll take you down to see the boats."

"This money, this five hundred seventy-five thousand dollars, is a life-changing event, Uncle Percy. It means you can leave the Gregory Home and live somewhere else if you want. Otherwise, if you stay there, they will hold the money, and you will pay for all of your care as time goes on."

"What does Margaret say about it?"

"She's very happy for you. And she says it's nice that you have so many options."

"Options, yes, our Margaret is very big on options. 'Keep your options open, Percy, keep your options open.'"

"So we need to make some decisions, Uncle Percy. First, do you want to sell the land for what they have offered? Five hundred seventy-five thousand dollars?"

"Do you want me to?" he says, his pale blue eyes focusing on me.

My heart hurts again. "Yes."

"Then I'll sell it."

"Okay," I say. "Now, the next question is, what would you like—" I stop, seeing mild panic in his eyes. I take his hand again. "What is it? What's wrong?"

"I don't want things to change," he whispers.

"Things don't have to change. You don't have to leave the Gregory Home. What we can do is switch you over to what they call the 'fee for service' program. They'll hold the money and deduct expenses as you go."

"What if I die after fifty thousand dollars?"

"The rest of the money will go to whomever you choose."

"I'd like you and your mother to have it. I love your brother, but he'd lose it all in a dice game."

I smile. "Uncle Percy, we don't have to decide everything right this minute. But you should know that Mother and I have all the money we need. I'm doing very well at DBS. I can help Rob if he needs it. So you can do what your heart tells you to do with the money."

"I want the Gregory Home to have it," he says. "They've been very good to me. And I didn't have any money before."

"That's because of the endowment," I say, nodding. "Their endowment spins off money to underwrite the services."

"They don't take Medicare, you know," he tells David. "It gets everything all balled up, Margaret says. Unless you have to go to the hospital. They take Medicare."

I think of what Margaret Kennerly explained to me, that if Uncle Percy is on the fee-for-service plan and goes into the hospital, if the bed is needed at the Gregory Home for someone who has no money at all, that bed will go to that other person and Uncle Percy and his money will have to go elsewhere. But this is too much information right now. What I need to determine for sure is whether Uncle Percy is okay about selling the land and that he understands that his options in life could change significantly if he would like them to. But he wants to stay on at the Gregory Home, which surprises me not in the least, and I know Mother and I will do whatever we have to do to make sure he always has a place there.

Uncle Percy frowns. "I remember Grace got some money and she left. And she hated it. She wanted to come back. And then she died."

"You're very healthy, Uncle Percy, and you have a lot of good living to do. This is a good thing that's happened, not a bad thing."

He looks at me, cringing slightly.

"Please," I say, squeezing his hand, "tell me what you're thinking. It's very important that I know how you feel."

He meets my eyes, looking fearful. "I want things to stay the way they are."

"I'm sorry," David says, leaning forward, "I didn't hear that."

Uncle Percy straightens up a little, as if what he said has lifted a burden. "I said, I want things to stay as they are. I want to give the money to the Gregory Home."

I don't know whether to laugh or cry, but if this is still what he wants to do after he's taken some time to think it over, then that is what we will do. David brings out a manila envelope containing the finished documents that were faxed to the condominium regarding the sale. "We're going to need the nurse and the other guy as witnesses," he says to me. "Well, Mr. Harrington, this is a great deal of money you'll be receiving."

"Yes, isn't it wonderful," he says, happy now, pale eyes shining. "Margaret can put it in the endowment fund. It will help a lot of people for a long time."

I lean forward to kiss his cheek. "Yes, it will."

"I don't want to hurt your feelings," he says then, "but you

are one scary-looking babe, Sally. It's like being kissed by that
guy with the cape and the organ."

"The Phantom of the Opera?" I say.

While David finishes up with Uncle Percy and the witnesses, I take my briefcase with me and head down to the
boardwalk and walk for several blocks before I sit down on
a bench. I know I'm not supposed to be in the sun with open
wounds, and I know everyone is staring at me, but I sit back
for a minute anyway, closing my eyes against the brightness.

In my briefcase I have twelve typewritten pages of notes
about World Sound Industries. The report outlines who they
are supposed to be and my suspicions regarding who their fi-
nanciers may really be. It has a list of their other industrial
properties in the United States and a long list of their pollution violations. There is information about the nature of the
pollutants that would spew from the proposed Hillstone Falls
plant, the radius of the pollution, and it cites the lawsuit the
attorney general of Connecticut is preparing in an effort to stop
the plant from being built.

In other words, it is, from soup to nuts, a convincing reminder
that upstate New York is about to let someone poison the air of
at least three neighboring states and the land and water for an
entire region. I also included a list of famous people who own
significant land holdings along the Hudson that will ultimately
be affected: actors and directors, venture capitalists and ty-
coons, horse breeders and dress designers, all of whom, evidently, are unaware of what is about to happen in their backyard.

If I saw these notes for the first time, I know I would investigate the project. There is no hint of murder or the mafia,
of corrupt politicians or international money laundering. No,
there's no earthshaking scoop here, just the facts on the pub-

lic record, which, for some reason, haven't come to the attention of the public.

I slip the pages back into the manila envelope and seal it. I check the address and make sure the postage is properly affixed. Then I walk to the end of the block and drop it in the mailbox.

I'm mailing it to ABC News with no return address. Consider it an anonymous lead.

CHAPTER THIRTY-ONE

"**M**aybe it's too soon to be at work," Paul says.

"No," I tell him, "I feel much better. Really. As soon as I heard Roderick was going to be okay, I felt like a new person." Yeah, well, maybe. (Someday I'm going to have to start telling the truth.)

I touch the edge of my computer keyboard absently, thinking about the news I received when I arrived at West End this morning: that Roderick Reynolds has filed a multi-million dollar suit against *Expectations* magazine, DBS News, *and* me. I can't really blame him; I may even be envious that he can get back at anyone. I don't have anyone I can go after—rather, I have no *way* to get back at anyone. At least not for the moment.

I pretend not to see Alexandra flying into my office until she is standing over my desk, glowering at me. Reluctantly I tell Paul I have to go, hang up and swivel my chair in her direction.

"It's one thing to claim your family was in some type of danger," she begins.

"They were," I tell her.

"But attorney-client privilege with my *brother?*" the anchorwoman cries.

"Given the circumstances, who better?"

After a moment, she sighs, letting her shoulders sag, and sits down into the chair with a thump. She has already changed for the newscast and, I can see, made it as far as hair and makeup before hearing I was in the building. She looks good. (Well, who doesn't in comparison to me?) She's wearing a blue suit, blouse, pearls and simple gold earrings, her standard newscast kind of outfit.

The way Cleo does her makeup reaffirms her eyes. "You look truly horrible," she tells me.

"Everyone's being so nice to me, I can't stand it."

"Tell me to let this go," she tells me.

"You have to let it go," I tell her. "Because there is no story. Speaking of which—" I gesture to my computer "—I just fixed that horror that was passing for a business report."

"The nephew's still here," she says. "I'm going to have to bribe Dale Earnhardt Jr. myself to get rid of him." Her eyes come back to me. "How are you really?"

"I'm okay. And your brother was a lifesaver. I really owe him."

Her head kicks up and she smiles one of her more dazzling ones. "So you like him?"

"Who wouldn't? He's amazing."

"I mean—" She catches herself.

I knew it, I think. *She threw him at me.*

"He thinks you're very special, too. That fact evidently was not included in your attorney-client privilege," she adds.

I laugh, but inside I am a mess. Once I knew that things might be okay, and that my family was off the hook and that Roderick would recover, I found myself fixating on David. I keep thinking about him, trying to replay our time together, rerun things he said, and as different scenarios play out in my mind, so do all kinds of emotional and physical reactions.

"I love him very much," Alexandra says. "He's been supportive of me in ways you cannot imagine."

I don't tell her that I know why she and Georgiana spent the Christmas holiday in Scotland instead of Kansas, about her brother being here for sperm donation, or about how the separation from his wife finally came about. *Supportive?* I'll say. I still wonder what she's thinking will happen with the network when Georgiana bears a child that looks like Alexandra.

Well, we'll see. Perhaps Alexandra will show the world how it can be done.

"I do have one story I'd like to assign," I tell her.

She raises her eyebrows.

"My stalker, Luke Jervis. This guy has a history beyond belief. His mother was in prison when she gave birth to him, he was diagnosed as severely emotionally disturbed by age seven, he was institutionalized at fifteen, had multiple suicide attempts, was arrested for assault, but was found insane and put in a mental hospital and then was released ten months later because the state laws changed regarding mandatory institutionalization."

"Yikes," the anchorwoman says quietly.

"So for the past nine years, he's been receiving treatment, has been picked up twenty-three times for—"

There is a brief knock at the door and David appears. "Speak of the devil," Alexandra says.

"Benjamin asked me to tell you that it's time," he says to his sister.

She gets up.

"I'll come, too, if you want," I offer.

"No, you relax," Alexandra says, waving me down. "This is your last day of medical leave." She turns toward the door. "Thanks for the business report, by the way."

The Warings leave my office together and I touch the edge

of my desk. While David was here I was perfectly fine, but the moment he left, just now, I started feeling strange again. A kind of hollowness and excitement.

It's the rapport we've had from the beginning, that sense of connection and conformability, and of an all-at-once feeling of coming home and yet launching upon an adventure at the same time.

Definitely uncharted territory.

I swivel my chair toward my computer, when there is another knock.

David. He closes the door and walks across my office to stand in front of my desk.

I don't say anything. He doesn't either. We just look at each other. Then he holds out his arms and I find myself going around my desk to walk into them, resting the side of my face against his chest and feeling his arms gently close around me.

His heart is pounding, too. "I'm going to be alone at the farm this weekend," he murmurs. His arms tighten slightly. "Would you come with me?"

I can rationalize saying yes. I can tell myself that we will simply get to know each other and will take walks and maybe ride horses and go to a movie.

But that's not what would happen. I would go with him to fall in love. I would go to give him everything I have. I would surrender, I would do anything, and I could never look at myself in the mirror again.

He is someone else's husband.

I feel choked with disappointment. Then I feel miserably depressed, and the tears start to fall on their own. I pull back from him, covering my face with my hand. "I'm sorry, but I can't. I want to, but I can't. Not with the way things are."

He steps forward to put his arms around me again and I let him. "Then I'm going back to California this afternoon."

My depression deepens. I feel cheated, punished. I swallow and nod against his chest. "Okay."

Finally I pull away and move over to look out my window. A few moments later, I hear my office door open. And softly close.

I continue looking out the window.

About the Author

Laura Van Wormer grew up in Darien, Connecticut, and graduated from S. I. Newhouse School of Public Communications at Syracuse University. In high school and in college she worked in bookstores, and after graduation joined Doubleday as secretary to the editor-in-chief. She worked her way up to becoming an editor and later left to pursue her own writing career.

Riverside Drive was her first novel, followed the next year by *West End,* which introduced the characters of Cassy Cochran and Alexandra Waring. Heroine Sally Harrington would later come to work for Cassy and Alexandra at DBS News. (Other DBS News novels before Sally made her debut are: *Any Given Moment* and *Talk.*) The Sally Harrington books are, in order: *Exposé, The Last Lover, Trouble Becomes Her, The Bad Witness* and *The Kill Fee.*

Laura divides her time between Meriden, Connecticut, and Manhattan. She is a member of The Authors Guild, Mystery Writers of America, Sisters in Crime, Friends of the Library and Rotary Club.

She cordially invites you to visit her at LauraVan-Wormer.com.